# Kris Bock

# Valley
# of Gems

Pig River Press

# Pig River Press

Copyright 2015 by Chris Eboch
ISBN: 8554343162
ISBN-13: 979-8554343162
(previously published as *The Dead Man's Treasure*,
ISBN 0692371672.)

Action and romance combine in this lively
Southwestern adventure, complete with riddles the
reader is invited to solve to identify historical and
cultural sites around New Mexico.

If you would like to try to solve the clues yourself,
you can download a printable copy from the
Romantic Suspense Novels page of the Kris Bock
website at www.krisbock.com. That document also
includes some of the Southwestern recipes
mentioned in the book.

For book news & sales, sign up for the Kris Bock
mailing list: sendfox.com/lp/1g5nx3.

Visit The Southwest Armchair Traveler blog -
http://swarmchairtraveler.blogspot.com/ – for
Southwestern travel tidbits, recipes, quirky
historical notes, and guest posts.

# Valley
# of Gems

Note: chile is the preferred spelling for the
New Mexico variety of the chili pepper.

# *One*

Rebecca peered through the small, cloudy window into the machine shop. Inside, someone held a flaming welding torch to an odd jumble of metal. She couldn't see the person's features beyond the face shield, but a glimpse of tousled, dark blond hair suggested it might be the woman from the article. The treasure hunter.

The woman who could help. If only she would.

Rebecca made sure her blouse was neatly tucked into her skirt and pushed through the door. A burning, metallic smell hit her. The new angle gave her a glimpse of the welder's shoulders and she reversed her opinion. That was no woman.

He turned off the torch and removed the welding helmet. "Hey." He was average height, with sun-streaked hair and a killer smile. Sweat glistened on his face and lean, muscular arms. He was sexy in an athletic way, though she preferred the work-obsessed brainiac type.

Rebecca gave a brief nod of greeting. In the clutter of odd machinery, it took her a moment to spot the woman leaning against a long metal table. Curly blonde hair, curvy figure in jeans and a tank top. That was whom she'd come to see. "Camille Dagneau?"

"Call me Camie." The blue eyes studied her with open curiosity.

Rebecca forced a smile, hoping her fatigue and anxiety didn't show. "I'm Rebecca Westin. Can we talk?"

"Sure, go ahead."

Rebecca glanced at the man, but he was poking at his project, testing the weld or something, and it would be rude to insist he leave in the middle of his work. He was probably a student, though he looked close to thirty, and the metal thing looked more like an artistic sculpture than an engineering project.

She moved closer to Camie and spoke in a low voice. "I read about you in a *National Geographic* article. And when I found out you were here, in New Mexico ... Well, it seemed like too good a coincidence to pass up. I'm hoping I can convince you to help me find another treasure."

Behind her, the man said, "Wait a minute, if this is a treasure hunt, I want in this time."

Rebecca shot him a frosty look, but he kept smiling. He was probably used to getting whatever he wanted with that smile. But this wasn't a game. Her future was at stake. She turned back to Camie, shifting slightly to block out the man, and waited for a response.

"You want to hire me as a treasure hunting guide?"

Here's where things got tricky. "That's the thing. I don't actually have any money to pay you." She wouldn't explain why she was broke, why she needed more money. She didn't want pity. She tried to project a confidence she didn't feel. "But I'd like to propose a partnership. I supply the clues, and you supply the expertise."

Camie leaned back against the table and crossed her arms. "What makes you think this treasure is something I couldn't research and find on my own?"

"It's a family treasure. Not something from legends, like that other one you found. That's why I'm coming to you. I understand your partner is the historian, but you're the one who knows the desert."

"I'm intrigued. Can I see some ID?"

Rebecca blinked in surprise, then fished her wallet out of her purse and handed over her driver's license. Camie leaned over the table and made notes on a pad of paper. Rebecca rubbed her nose, which tickled from the acrid smells – burning metal and something like motor oil or grease, as near as she could guess.

After a minute, Camie tore off the bottom half of the paper and handed it to Rebecca. "Come to this address at six. We'll give you dinner and then we can talk."

Rebecca opened her mouth. She'd expected to explain a lot more, had been ready to persuade, to negotiate. But she closed her mouth and nodded. This was a start. No point in pushing it and maybe ruining things. Besides, she didn't want to go into detail with the strange man in the room.

She wanted to ask who "we" referred to, but it was probably Erin Mayer, the woman's partner from their big find the previous year. That was fair, although Rebecca didn't want to bring too many people into this. It was bad enough that she'd already be competing against her half-siblings. She didn't need strangers in the race as well. But she'd never win on her own.

"I'll see you then." Rebecca turned and left, without even a glance of acknowledgment at the man. Hopefully he got the message.

Outside the building, she walked slowly across the small college campus. It didn't look like any university she'd seen before. No massive brick buildings, no huge sports stadium. Just a dozen or so tan stucco buildings with red tile roofs. Nothing was over three stories high. At least it had grass under big shade trees, the green soothing and familiar. She'd been chilly that morning leaving Albuquerque, but now, eighty miles south and heading toward noon, it was time to peel off her suit jacket. If nothing else, a week in New Mexico in May made a nice vacation after a wet, dreary Seattle winter that seemed determined to hold on forever.

What could she do for the next few hours? She was in no mood for sightseeing, even if she knew what sights the area boasted. The drive south had been enough to make her feel like a fish very far out of water. All that desert, all those browns and reds. Even the distant mountains that paralleled the highway hadn't helped. They were the wrong color, and there were so many of them. She could see for miles, which proved how large the state was, vast plains and mesas and canyons. How would she ever find the treasure?

She paused as if looking at some flyers pasted on the glass door of a building, though really it was an excuse to stop her aimless wandering. She couldn't afford to waste time. And she'd make herself sick if she spent the afternoon worrying about whether that woman would help. Rebecca would simply have to persuade her. She'd never backed down from a challenge.

Her gaze shifted past the glass into the building – a library. Libraries had information. A local college library might have resources she couldn't find anywhere else. She had her plan for the afternoon.


Rebecca pulled up to the address Camie had given her. She was ten minutes early, since it hadn't taken much time to get across the small town. Her stomach gurgled. It was nice of them to offer her a meal, and it would save her a few dollars. Hopefully they'd have something better than the slice of cafeteria pizza she'd had for lunch. She needed to get back on a healthy diet. Her pants had started digging into her belly six months earlier. She'd recently bumped into an old coworker who had assumed she was pregnant. That was embarrassing for both of them.

At least she'd forced herself to run twice a week throughout the entire ordeal. It had been mainly stress relief, but it also burned calories. She quickly did the math in her head. Five hundred calories per run, twice a week, was over a pound a month. Without those jogs, she'd have added another dozen or so pounds and probably wouldn't fit into her clothes at all. And she certainly wouldn't be in any kind of shape for treasure hunting in the desert.

She glanced at her watch. Three minutes till six. She left the car and headed for the house.

A slim woman with short dark hair opened the door. "Hi, you must be Rebecca. I'm Erin. Come on in." Rebecca met her friendly smile with a silent sigh of relief. Whatever Camie had found out or decided over the course of the afternoon, apparently they weren't ready to laugh at Rebecca or turn her away – yet.

The fact that male voices came from the back of the house was less encouraging. How big was her audience?

Camie came out of the back room, probably the kitchen, carrying a pitcher of what looked like iced tea. "Good, you're prompt. I hate people who are late." She put the pitcher on the table. "I made my famous green chile stew. I hope you don't mind spicy food."

"No, I like it."

Camie grinned. "Points for that as well." She gestured toward a tall, lanky man as he came out of the kitchen. "That's Drew. He hangs around with Erin a lot, and for some reason she lets him."

The man shook Rebecca's hand and then draped an arm over Erin's shoulder. She looked perfectly happy to have him around, and Rebecca could see why. He was tall, dark, and handsome in jeans and cowboy boots. A man had been involved in that other treasure hunt as well, according to the article. A helicopter pilot. If this was him, he might come in handy after all. Not that she could imagine locating buried treasure from a helicopter, but at least it was less mind-boggling than heading into the desert on foot.

Rebecca's smile froze in place as the man who'd been welding came out of the kitchen. He leaned forward to put a plastic container on the table, and his forearms were sculpted works of art. His gray T-shirt showed those well-defined shoulder muscles, though he wasn't bulky overall. He was built like a professional dancer, but that seemed an unlikely profession in a small town in the middle of New Mexico.

He reached out take her hand in a warm, firm grip. "We didn't officially meet. I'm Sam."

Before Rebecca could respond, Camie said, "And I'm hungry. Let's eat." She slid past Sam, giving his sides a quick squeeze that made him jump and chuckle. They must be a couple. Good thing Rebecca hadn't been even ruder to him earlier.

The stew wasn't what she would have called chili. No tomato, just beef, onions, beans, and the local green chile, with sour cream, cheese, and cilantro served separately to sprinkle on top. It was delicious, even if it made her mouth burn and her nose run. Sam's plastic container turned out to be a tortilla warmer and he'd apparently made the tortillas himself. She'd never been a fan of flour tortillas, but these were light and flaky, not like the usual bland cardboard ones. They were perfect for soothing her tongue when the stew got to be too much.

It was a friendly, noisy meal, as the others joked and teased. No one brought up the treasure hunt or asked Rebecca any questions. She couldn't quite relax, knowing what was to come. She was an outsider, watching people who knew each other well, but at least she had a reminder of what life could be like. The last time she'd felt that kind of camaraderie had been in college, which seemed like lifetimes ago, not a mere decade.

*This. This is what I want. Someday.*

For now, it was enough that she could dream again. That she'd taken these first steps. If she found the treasure, it might not solve all her problems – but it would be a big help. Rebecca could pay off her debts and make sure her niece kept getting the best medical care. With enough money, she could take time off before looking for another job. Relax a little. Do something for herself for a change. Figure out her future.

Two years earlier, she'd been well on her way to her goal of being financially independent by age 35. She could've quit her job and started her own company, or thought about having a family. Now she was worse off than she'd been at twenty. No job, no home, credit card debt, and a gap in her résumé that would raise uncomfortable questions. The treasure would put her back on track, and then some.

Finally the meal ended and Camie waved everyone to the living room to "get down to business." Rebecca was tired of business in all its forms, but she couldn't slow down yet.

Erin and Drew sat hip to hip on the couch, with Sam sprawled next to them. Rebecca settled into one of the facing chairs.

Camie dropped to the floor, cross-legged. "Tell us what this is all about."

Rebecca gathered her thoughts. "I'm going to have to start with some family history." She didn't want to, but the rest wouldn't make sense without it. "My father, Arnold Westin Junior, grew up here in New Mexico. In Santa Fe, specifically. He married a woman called Isabel and had three children – Arnold the Third, Benjamin, and Tiffany. A few years later, Arnold left Isabel and moved to Oregon. I don't think he ever saw those children, or any of his family in New Mexico, again. However, his father, the first Arnold, was a wealthy man and took care of his daughter-in-law and grandchildren."

She took a deep breath, avoiding meeting anyone's eyes. The

story was sordid, but that wasn't her fault. Worse, though, it made them all look pitiful. "Arnold met my mother, and they had two more children, my sister Sophia and me, before he died in a car accident twenty years ago. We never heard from Dad's New Mexico family – until a few weeks ago. Arnold Senior died of cancer and left an unusual will."

Interest, which had been polite, sharpened. Now she had to hook them. "Apparently my grandfather was a collector. His house is full of antiques. But he particularly collected small items of very high value. Spanish doubloons. Old native jewelry." She shrugged. "I don't know what exactly. But enough treasure to fill a treasure chest."

Camie grinned. "And what, he lost it?"

"No. He buried it."

# *Two*

Camie laughed out loud. "I think I like your grandfather."

Rebecca managed to smile, though she wasn't so sure she agreed. She was spending hundreds of dollars on this venture and was more likely to lose it than make a high return on her investment.

Sam leaned forward, elbows resting on knees. "Please tell me he left a treasure map."

"Nothing so simple. But he left clues." When they looked at her expectantly, she added, "I'm sorry, but until we have a formal arrangement, I'd rather not tell you more." She held her breath, but her statement merely elicited shrugs and nods. Either they were very reasonable, or they weren't taking the treasure seriously.

"Before we commit to anything," Camie said, "I have a few questions about you."

Rebecca straightened. "Very well."

"I ran a background check on you this afternoon. You got dual degrees in computer science and math, and graduated in four years at the top of your class. You worked for Microsoft for five years before moving to a small but well-respected tech startup. Everything in your history suggests a hard-working, responsible, straight arrow. Until about a year ago. You lost your job, you sold your condo at a loss, and your credit rating tanked. So what's all that about?"

Rebecca stared. She'd expected some kind of check after Camie had asked for ID, but this was more than a quick Internet search. Her face warmed with embarrassment, but at the same time she had to respect someone who could, and would, handle things that way.

She thought her reasons were good enough. Hopefully these people would as well. "Last year, my sister Sophia had a baby, nearly four months premature. The baby, Lizette, was in the hospital for weeks, and my sister had health complications as well. And of course, so many baby things aren't covered by insurance. My sister and the baby needed extra care at home, and her husband couldn't afford to lose his job–"

She took a deep breath. She hadn't planned to tell them so much, but it had all come tumbling out. "Anyway, I used up all my leave, and they finally let me go. I sold my condo and moved in with my sister and her husband, since I was there most of the time anyway. I had enough in savings to help out for a while, but that's gone. My sister and the baby are doing much better, so it's time for me to move out. I've been looking for work, but the tech market isn't great right now."

She shrugged. "And then this happened. It seemed worth pursuing."

"So you flew to New Mexico, broke and without friends here, to look for a buried treasure based on a dead man's clues." Camie grinned. "You're a gambler."

"Hardly." She'd put the plane ticket on her credit card and didn't know when she'd be able to pay it off. It made her sick to think about it. Rebecca had to keep reminding herself that she was still young. She had decades to prepare for retirement. Yet some part of her feared she was turning into her parents, spending money faster than it came in and then wondering why the checks bounced.

"What I am, is angry." She'd hardly realized it until the words came out of her mouth. "If my loving grandfather wanted to leave us something, why didn't he simply do it? It would have been a godsend, but–" She wrestled for control. "My niece will need physical therapy as she grows. My sister can't work and also take care of her. This treasure could help, if I can find the darn thing."

Nobody spoke for a moment.

"It's not the best time," Camie said. "We're heading into finals week, and I have to be in the machine shop a lot so students can finish their projects. Erin's got a full load, too. I'm not saying no, but it will take some juggling."

Drew said, "I have a job lined up for the next two weeks, but I might be able to give you a few hours now and then."

"I'm in, if you'll have me," Sam said. "I've always wanted to hunt for buried treasure and I missed out on the last one."

That's why she hadn't seen him in the *National Geographic* pictures. Maybe he and Camie hadn't been dating then. Rebecca wasn't sure what he brought to the group, other than good looks, some obvious physical strength, and homemade tortillas. But she didn't want to lose Camie's help by turning away her boyfriend. Besides, Rebecca probably needed all the friends she could get.

On the other hand, it would be smart to protect her investment. "We'd better set down contract terms. I'm not willing to split the treasure five ways, especially if we're not all putting in the same amount of work."

"Consider me hired help," Drew said. "If we use the helicopter, I need to get paid for gas, but I won't expect a share of the treasure."

Sam grinned. "I'm in it for the adventure. You can keep the treasure."

Rebecca stared at him. She could see how treasure hunting would sound like an adventure, but it was still hard to imagine anyone doing it simply for the fun of the thing. When she realized she'd been holding his gaze for several seconds, she jerked away.

Erin spoke up. "Honestly, I'm not anxious to go running around in the wilderness again, and I have classes and grading. But I'm willing to donate my time as a researcher, if it's needed. Research is fun."

Camie shook her head. "Doing things is fun. But I guess that's why we make a good team."

"You're all being very generous," Rebecca said. She hoped it wasn't only because they felt sorry for her. And as much as she needed the money, she also wanted to be fair. Besides, if they weren't getting a reward, how hard would they really work? "How about this – I get ..." She almost said fifty percent, but apparently she was the only one who really cared about the money. Might as well shoot high and see what happened. "Seventy-five percent of whatever we find, since I'm supplying the clues. The other twenty-five percent you can divide up however you see fit."

"Okay, we're all agreed?" Camie looked around and everyone nodded. "Do you really need it in writing right now, or can we get to the important part and talk about the treasure?"

Rebecca studied the faces around her. Training told her to get everything in writing, but she didn't want to insult anyone. They were already placing their faith in her, giving time to what was probably a wild goose chase. In any case, she knew so little at this point that they'd hardly be able to steal the treasure from her yet. She'd write up a contract that night. She nodded. "All right. But I'm afraid it gets a little complicated."

"Of course it does." Camie chuckled.

Rebecca flushed. She wasn't trying to be difficult or keep secrets. It was simply hard to know how to explain everything. Everyone seemed to be smiling, though, so she went on. "I flew down yesterday for the reading of the will. The lawyer made it clear I had to be there in person. I think the other grandchildren expected – well, I won't try to read their minds." It had been pretty clear, though, that they'd been unhappy about the will.

She pushed the hair back from her eyes. "All his grandchildren have the opportunity to find this buried treasure. My grandfather seemed to think it was, I don't know, a way to bring us together. Or maybe a test." She shrugged. "Anyway, Sophia couldn't come down, so she's officially out – though of course I'd share with her. But I looked over the wording very carefully, and nothing says I can't get help from people outside the family."

"I take it you see your half-siblings as competitors, not allies?" Sam said.

She couldn't hide her grimace. "It's not so much how I see them as how they see me. I'd be happy for us all to work together. But they made it perfectly clear I'll get nothing from them, not one word of help and no portion of the treasure if they find it first. If this had happened a couple of years ago, I would have ignored the whole thing and let them have it. But at this point, Sophia and I need the money more than they do."

She sighed. "They don't want me involved, and I guess I can't blame them. But what my father did is not my fault, and I'm not willing to walk away from this just because they think I have no business being here."

"Of course it's not your fault," Erin said gently. "And it's unfortunate that they can't be pleased to meet a new sister. But that's the way some people are."

Rebecca nodded and hoped that a few quick blinks would hide the moisture in her eyes. She'd been shocked at first to find out she had half-siblings, but then she'd looked forward to meeting them. Had even hoped they might grow close someday. Now she dreaded facing them again.

Erin frowned. "It's possible they'll change their minds about you in time, but we certainly can't count on it. So for now they're against us."

"We have competition." Camie looked delighted.

Rebecca had to smile at the way this woman embraced challenges. "I'm afraid so. And we don't get all the clues at once. More like one clue leads to the next, from what I gather, and they're hidden in different places."

Sam said, "Then it's possible if we don't figure out the first clue before they do, we won't get any of the others. This may be a very short adventure."

Rebecca shrugged. "I'm not sure what form the clues take. The lawyer made it clear that we're all supposed to leave the clues in place for the next people, but ..."

"But we can't trust your relatives," Camie said. "We'd better get started!"

Rebecca grinned outright. "It's not quite so desperate as that. The first clue will be revealed tomorrow. We're all meeting at my grandfather's house at eleven a.m. We can't do much until then."

Erin leaned forward. "Rebecca, I'm curious. You came down here to ask for our help before you've even seen the first clue. What if it's something you can figure out on your own?"

"I don't know anything about New Mexico. I don't know anything about my grandfather or his family. Plus, it's three against one. Actually, more like one against dozens, because you can bet their mom is on their side, and probably other relatives and friends."

"A wealthy family that's been around for years?" Sam said. "They could have the full old-boys' network on their side."

"And I'm on my own. Even if by some miracle I know

exactly what the first clue means, what then? I don't know my way around. I don't understand how things work here. I have so many disadvantages–" She stopped herself. She didn't want to make it sound impossible, even if it was. "I figured it was worth getting some help if I could."

Camie nodded. "You made the right choice."

Sam leaned back on the couch, his legs crossed at the ankles. "I don't know if we'll find the treasure, but it should be fun to try." He met her gaze with a smile.

Fun. That was the last thing on her mind. This wasn't about having fun. Still, if that's what it took to get them involved, they could have all the fun they wanted.

"Your grandfather's house is where, Santa Fe?" Camie asked. When Rebecca nodded, she made a face. "I can't get away tomorrow. Two students with projects they should have finished a week ago have scheduled shop time."

"And I have classes to teach," Erin said.

"I'm free." Sam grinned at Rebecca. "Want an escort to that meeting?"

It figured it would be him, when she would've felt more comfortable with one of the women. What did he do that he had no work on a Friday? But she nodded. Any help was better than going alone.

"It's about two hours to Santa Fe, but why don't we meet at eight so we have plenty of time to find the house or deal with construction delays."

Rebecca nodded again. She'd better come up with some conversation by the next day, if they were going to be in a car together for hours.

Camie rose. "Now, if you'll forgive me for saying so, you look exhausted. Do you have a place to stay?"

Rebecca shook her head. "I wasn't sure if I'd be going back to Albuquerque or what."

"Take the guest room upstairs," Erin said. "For as long as you're here."

That would definitely help her budget. "Thanks, I appreciate it." She quickly covered a yawn. Somehow knowing she had help with the treasure must have relaxed her enough that the fatigue was hitting hard.

"Get your things and go on up to bed." Camie rubbed her hands together. "And in the morning, we'll work on that treasure!"

Rebecca could only envy Camie's enthusiasm, but she felt herself smiling. Yes, she'd made the right decision. She'd found allies with brains, skills, and energy. She could almost believe they might win.

# *Three*

Sam dashed back downstairs after seeing Rebecca settled in her room. She'd looked surprised and rather confused when he'd carried her bag up for her. He found the others in the kitchen, putting away food and doing the dishes.

"Well, what do you think?" Camie asked. "Was I right about her?"

"I like her," Erin said. "She's smart, she works hard, and she's in way over her head." She grinned. "I can identify with that last part."

Drew bumped her gently with his hip. "You can identify with all of it."

Sam stepped out into the dining room and checked that Rebecca was still safely tucked away upstairs where she couldn't hear them. He turned back to his friends. "She's wound pretty tight. She must be holding things together with sheer willpower. This treasure hunt might not be a vacation, but at least she'll get some fresh air and exercise. And maybe put on some more comfortable clothes."

Camie snorted. "No kidding. I hope she has some jeans or shorts and hiking boots. At least her pumps had low heels. She's not entirely impractical."

"She was coming to a meeting, and that's how people dress for meetings out there in the rest of the world," Erin said. "Sounds like she's had a rough time lately."

"I hope she's fit enough for this adventure," Camie grumbled. But Sam knew his friend wouldn't have invited Rebecca over for dinner if Camie hadn't taken an immediate liking to her.

"Do you think there's any chance we'll find the treasure?" Drew asked.

Camie gave him a haughty look. "How can you doubt it?"

"It isn't going to be easy," Erin said. "Her other relatives have a big advantage. They knew the grandfather. How he thought, where he went."

"Yes, but Rebecca has us," Camie said.

Sam smiled at her confidence. "I hope it's enough. She needs something good to happen for her."

"She wouldn't like you feeling sorry for her," Erin said.

He considered. "Probably not. Too much pride." That wouldn't put an end to his sympathy, but he'd have to be careful about how he expressed it. He wanted to be part of the treasure hunt. He didn't have a good excuse to butt in, so he'd have to prove his value. And remember that while it might be merely an adventure for him, it meant a lot more to her.

He grinned as he wiped down the dining room table. He had a feeling the next week was going to be quite entertaining.

Rebecca double-checked her tote bag. Wallet, tissues, makeup to touch up her face when they got to Santa Fe, emergency granola bar, tablet computer. She'd skipped the black dress she'd worn to the memorial and yesterday's business suit in favor of comfortable jeans and tennis shoes, with a turquoise top and lightweight black sweater. She had no chance of impressing her new relatives no matter what she wore, so she might as well be comfortable during the long drive. Her sweater could go in the bag later if it warmed up.

Sam wore a sky-blue T-shirt that set off his tan, cargo shorts, and trail runners, so at least she wasn't underdressed compared to him. New Mexico seemed to be even more casual than Seattle.

Erin handed her a bottle of water. "Take this, and drink it. Seriously, it's dry here, and you'll be getting dehydrated even if you don't feel thirsty."

"Thanks." Rebecca tucked it into her bag.

"Ready?" Sam asked. "If you like, I can drive, so you can check out the scenery."

"Sure." She didn't care about the scenery, but she was anxious enough without having to drive in an unfamiliar city.

Sam filled a big travel mug from the coffeepot. "You sure

you don't want one for the road?"

She shook her head. The green chile cheese bagels they'd had for breakfast had been good – though not exactly a start to a healthier diet – but now her stomach churned. She didn't need anything else working on her nerves. "I just want this day to be over." She'd spoken softly, mostly to herself, but Erin shot her a sympathetic glance, and Sam gave her shoulder a light squeeze as he passed her, heading for the door.

Once in the car, she closed her eyes and did a short meditation exercise as Sam pulled into the street. Everything would be fine. She would make sure of it. And if this whole adventure blew up in her face, well, she would find a job and build herself back up, day after day and year after year.

But she wouldn't think about that possibility now. It made her want to crawl back in bed and drag the covers over her head.

After a few blocks, Sam turned onto the highway on-ramp. "Keep an eye on the dirt beside the road, and you might see a prairie dog."

"Really?" She'd never seen one and didn't know much about them, but somehow the idea of prairie dogs made the area seem friendlier. She saw a few holes, but the car was quickly accelerating and she couldn't be sure if the brown lump she spotted was an animal or a clump of dirt.

Sam fiddled with the radio and tuned it to a station playing classic rock. Since he was driving, and he didn't seem inclined to conversation, she could ... do what?

She could pull out her computer and check e-mail, but she didn't get much e-mail anymore, and it would be better to save the battery. For the two hours of the drive, she didn't have to do anything. In fact, she *couldn't* do much of anything.

When was the last time that had happened?

Rebecca gazed out the window. The morning sun caught the desert at an angle, showing wave after wave of undulating hills and valleys stretching toward the distant mountains. When she heard the word desert, she thought of sand dunes, but this wasn't like that at all. It was kind of pretty, with all the soft greens and pinks, and the blue sky above, with a few puffy white clouds like something out of a cartoon.

Sam sung softly along with the radio. His voice was

pleasant, though not quite in tune. It was rather endearing, that he was willing to sing in front of her, even if he wasn't very good. She wished she had the nerve to do things like that.

Sam grabbed his coffee mug from the cup holder and took a sip. "Don't forget to drink your water. Erin was right about that."

"I will, in a while. If I start now, we'll have to stop on the way there."

"Hey, we can find a rest stop if we need to. Better that than you getting dehydrated and feeling lousy during the meeting. We'll need to stay sharp. But honestly, you probably won't have to pee as much as you think you will."

She couldn't believe she was talking about peeing with a man she barely knew. She nodded toward his coffee mug. "That stuff dehydrates you, you know."

He grinned. "That rumor is exaggerated. Anyway, I'm used to being here, you're not. Trust me."

She sighed and pulled out the water bottle. That was why she had asked for help, after all, because she had no experience in New Mexico. No point in asking for advice if she wasn't going to take it on something as simple as drinking water. She drank a quarter of the bottle and then leaned back and watched the world pass by.

She must have dozed off, because the scenery had changed and Sam was saying something that hadn't registered. "What?"

"Next exit, Santa Fe. The GPS says we're only twenty minutes from your grandfather's house, so we have extra time. Do you want to stop somewhere or head straight for the meeting?"

She yawned and stretched. "Um, find a gas station, I guess." She hated gas station restrooms, but if she had to face her half-siblings, she wanted to look and feel her best, or at least the best she could these days. And she should have a small snack so her blood sugar didn't drop too low and make her cranky. The meeting would do that well enough. "I'm sorry I fell asleep. I hope you didn't need me to navigate or anything."

"No, it's a straightforward drive. I'm flattered, actually, that you were relaxed enough to fall asleep." He flashed a grin. "Maybe it was simply exhaustion, but I prefer to take it as a compliment."

She found herself smiling back. "Hey, whatever works for you." It was odd that she had managed to doze off two feet away from a man she barely knew. Odd that she felt relaxed enough to sleep at all, with the stress of the upcoming meeting. Maybe having someone to help made that much of a difference. Or maybe she had been carrying so much stress for so long that her body couldn't take it anymore.

Instead of a gas station, Sam found a café and bakery. Rebecca's stomach didn't need much persuading to believe it was time to eat again. It had been two and a half hours since breakfast. A pastry and green tea should give her the energy to face her half-siblings.

Rebecca freshened up in the restroom, and then, a little too soon, they were pulling up to her grandfather's house. As she got out of the car, a man hurried toward them.

"That's the lawyer," Rebecca told Sam. "He's all right."

The man took Rebecca's hand in both of his. "Good, you're here! I had to step outside for some fresh air. The atmosphere was getting a little, er, stuffy inside." He was a small man, several inches shorter than she was, with wispy hair and thick glasses. He turned to Sam, and before Rebecca could introduce them, said, "Luis Ruiz, Mr. Westin's lawyer."

Sam introduced himself, which saved Rebecca from having to decide how to identify him. She hadn't even known his last name.

"Is it all right if I accompany Ms. Westin?" Sam asked.

"Yes, certainly, and she'll be happy to have a friend here." Mr. Ruiz turned to her. "Not that we aren't all your friends, my dear."

She managed to smile, despite the three people who came out of the house to stand on the front porch. Tiffany, plump, dark-haired, and in a flowered dress, raised her hand in a slight wave. But then she glanced at the two men near her, folded her hands, and looked down. Rebecca's oldest half-brother, Arnold the Third, was a barrel-chested man whose belly pushed out above his ornate belt buckle. He glared at Rebecca for a few seconds before ostentatiously turning his back and going in the house. Her other half-brother, Benjamin, not quite so big but heading in that direction around the stomach, studied her a while longer. She couldn't read his expression from that distance. He took Tiffany's arm and led her into the house.

She didn't know if it would ever be possible to break through their animosity, but she knew she didn't yet have the energy to try.

The lawyer led them toward the house, a gorgeous, sprawling structure with a red Spanish tile roof and stucco walls tinted a soft peach.

Sam asked, "You knew Mr. Westin well?"

"Oh yes. Since we were boys. A great one for the pranks, Arnie was. Back then, and later in life as well, he always had his little jokes. 'Lighten up,' he would tell me, 'it's bad enough you're a lawyer; you don't have to be serious as well.'"

The little man chuckled as they paused on the porch. "Yes, he had quite a sense of humor. But he was clever, too. Sharp as a tack. People didn't always realize it at first, and he used that to his advantage. But he was a genius with numbers. Those puzzles, what are they called, Sudoku? He loved those. Any kind of puzzle, really, but those were his favorites."

Sam glanced at Rebecca with raised eyebrows, and she realized his question had not been idle conversation. Anything they could learn about her grandfather might help them. She needed to get her mind off her unfriendly relatives and her hurt feelings, and focus on practical matters – finding the treasure.

"I wish I could have known him," she said.

It was a vague statement, but enough to get the lawyer talking again. "Oh, I know he would have liked that as well. You two would have gotten along like a house on fire. I understand that you have degrees in math and computer science. I'll bet you got that aptitude from your grandfather."

Rebecca hadn't thought of it, but it might be true. Neither of her parents had shown much skill with numbers, at least when it came to the family's finances. Her own interest had been driven by desperate necessity, as the only one who grasped the concept that income should exceed expenses. But math also came easily to her, and she loved Sudoku. How strange that her affinity might have come from her mysterious grandfather.

"If he'd been a younger man, I'll bet your grandfather would have been head of one of those technology startups," Mr. Ruiz said. "As it was, he got one of the first computers and always had to have the latest gadget." He gave her a sweet smile. "Not all of us older folk are anxious to learn new things, you know. But your grandfather, he was on the cutting edge, one of those, what do you call them, the first users?"

"Early adopters," Sam supplied.

"That's right." Mr. Ruiz reached for the door, but Sam stopped him with a hand on his arm.

"If Mr. Westin wanted to meet Rebecca so much, why didn't he contact her sooner?"

She'd wondered the same thing but hadn't been willing to ask.

"He only found out about the girls when he was already quite sick with cancer. And when he found out about their, er, situation, with the baby, he didn't want to add a burden to them."

And this farce wasn't a burden? Rebecca shrugged that off and followed Mr. Ruiz into a large foyer floored in dark red tile. The others were clustered together ten feet away. Arnold glared at the lawyer, who either didn't notice or didn't care. Benjamin kept his attention elsewhere. Tiffany looked away quickly when Rebecca offered a tentative smile.

Mr. Ruiz introduced them to Sam. No one offered to shake hands.

"What's he doing here?" Arnold demanded.

"He's accompanying Miss Westin."

"He can't do that!" Benjamin said. "You told us only the people named in the will could do this, and they had to show up for the service. That's why the other one, her sister, is out." The look he gave Rebecca said clearly he wished she'd failed to turn up as well.

"I said the Westin family members mentioned in the will could only participate if they attended the memorial service." Mr. Ruiz added gently, "However, there's nothing to prevent Miss Westin from bringing a friend."

"That's not what Grandpa meant!" Arnold said.

"Perhaps. But that's what he said, and it's important to say what you mean." Mr. Ruiz gave them a cherubic smile.

"Particularly when working with lawyers."

"That means we can bring in other people as well," Benjamin said.

"Certainly." The lawyer paused before adding, "Of course, I recommend you determine in advance what they get for their assistance, and get it in writing. You don't want someone suing you for a share of the treasure later." He turned and led the way into the next room, with the older Westin siblings grumbling along behind.

Sam winked at Rebecca and they followed. It looked like they had an ally on the inside. No doubt the lawyer would only do what was allowed by the terms of the will, but at least he wasn't working against her.

The large sitting room they entered had tan tile, partially covered by scattered woven rugs in patterns dominated by red and black. Shelves, wooden side tables, and pedestals held a variety of beautiful objects, from intricately woven baskets to painted pottery to stone sculptures. Mr. Ruiz gestured for them all to sit on the brown leather couches and chairs. Rebecca sat, and Sam stood behind her chair.

The lawyer didn't waste any time. "As you know, the will stated that your grandfather took some of his most valuable small items, placed them in what he charmingly called a treasure chest, and hid it somewhere in the state of New Mexico. You will receive clues to help you find this treasure. The first clue is hidden somewhere in this house. You have three hours to find it."

# *Four*

After a moment of stunned silence, Benjamin squeaked, "What, you mean starting right now?"

"As soon as I play a video." Mr. Ruiz crossed the room to a wooden cabinet and opened the doors to reveal a large-screen TV. He pushed some buttons and Rebecca's grandfather appeared on the screen in high-definition color, his face two feet across. She stared at the man smiling out at them. She'd seen a few pictures online and at the memorial, but a shiver ran through her as he spoke, a voice from beyond the grave. She shook off the feeling to focus on his words. She couldn't afford to miss anything.

"I'm glad you have gathered here today. I hope you are all here."

Mr. Ruiz shot Rebecca a sympathetic glance, reminding her of her missing sister. Too bad she and Sophia couldn't be doing this together. At least she wasn't completely alone. She glanced over her shoulder and gave Sam a grateful smile before turning back to the TV.

"All my grandchildren. You may have different mothers, but you are the children of my son. He wasn't the greatest father, I know. Maybe I have some responsibility for that. But none of you have any responsibility there. So I hope you will put aside any differences and work together."

Rebecca didn't look at her half-siblings. She didn't need to see their disdain again. Her grandfather cleared his throat and took a sip from a mug. His voice had a pleasant low rumble, but it seemed weak. How sick had he been when he made the video?

"If you follow my instructions, and I sincerely hope you will, one thing will happen for certain. You will get to know this state, this land I love, better than ever before." He smiled. "This is true even for those of you who grew up here. Another thing I hope will happen–"

"We'll find the treasure," Arnold the Third growled.

"–you'll become a family," Arnold the First said on the video. "I have designed a series of clues to use the knowledge and expertise of each of you. You will save time and have a better chance of success if you work together. You will also get to know each other." He leaned forward. "Those of you who think you know each other well, even you have things to learn."

Without turning her head, Rebecca glanced at her relatives. The men were looking at each other with surprise, while Tiffany dropped her gaze to her hands clenched in her lap. Was her grandfather implying that they had secrets? If so, were they the minor embarrassments that anyone might want to keep quiet, or something more serious? Could she use them if she found out the truth, and did she have any right to do so?

On the video, Grandpa said, "Rebecca and Sophia, I'm sorry I never got to meet you in person. Maybe if I had more time – but they tell me it's a matter of weeks now. I don't think you're ready yet, and I don't want you to see me only as a weak, dying old man. I'll be watching over you – all of you, including the new generation. My old friend Luis Ruiz will make sure my wishes are carried out. To start, you have to find the first clue. I made it simple."

He grinned mischievously. "It's in this house, my house. To find it you have to understand my history. History is important. It tells us about our country, our ancestors, our family, ourselves. What can you learn from my history? That's your first task. But don't forget the future. That's important, too. The future is already happening, and unless you realize that, you won't understand the past. Don't neglect your family. Family is everything, even if you don't know them."

He looked at his desk and seemed to be thinking. He looked up and shrugged. "I guess that's about all. Goodbye and good luck." He fumbled for a remote control on his desk, and the screen went black.

Benjamin shot to his feet. "That's it? That's no help at all!"

"Old fool," Arnold mumbled. "He must've been getting senile."

Tiffany shot him an angry look but didn't speak.

Benjamin started pacing. "This is ridiculous. I don't have time for this nonsense. I'm a businessman, I have things to do."

"You are, of course, welcome to go do them," Mr. Ruiz said, and Benjamin lapsed into frustrated silence. The lawyer glanced at his watch. "Three hours, starting now."

"No time to lose." Benjamin looked wildly around the room. "History. He has shelves of history books."

"Or the artwork," Tiffany whispered. "Maybe something hidden in one of the pots or baskets? That's more like family history."

"Quiet," Arnold snapped. He rose and loomed over Rebecca. "We're starting in this room. You can start someplace else."

She met his gaze as she rose. She turned and left the room without a word, but she was trembling when she reached the hallway. She didn't notice Sam behind her until he rubbed lightly between her shoulder blades. "I'm sorry you have to put up with that kind of rudeness."

"It's all right." Her breath heaved in and out. She buried the hurt and humiliation under anger. "Actually, it makes things easier. I won't feel a bit sorry for them when we find the treasure!"

Mr. Ruiz came out and closed the door behind him. Sam turned to him. "Do we have access to the entire house?"

"Yes, wherever you like. I'm going to make a pot of coffee. It will be in the kitchen if you need some." He shuffled off.

"Do you have any ideas for where to start?" Sam asked Rebecca.

She sighed. "I have a feeling that to understand his clues, we'll need to think like him. But how can we?"

Sam put his hands on her shoulders. "Mr. Ruiz said you're a lot like your grandfather. Try thinking like yourself."

She stared at him, and then she laughed. "All right. I suppose I don't have a better plan, and that one has the virtue of being easy." She thought a moment. "In that video, he was at a desk. Maybe he has an office in the house. That's where I'd hide something, not in a room where guests visit."

"Good thinking," Sam said. "I'll do a quick overview of the whole house. I don't know if I'll find a clue, but at least we'll learn some more about your grandfather. Hmm, he did say the clue was *in* the house, right?"

"Yes. So assuming he was precise with his language, we can forget about outside." Rebecca glanced around the entrance hall, with four interior doors and a stairway visible. "Three hours!"

"Focus on what he said – family, history, and the future. Those concepts seem to be key."

She nodded and headed upstairs. Sam stayed below to take a closer look around the first floor. The kitchen led to a screened porch at the back of the house, with a laundry room tucked to one side. He also found a large dining room and a library with shelves full of books.

The elder Mr. Westin seemed to have had a broad range of interests. One bookcase held rows of hardcover mystery novels. Sam shook his head, smiling. No wonder the man thought a treasure hunt would be a good idea. He was probably the type to have murder mystery dinner parties.

Most of one wall held history titles, but Sam didn't think it was worth removing the books and shaking out the pages unless they had more specific info to go on. The old man was supposed to like puzzles. A random search wasn't much of a puzzle.

He sensed more than heard someone behind him and turned to see Tiffany hovering in the doorway. She didn't meet his gaze as she cleared her throat and said, "What's Rebecca doing?"

"What do you think?" he snapped. "You haven't been very kind to her."

The vague response worked to put her on the defensive, without giving away any useful information. She flushed. "I know. It's ... hard."

"Harder for her."

"Maybe," she whispered. "I don't hate her, you know."

Sam sighed. He couldn't keep harassing someone who looked so vulnerable. Besides, if she fled, she might interrupt Rebecca. He gentled his tone. "Your brothers seem to hold a pretty big grudge."

Tiffany sank into a chair. "Arnold does. Benjie mostly follows his lead."

"And you?"

She shrugged and looked down. "I don't know. So, um, where is she?" Tiffany still wouldn't look at him.

"Why?"

"I just thought you two would be together. And I wondered if, that is …" She mumbled something about Arnold.

"You wanted to spy on us."

She flinched. "Arnold said … I know it's not … But he …"

Her timidity was tiring. "What do *you* think?"

She finally met his gaze. "I don't know. This whole thing. I don't care about the treasure."

Interesting. "What do you care about?"

She straightened her shoulders. "I care about my family. You're not seeing my brothers at their best. But they are decent men. They're upset and hurt. Angry that grandfather is making us go through this. That they have to prove themselves."

"It does seem like a lot of work, especially if you were figuring on inheriting outright. Why do you think he did it?"

She shrugged and a small smile played about her lips. "Grandpa liked to tease. And I think … I think he wished we were more like him. More … playful. You must look around and assume we grew up privileged, and in some ways we did. But it was hard, too. I barely remember my father, but the boys do, and I think they've spent their whole lives trying to prove something. I think they believed that one day he'd come back, and he'd be proud of them, of the men they'd become. They worked hard for that, even though they didn't need the money. We only found out a few weeks ago that our father was dead. A lot of dreams died that day, dreams maybe we hadn't even acknowledged we had."

Sam studied her. There was more to Tiffany than a plump, vaguely pretty, quiet younger sister. "I wish you were having this conversation with Rebecca."

She smiled. "Maybe someday I will. Arnold told me to keep an eye on Rebecca, in case she found something. But that's not right. Grandfather was very big on playing fair. No cheating! Oh, he didn't mind if you found a loophole, if you could make a good case for it. A clever argument counted for a lot. But so did fair play and honor. I'm sorry my brother has forgotten that for the moment."

"Your grandfather sounds like an interesting man."

"He was." Her eyes filled and she blinked rapidly. "He was lovely." Her voice broke and she ducked her head. Sam gave her shoulder a gentle pat and headed out of the room, giving her privacy for her grief.

Upstairs, Rebecca had finished a cursory glance through the small office. A bookshelf held computer manuals, an almanac, dictionary and thesaurus, and books of puzzles: crosswords, cryptograms, Sudoku. She pulled out a few and flipped through them. All the puzzles had been done. She hoped they wouldn't have to resort to looking through those for some sort of clue. That was more than a three-hour job.

She checked the desk drawers, which held the usual office supplies. Nothing immediately jumped to mind as a hiding place. She sat at the desk, trying to imagine her grandfather in that office, making his plans. The computer sat silent and dark in front of her. On a whim, she turned it on. Mr. Ruiz had said her grandfather liked technology. Maybe he kept his plans in his computer files. It seemed too obvious, but one never knew.

The screen asked for a password. Drat. She was no Hollywood computer hacker who could break into a secure system in a matter of minutes. The most she could do was guess.

On the other hand, older folks often didn't use complex passwords, the recommended kind with a lot of random letters, numbers, and symbols. For that matter, a lot of her young colleagues had relatively simple passwords, if you could figure out the starting point. Some of the computer testers made a game of trying to break into people's computers, to teach them a lesson.

Many people used a familiar name or word they could easily remember. Surely her grandfather knew not to use something as obvious as his birth date, phone number, or Social Security number.

What else? Family members, maybe. She typed in the names of her three half-siblings. No luck. When she tried her own name, she got a message that the computer was locked. Right, she would have to wait sixty seconds before she could try again with three more guesses. And at some point, if she made too many wrong guesses, the system would likely shut her out completely.

She leaned back with a sigh. A lot of people wrote down their password and kept the note near the desk. She did a thorough search and found nothing. That meant he must have it memorized. At least that gave credence to her idea of a familiar name or word, and she'd used up the sixty seconds wait time.

She tried her name and her sister's. Nothing. She realized her disappointment was more than the failure to get in. Some part of her had hoped he might care enough to use their names. It had a certain logic to it, since anyone could find out his other grandchildren's names, but probably wouldn't know about Rebecca and Sophia. She tried " RebeccaSophia" but that failed as well. And her three tries were up, with another sixty seconds to wait.

She peeked behind the paintings on the walls, but saw only blank wall.

Back to the computer. Her father's name was the same as Arnold's, unless Grandpa had gotten fancy and used Junior. And if so, was that "Junior" or "Jr"? Too many options! Then there were family nicknames, or names in combination. And if she had to come up with name and number combinations, she could be there all day – or until the computer locked her out.

But if the clue was in the computer, then his grandchildren were supposed to be able to get in. It couldn't be too complex.

Or maybe she was on the wrong track completely.

She leaned back, trying to ignore the rumble of voices from downstairs that suggested the others had left the first room. She had to think. What had he said in the video? A lot of stuff about history and family, with a theme of forgiveness. She tried *family*, *forgive*, and *forgiveness*. Nope.

She should have taken notes during his talk. She closed her eyes and tried to remember his wording as closely as possible. He talked about getting to know the state and each other. The secrets they had. Becoming a family. He would be watching over them. She resisted the urge to glance over her shoulder. Something about the next generation and the future.

She sat up straight. She hadn't tried the name of some family members: his great-grandchildren. At the end, he'd said family is everything even if you don't know them. Had any of her half-siblings even bothered to wonder about their baby niece? Trembling, she typed the name of her sister's daughter, the youngest great-grandchild, Lizette.

Nothing. Drat!

She was about out of ideas. She closed her eyes and pictured her baby niece. Sweet little Lizzie. She needed the money more than her rich New Mexican aunt and uncles.

Voices mumbled in the distance. How much time did she have alone up there? She had to make every moment count.

Rebecca held her breath and typed in Lizzie.

She got in.

She smiled at the computer. This clue had a computer angle and a password that only Rebecca and her sister would be likely to know. For the first time, she felt like maybe her grandfather wanted her to succeed.

Of course, the rest of the clues might be weighted towards the others. He did say he wanted them all to work together. But at least she had a head start – at least if the computer was relevant, and not a coincidence. It was entirely possible he'd used that password only because he changed his password frequently and had already used all the other names. Getting on his computer might wind up being a dead end rather than a step forward.

She closed her eyes again, her fingers still hovering over the keyboard. *Don't just search randomly. Think!* He said they had to know his history. Everyone assumed he meant his past, but history had a computer meaning as well. If she was looking for his computer history, she had two options: his Internet browser history, or his files. Files were more permanent, and therefore more likely.

Footsteps came rapidly up the stairs. She needed more time. Should she sign out, to make it harder for anyone else to get on the computer? Jump away and pretend she'd never been on it? No, it would take too long to shut down.

Before she could decide, Sam appeared in the doorway and whispered, "How's it going?"

She grinned with relief. "Promising, I think, although I could be on completely the wrong track."

"Keep it up. I'm going to take a quick look around up here. The boys are done in the sitting room, though. Hopefully they'll stay busy in the library for a bit, but we may have company before long."

She nodded, her gaze already back on the computer. She opened the document folder and organized by "date modified." The last file was titled "Congratulations."

# *Five*

Arnold's voice came from downstairs. Rebecca couldn't hear what he was saying, but the tone sounded accusatory. Of course, she'd never heard him sound any other way. She opened the document, typed the command to print, and began shutting down. Heavy footsteps came up the stairs.

Hurry up and close!

Rebecca snatched the paper from the printer, folded it, and jammed it in her back pocket.

Arnold's voice came from the hallway. "Where is she?"

"Your sister?" Sam answered. "She was down in the library last I saw her."

"Not her! Out of my way."

Rebecca hit the final commands to shut down the computer and pushed away from the desk. Sam strolled past the doorway, glanced in, and raised his eyebrows as she came toward him. Rebecca smiled. She stepped into the hallway as Arnold barreled out of the next room.

"She's not in–" He stopped when he saw Rebecca.

"No one said she was." Sam put his arm around her. "She's right here, obviously."

"But you were blocking that doorway, like– Never mind." He turned to Rebecca and demanded, "What have you been doing?"

Rebecca shrugged. "Trying to figure out my grandfather, but he's quite a puzzle." She tried to look defeated. "I'm tired and I have a headache. Mr. Ruiz said something about coffee?"

Sam nodded. "It's all right, we have plenty of time. Maybe a break will help you think better."

Rebecca avoided looking at Arnold as she ducked past him,

afraid she would break into laughter. She hurried to the kitchen but jerked to a stop when she saw Tiffany seated at the table beside Mr. Ruiz. Had they seen her grin before she hid it?

Sam edged past her. "Don't tell me you've given up." His tone was friendly.

Tiffany returned his smile. "I'm avoiding my brother. The loud one. He's not too happy with me right now." She glanced at Rebecca and then quickly away. "Anyway, I have no idea where to look or what I'm looking for. I know Grandpa meant this to be fun, but ..." Her voice trailed off.

Mr. Ruiz patted her hand. "Don't worry, my dear. I shouldn't tell you this until the three hours are up, but I don't think it will hurt to have a little hope if you ladies are stuck." He glanced up at Rebecca, but she wasn't about to mention that she might have found the clue.

He went on. "If no one finds this clue, or rather if not everyone finds it and you don't decide to share, it's not over. Tomorrow at noon, I have a copy of the clue that will be given to everyone. So you see, if you don't find it, it's not the end of the world! Finding it simply gives you a head start."

Rebecca managed to smile even as her heart sank. She'd been hoping she was a big step ahead of them. But if no one else found the clue, at least she and her new friends had a few extra hours. And since she hadn't actually had a chance to look at the clue, this would save her if it turned out that she'd printed a card for someone's graduation or something.

She clenched her hands to keep from reaching for her back pocket. Did she have the clue or not? If so, she couldn't give any sign of it. If not, she should be searching, not chatting.

Mr. Ruiz pushed a plate toward her. "Biscochitos?"

"Um, yes, sure." They looked like oval sugar cookies but had a different taste. Licorice? Sam filled a cup of coffee and handed it to her. She nibbled the cookie between sips, but she didn't sit. She wanted to get out of there, go someplace quiet, read the page she'd printed, and think. But once she left the house, she might not find it easy to get back in. What clues would she miss then?

"I have to go to the bathroom!"

They gaped at her, and she blushed. She'd spoken loudly the

moment the idea had popped into her head. Tiffany gestured out the kitchen doorway. "First door on the left."

Rebecca was lightheaded by the time she got there. She'd forgotten to breathe. She locked the door, leaned back against it, and studied the document she'd printed.

> The Western Trail takes you past
> At 106 degrees
> 42 minutes will get you there
>
> Pass the mountain to the north
> To where the ladies gather
>
> The end is amazing
> Where people smile and dance, and rock
> These eyes have seen 500 years
> Do not avoid their gaze, but meet it closely

That certainly seemed like a clue. If not, it was really bad poetry. Unfortunately, she had absolutely no idea what it meant. Each line sounded random and unconnected. Only one thing seemed moderately clear, that whatever they were supposed to find was probably not in this house.

So what next? Get out of there, share the clue with Sam, and hope he had some ideas? Or use their remaining time to explore the house more? She took advantage of the bathroom, but still hadn't made a decision when she headed back to the kitchen. Maybe she could get Sam alone and ask his opinion.

When conversation paused, she started to speak. The doorbell rang with a *bong* that echoed through the house. Rebecca and Tiffany both jumped and then exchanged a sheepish glance. Footsteps tapped in the hall, and they heard the front door opening.

Tiffany started to smile at Rebecca. A man's voice called out a hello. Tiffany's eyes widened, and then she squeezed them tightly shut.

A moment later Arnold pushed into the kitchen with another man. Benjamin trailed behind. The new guy looked to be in his late thirties, a businessman to judge by his tailored suit and tidy haircut. He turned a warm smile on Rebecca. "Hello, you must be Rebecca. So nice to meet you." He offered his hand and she took it automatically. His dark eyes held hers in a friendly gaze until she was forced to blink.

She drew her hand away, and he turned to Sam. "I'm Rick Mason, Tiffany's husband. And you are?"

"Sam." They shook hands.

The man rounded the table and leaned down to kiss Tiffany's cheek. She whispered, "What are you doing here?"

"I'm here to help. Arnold called me."

Tiffany glared at her brother, but Arnold simply looked smug. "Now Tiffany, Rick told me all about your little misunderstanding. You know you'll make up, you always do. If you would talk to him rather than running away–"

Tiffany broke in, her voice shrill. "I don't think this is appropriate to talk about right now!"

"Quite right. We'll have plenty of time later." Rick put his hand on Tiffany's shoulder. She ducked her head so her hair hid her face, but her posture radiated misery. Embarrassment at having witnesses to her marriage trouble? Guilt over the "misunderstanding," whatever it was? Or something else?

Rick added, "Right now I want to get to know your lovely sister and her friend." His smile was charming, and under normal circumstances Rebecca might have been flattered by the friendly attention, or at least relieved that this one new family member wasn't treating her like the enemy. But the atmosphere of the room was getting too tense. Besides, time was ticking away, and the others didn't know she'd already found something. Rick Mason's presence seemed designed to distract her.

To her left, Benjamin whispered, "Does this mean we have to share with him as well?"

"Don't be a fool," Arnold hissed back. "He's married to Tiffany, he shares her portion. We might as well get some help for it." He added gleefully, "And he's not a *Westin* relative, so we can use him!"

Rick came toward Rebecca, smiling. Arnold and Benjamin were still whispering. Suddenly Rebecca had had enough, and never mind the consequences of leaving early.

She backed toward the doorway. "Actually, I think we'll be going."

Tiffany sat up straighter. "Already?"

"You found something in the office," Arnold growled. "I knew it."

Sam said, "I believe Mr. Ruiz has something to tell you about the clue." As everyone turned to look at the lawyer, Sam followed Rebecca out the kitchen doorway. They hurried through the entrance hall and a minute later were climbing into the car.

Leaving might have been a mistake, but for the moment Rebecca felt only relief.

# Six

Sam glanced at the house as he started the engine. No one had followed them.

Rebecca leaned back. "Whew! That was getting intense. Am I a fool for not making use of the remaining time we had access to the house?"

"Did you find the clue?"

"Yes."

"Then I think our time is better spent elsewhere." He pulled out of the driveway. He wasn't yet sure where they were headed, but he could backtrack out of the neighborhood and start in the direction of downtown Santa Fe and the Interstate. "I got pictures of every room, so we can refer to those if necessary. I took a video of your grandfather's little speech as well."

"You did? I didn't notice."

"Hopefully no one did. That's why I was standing behind you; I made sure your head was blocking everyone's view of my phone. But I thought we might want to know Grandpa's exact wording at some point."

"Smart." She smiled at him. "I obviously made the right choice in asking for help, and in letting you ... what did you call it, join the fun?"

Sam nodded. "Though your grandfather had a strange sense of fun. What did you think of Tiffany's husband?"

"I don't know. He seemed friendly, at least compared to the rest of the family. But ..." She couldn't think how to put it in words. "He didn't blink often enough."

Sam chuckled. "He certainly tried to turn on the charm. I wonder what he does. As a general rule, I don't trust people who wear suits."

"That probably says more about you than him."

He grinned. "True enough. You want to share that clue?"

"If you don't mind terribly, I'm going to keep you in suspense a little longer." She pulled out her tablet computer. "If I look at the clue again, I'm going to be distracted by trying to figure it out. I want to make notes on everything we learned while it's fresh in our minds."

"Okay." He described the house, with a focus on what they could learn from the content. Grandpa Westin was obviously wealthy, collected New Mexico art and artifacts, and loved mysteries and puzzles of all kinds. That didn't tell them anything new, but Rebecca noted some of the specific things they'd noticed, in case the information came in handy later. They had the pictures, but it was good to get their mental impressions down as well.

As Sam described his conversation with Tiffany, he tried to study Rebecca from the corner of his eye while paying attention to traffic. He hoped she'd be happy to hear her half-sister wasn't as much of an enemy as they'd thought.

Rebecca was silent for a minute. Finally she asked, "Do you believe her?"

"About what? Oh, you mean was she really sorry?" He considered. He wanted Tiffany to be sincere. He wanted to think that she and Rebecca might become friends someday. But he had to admit, "I suppose it could be part of a plan to befriend you. A sort of bad cop/good cop act with her brothers. She's not a very skilled actress if that's the case. She acted guilty and uncomfortable. I assumed that was because of the way they were treating you, but it could be because they were trying to trick you, and she felt awkward."

Rebecca nodded and looked out the window with a sigh. "I don't think we can take the chance of trusting her. And I don't trust her husband." She didn't want to admit that she'd found the man attractive despite that. He had a warmth and charm that were unnerving, although maybe her lack of a social life had made her overly susceptible.

She wondered what he did. Whatever it was, he was probably good at it. Most politicians would sell their soul for that kind of presence. It was no wonder that Tiffany had fallen for him, even though she seemed plain and dull next to him. People probably looked at them and wondered why he didn't have a gorgeous young wife, and no doubt a few women were ready to volunteer. Maybe that was the cause of their problems, whether he cheated or whether Tiffany was simply afraid he might.

If she could be confident that Tiffany was really friendlier than her brothers, Rebecca might be willing to attempt a divide and conquer strategy, to see if they could persuade Tiffany to help. But Rick Mason was a wild card. Arnold had called him, not Tiffany, but he would still have influence over Tiffany. He was better avoided. Sadly, that meant her half-sister was better avoided as well.

She gazed out the window. She had a vague impression of lots of stucco buildings, but she couldn't focus on what she was seeing. All the thoughts, sights, and conversations of the last few hours swirled in her mind. The car suddenly seemed stifling, and she felt lightheaded.

Sam said, "I admire your discipline in wanting to take notes first, but will you think I'm too impatient if I beg you to tell me about that clue right now, pretty please?"

She snorted. "You're the most relaxed person I've met in ages. I know I'm uptight; you don't have to tell me."

"I said disciplined, not uptight. It wasn't a criticism."

"Whatever." Rebecca took a few deep breaths. "Sorry, I'm wound up from all that tension."

"I don't blame you for that, but I'm on your side."

"I know." She managed to smile. "I'll try not to take my anxiety out on my partners."

"Partner and friend, I hope."

"Sure." She wriggled so she could pull the folded paper out of her pocket and spread it on her lap. "It's a poem of sorts, but it sounds to me like complete nonsense. I don't know what we're going to do about it. What was I thinking, coming here?" She was tempted to crumple the paper into a ball and throw it out the window. She closed her eyes and rubbed her forehead.

Sam said, "You really have a headache?"

"I'm getting one. I think my brain is full."

"Maybe some food will help."

"Why does everyone keep trying to feed me? I was hoping to lose weight on this trip."

"You don't need to lose weight."

"I wasn't fishing for a compliment," she snapped.

"Just making a statement." His voice had that cool, neutral tone of someone trying to be reasonable against great odds. "You shouldn't be dieting while you have so much to do and think about. You need to keep your energy up."

After a long pause, she said, "Is this your subtle way of telling me I'm being a brat, and maybe eating something will help?"

He gave her a sideways glance. "I wouldn't dare suggest something like that."

She chuckled. "Because you would be right. I have some issues with my blood sugar. If I go too long without eating, it drops, and I get irritable." She sighed. "And one of the side effects is that once I get into that low blood sugar state, it's hard to make decisions or recognize that I need to eat. I know I do, but some part of my brain takes over and gets rebellious."

Sam smiled. "You know, when I was twenty, I could go rock climbing for six hours with nothing more than a couple of beers to sustain me, and then afterward eat a whole pizza. Now that I'm thirty, my body is telling me that's not appropriate behavior anymore."

"It doesn't seem like I should need food already, when I just had a cookie." She glanced at the clock on the dashboard. "But I guess more time has passed since our mid-morning snack than I thought, and a cookie and coffee aren't exactly slow-burning energy foods." She normally tracked her meals closely, but traveling and stress had interfered big-time.

They paused at a red light, and he reached over to touch her arm. "Camie, Erin, Drew and I, we all want to help you, but this is going to be a lot harder on you than on any of us. Camie will run you into the ground if you let her. You have to tell us if you can't handle something, or if you need a break. Don't be embarrassed about it. This is your show. You're not used to the altitude here, the dry air, the desert where everything is ready to bite or stab you. Plus, it's a lot more emotional for you. Take it easy on yourself."

She nodded, feeling choked up, but that was probably in part the low blood sugar emotions.

The light changed and Sam pulled forward. "In any case, there's no reason for us to leave Santa Fe until we have some idea of where we need to go next. A late lunch will give us time to study the clue. Do you have a preference for food?"

"Not really."

"Whenever I get to the big city, which around here means Albuquerque or Santa Fe, I like to get something I can't get back in town, which means basically anything besides New Mexican food, pizza, or burgers. I see a Thai restaurant, or we can keep looking."

"Perfect." She knew if she had to consider multiple options, she'd find it impossible to make a decision. That was another side effect of low-blood-sugar brain.

He pulled into an outdoor shopping center. A few minutes later, they were in a booth in a small, cozy restaurant and a Thai iced tea was soothing Rebecca's nerves. She pulled out the poem and read it aloud. "Mean anything to you?"

Sam moved around the table to sit next to her, so they could both see the paper. "All right, let's take this one piece at a time."

Rebecca ran her hands through her hair. "The Western Trail takes you past. Past what? Or did he mean to the past, like something historical? Like 'Go West, young man'?"

"That's pretty broad." Sam leaned closer to read the text. "Western Trail is capitalized. Maybe it's a specific route, a hiking trail or road or something."

Rebecca pulled out her tablet computer and quickly did a search. "There is a Western Trail Drive in ... how do you say this?" She pointed to the word *Tijeras*.

Sam said the name, pronouncing the j like an h. "That's a town east of Albuquerque, I think. I'll make a note, but before we go tearing off there, what else do you have?" He peered at the screen. "There, Great Western Cattle Trail sounds promising."

Rebecca clicked on the link and scanned the page. "Nope, doesn't go through New Mexico. Grandpa did imply we were going to get to know *this* state. That's a broad enough search area, so I hope we can avoid crossing state boundaries." She clicked back to the search page and scrolled down.

"What's that one? A business on Western Trail in Albuquerque, and it says across from the Petroglyph National Monument." Sam scribbled on the printout. "Petroglyphs are definitely from the past."

"Promising. Let's see what else we get for Western Trail before looking further." Rebecca went to the next search page. "The Great Western Trail again. This source says it includes New Mexico. I guess that could be it, if the rest of the clue narrows it down to the New Mexico part of the trail." She glanced over the clue again and sighed.

Sam made a note. "Anything else?"

"A vet in Moriarty ... educational company in Albuquerque ... Actually, I'm surprised there aren't a lot more, with such a basic name. Here's one for a hike." She clicked the link. "It's from a book. No, looks like it's referring to the western trailhead, not a specific trail name. I'm getting a few more for the petroglyph place. I want to take a closer look at that Great Western Trail thing first, though."

She followed a link to a forest service site. Sam's shoulder brushed hers. Rebecca forced her attention back to the screen, skimmed the information which had to do with a trail in Utah, and then checked a few more links. She cleared her throat. "There's some evidence the trail did cut through New Mexico, but it seems to be accessed only in other states. Of course, that's based on a five-minute search."

"How about a map search?"

"Right." She should have thought of that. Would have, if she'd been concentrating fully on the search and not getting distracted by the warm shoulder and spicy smell of the man next to her. She was pretty sure her own deodorant had broken down under the stress of dealing with her relatives. She tried to keep her elbows close to her sides as she typed in new search terms.

"Okay, these maps aren't showing New Mexico."

"Good, I think we can dismiss that one." Sam leaned back and Rebecca let out a sigh of relief. Hopefully he would think it was because they now only had one lead to follow. It had been too long since her last date if she was feeling aroused by sitting next to a man while doing a computer search. Not that working on a project together wasn't sexy, when you were in sync ...

*Focus!*

"The petroglyphs seem like our best bet, then."

Sam was studying the clues. "Yes, especially considering this bit about five hundred years. That must be about right for how old the petroglyphs are. The first Spanish settlements were around sixteen hundred AD, so anything much older has to be native."

Rebecca browsed the National Park Service page for the monument. "Hey, the visitor center is on Western Trail! That's a good sign." She glanced at the clues. "What about that 42 minutes thing? Is that how long it takes to get there, or from there to where we're actually going? And the temperature, he couldn't predict what it would be during our visit. Are we going to have to compute some mathematical formula for travel time at a different temperature?"

"I hope not, because unless we're supposed to take a hot air balloon, I don't know how the temperature matters."

She scrolled down the directions page, skimming the information. She almost skipped over the directions for GPS users, but a number caught her eye. "One hundred and six ..." She laughed. "It's not time and temperature, it's degrees and minutes for a GPS. The visitor center is at one hundred and six degrees, forty-two minutes west."

"Oh good grief, I should've recognized the minutes and degrees reference. That confirms it! It can't be a coincidence."

"Thanks, Grandpa."

The waiter brought pad Thai noodles and yellow curry. Rebecca pushed aside her tablet and Sam moved to the other side of the booth. "I think we have our next stop," he said. "The petroglyphs are near Albuquerque, so we can go this afternoon. That should put us a good jump ahead of the others if they don't find the clue on the computer."

Rebecca grinned and dug into her food. Her headache had completely vanished.

The hunt was on.

# *Seven*

They got back in the car and Sam brought up the Petroglyphs on the GPS. He headed out of Santa Fe on the highway. "We've got about an hour."

Rebecca pulled out the clues and frowned over them. "The next section says 'Pass the mountain to the north.' Do you think we have to go all the way around a mountain after we reach the petroglyphs? And this ladies gathering part. Like at a, I don't know, spa or teahouse or nunnery or something?"

"Maybe they aren't real ladies. There's a rock formation known as The Three Sisters in one of the climbing areas I like. Could be something like that. But you know what I think? We should stop worrying about it for a while. Enjoy the scenery," Sam suggested. They had already left the city behind, and he gestured toward the desert hills around them. "In some places, you can spot signs of the Camino Real."

"The what?"

"Camino Real, it means royal road. It went from Mexico City through El Paso and up to Santa Fe. The Spanish used it, the traders and colonizers and conquistadors, starting in the late fifteen hundreds. It hasn't been used much in the last century, but in some places you can still see the signs of it. The ruts of the wagon tracks cutting through a hill, and the different kind of vegetation that grows in them."

It took her a moment to process what he'd said, but the information was intriguing enough to distract her. "This road hasn't been used in over a century and you can still see it?"

"Hey, things move slowly out here. But archaeologists can often spot old settlements because of the different kinds of plants that grow above the ruins."

"Are you an archaeologist?" That could explain the casual attire and flexible schedule, not that she knew much about how real archaeologists worked.

He laughed. "No, I just collect useless trivia."

She gave in to curiosity. "So what do you do?"

"Basically, I fix things. Plumbing, electricity, mechanical stuff."

"You're a handyman or some kind of contractor?"

"Something like that."

She studied his profile. His smile suggested a secret joke. Or was he laughing at her, assuming she'd think poorly of someone who worked with his hands? "That's cool. I'm not good with that kind of thing. I wish I was. It would be easier than always calling for help." She backpedaled quickly, lest he take offense. "Not that I'm suggesting the work is easy. Just, you know, it would be nice not to depend on other people." Or to pay the outrageous rates plumbers charged.

"My mom says everyone, boy or girl, should know how to make a good meal, clean a house, change the oil in a car, and fix a toilet, before they get out of high school."

She wrinkled her nose. "My cooking is passable. I hate cleaning, but I can do it. As for the other stuff ... I guess your mother wouldn't approve of me."

His gave her an affectionate glance. "Oh, she'd like you fine."

She tried to ignore the fact that her heart rate had sped up. "How can you say that? You barely know anything about me."

"You think? Camie likes you, and she's the smartest person I know. And Erin likes you – though she likes everyone unless they give her a good reason not to."

Rebecca waited, but he didn't continue. It didn't matter what he thought. She didn't normally depend on the opinions of men, or of casual acquaintances of either sex, to make her feel good about herself. And yet, she wanted to hear him say that he liked her and give a reason for it.

Before this past year, it wouldn't have mattered what Sam thought. She'd had her job, and before that her academic success, to prove her worth. What did she have now?

Nothing.

She needed to get out of her sister's house and back into the real world. Maybe not go back to what she was doing before. That had been great, but she didn't really miss it. Oh, she missed doing interesting work, and being around people who were passionate about their jobs. But the long hours, going home alone every night, that no longer appealed. Maybe she was simply too tired. But she needed to rebuild her finances, her security–

Sam finally spoke, without turning to look at her. "Do you want to know what I know about you?"

She glared at him. It shouldn't matter. She sighed and gave in. "Fine, I'm bursting with curiosity. Please tell me."

He grinned. "You're kindhearted and generous, because you gave up a year of your own life to help your sister and her family. She's your younger sister?"

"Yes."

"And you've always taken care of her."

Interesting that he would guess that. "Yes." She didn't resent it, though people sometimes thought she should.

He shot her a glance. "Who takes care of you?"

She stared at him. What an odd question. She was a healthy, single adult. She couldn't remember the last time anyone had taken care of her. At last she said, "I can take care of myself."

He smiled and nodded, as if he'd learned something more, but she couldn't imagine what. He said, "I also know you have nerve, because you're pursuing this treasure despite the people who don't want you here. And you're smart, because you asked for help."

She studied him, pondering what he'd said. Interesting that he would think of asking for help as a sign of intelligence. She knew she wasn't stupid, but she'd always thought her success was more a matter of hard work than being smart. "Asking for help is simply logical."

"Maybe, but plenty of people would struggle along on their own, or want to keep the whole treasure for themselves, no matter what. Look at Arnold – he only wants help if he can get it for free."

"He already has help," she grumbled.

Sam said, "So do you now."

She thought about what he'd said, glad they were in a car and not face to face. Compliments made her feel awkward, but she tried to consider his words rationally, as if hearing about someone else. She hadn't thought of helping her sister as kind or generous; it was simply necessary. But if someone else had done the same, what would she think of them?

A few years earlier, she might have thought the person a bit of a fool to give up a career to take care of someone else's baby. She was sure some of her coworkers had thought Rebecca a fool for her decision. But life was more complex than that. She'd done what she had to do to help her family survive. She hadn't been concerned with anyone else's approval, but it was still nice to get it from Sam. He really was sweet.

She studied his profile surreptitiously. He was cute, too, if you liked the laid-back type, which to her surprise, she apparently did. Too bad he was taken.

Or was he? She'd made that assumption on little evidence. She couldn't ask him flat out, but she might be able to nudge a bit, or find out from Erin.

Not that it mattered. She would only be in New Mexico for a week or so, and they'd be too busy to have a fling. Though she liked the sound of that word – fling. It sounded so playful, so free. She'd never had one before, unless you counted the time she had too much to drink at an office party and gave in to the advances of an equally tipsy coworker. It had taken them a week to figure out, with relief on both sides, that they were better off as coworkers and friends.

It didn't matter. Sam was being really nice to her, but that didn't mean he was attracted. It would be fun to have a safe little fantasy about him, but she would feel guilty if it turned out he was Camie's boyfriend.

Her gaze wandered down his arms to his hands on the wheel. She'd never seen forearms and hands like that, as if a sculptor had designed them to show every little muscle and tendon. She'd always been attracted to brains, but now she saw the appeal of a man who worked with his hands. She gave a little sigh. He would probably be really good at a fling.

She let her mind drift and enjoyed the scenery. Strange how she was able to relax here, despite all the things that should be stressful. Maybe it was a sign that she'd worn herself out so badly she had no choice. But she didn't think that was the whole story. There was something peaceful about New Mexico. The intensely blue sky, completely cloudless now. The rolling foothills with low vegetation, all muted tans and browns and greens. The distant mountains, not snowcapped and forbidding like the Cascades, but a soft reddish brown, the tops nearly flattened from erosion. And the traffic was nothing compared to the chaos in and around Seattle. Life really did move more slowly here. If only she could adjust to that rhythm, maybe even take it home with her when she left.

As soon as they reached Albuquerque, they left the interstate and headed west. Ten minutes later they were on Western Trail, pointing away from the city. They passed some newer developments and stopped at a light. The landscape ahead seemed almost empty of human presence, but a sign confirmed that the Petroglyph National Monument was ahead.

When the light changed, Sam pulled forward. "Let's start at the visitor center. I think there are a couple of different places where you can find petroglyphs, but we'll be able to get maps and brochures here."

They parked and headed to a low building nearby. Inside, Rebecca glanced around the shop while Sam chatted with the Park Service employee. She joined the two men as they leaned over a park map on the counter. Sam looked up at her. "There aren't any petroglyphs right here, so we have to drive to one of the trails. We have three options: Rinconada Canyon, Boca Negra Canyon, and Piedras Marcadas Canyon."

Rebecca nodded, though she wasn't sure how they were supposed to choose. While the employee described hiking times and what they would see on each trail, she eased the clue out of her bag.

Pass the mountain to the north

To where the ladies gather

Maybe one of the names for the trails offered a clue. She glanced again at the park map. The only word she recognized was "Canyon." A canyon sort of implied a mountain around it, but all three trails had canyon in the name. She smiled at the man behind the counter. "What do these trail names mean?"

"They're all Spanish." He tapped a finger on the map as he explained. "Boca Negra translates to black mouth. Rinconada refers to a corner. Piedras Marcadas means, essentially, marked stone. That's what the petroglyphs are, of course."

Hmm, no help. "What's this over here, Volcanoes?" That sounded strenuous.

"This is an ancient volcanic area. You can see it in the rocks; the black porous ones are volcanic. If you hike over there, you can visit several hills that are extinct volcano cones. But you won't see petroglyphs there."

Sam was still studying the map. "So if we drive north past *mountain* – I mean Montano Road – and keep going past Paseo del *Norte* ..."

Rebecca caught on and leaned next to him. "That takes us up to Piedras Marcadas Canyon. Hey, look, there's a Jill Patricia Street over there. What a coincidence."

The Park service employee raised his eyebrows as if waiting for her to explain, but when she only smiled, he said, "That's the one I'd recommend if you want a little more of a hike. You'll see hundreds of petroglyphs." He pulled out another map that showed a close-up of the trail. "It's six miles from here, and the parking lot is in this neighborhood. The trail is easy to follow from there."

The parking lot was right off Jill Patricia Street, and nearby streets were labeled Marna, Lynn, Shelly, and Rose. A gathering of ladies. Rebecca grinned at Sam. "Sounds perfect."

Back in the car, Rebecca compared the map and the clues. "The end is amazing, where people smile and dance, and rock. Hopefully that will make sense when we get there. It sounds like it could be referring to specific petroglyphs."

Sam flashed her a grin. "If it's all this easy, we could have your treasure in a couple of days."

She laughed, but her excitement was tinged with regret. She was actually starting to have fun. Would it be so bad if the chase lasted a little longer?

As Sam pulled the car forward, Rebecca glanced back toward the visitor center and caught a glimpse of a man who looked something like Rick Mason, Tiffany's husband. Then a bush blocked her view. She shook her head. The guy had only a superficial resemblance to Mason. No reason to think the others were so close behind them.

But it was possible, if they'd found the clue on the computer soon after Rebecca and Sam had left. If the chase lasted longer, Rebecca could miss out on a small fortune. She needed to stop daydreaming and focus. She'd gotten mentally lazy being out of work so long.

She went over the clue again but didn't make any breakthroughs. "The end" might suggest going to the end of the trail. At least the trail was only one and a half miles, and rated as "easy to moderate." Thank goodness she'd worn jeans and tennis shoes.

She waited impatiently as they drove past housing developments on their right, with mostly empty land on the left. Traffic was light, but the drive seemed to take forever. She glanced at Sam when they turned right and entered a busier part of the city. This did not seem like it should be bringing them closer to ancient rock art. But a glance at the map showed the route was correct, and a couple minutes later they were pulling into a small parking lot in a suburban neighborhood.

Sam cracked the windows, turned off the car, and looked at her. "We should have brought sunscreen and hats. I wasn't expecting to go hiking."

"I have sunscreen." Rebecca pulled it out of her bag. "I bought it the day I arrived, when I was feeling pink after half an hour outside." She applied it to her face, neck, and ears, and handed it to Sam.

He sighed. "I hate this stuff."

Rebecca hid a smile at the disgusted face he made while rubbing goop into his skin. The car was already heating up with the air-conditioning off, so she got out. Something moved at the edge of her vision and she glanced over her shoulder. A gray car with tinted windows had paused at the entrance to the parking area. It looked poised to turn in, but then the driver straightened out and pulled past, out of sight.

Strange. Her nerves prickled. Only one other car was in the lot, so this place must not get a lot of traffic. Maybe the driver had been lost, or wanted solitude and decided not to stop when he saw them.

She shouldn't go jumping at shadows. But maybe she would keep an eye out behind them, just in case.

Sam got out of the car. "Got your water bottle?"

"Oh, right." She retrieved it. It wasn't that hot out, really, until she remembered it was early May. It felt like Seattle in July. A warm July, too, not like the last one where she'd needed a sweater most days.

She drank some water and saved the last third of the bottle to carry along. She had the clue and the trail map as well. They headed up a sidewalk and a minute later passed a gate into desert scrubland. The soil was sandy, with low bushes and wildflowers. A hill rising on their right was covered with jagged black boulders, each a few feet across. Volcanic rock, Rebecca remembered.

They reached a numbered sign and paused. Rebecca glanced at the map. "I guess there's a petroglyph here."

"Several." Sam pointed.

Rebecca squinted. At first she didn't see anything. Then she tuned into the lighter marks on a black boulder twenty feet away. She couldn't tell exactly what the squiggles and lines were, but they were clearly not random. As she looked around, she spotted more and more petroglyphs.

Sam had moved farther down the trail. "Here are some humanoid figures. Kachinas, maybe."

Sure enough, one little figure had a circular head and was holding something – staff, sword, stick, she couldn't tell. Another small figure had a triangle-shaped head with straight lines sticking up like hair. "Kachinas, those are dolls?"

"They make kachina dolls, but they're also spirits. It impossible to say what the people who made these petroglyphs meant by them, but humanoid figures might represent gods or spirits." He shrugged. "Or not."

Rebecca glanced at the poem. "Where people smile and dance. Would you say those people are smiling?"

"Not really. I only see eyes, no mouth. And remember, there are about five thousand images along this trail, several hundred easily visible from the path."

Rebecca groaned. "If we have to look at every one of them …"

Sam leaned close and looked at the poem. "'The end is amazing.' Let's head toward the end. We can get an overview on the way, and if we don't find something at the end, we'll take a closer look as we come back."

They moved forward, but it was hard to hurry. Every few feet Rebecca wanted to pause and study one of the petroglyphs. There were so many! Handprints, geometric shapes, squiggly lines, and human and animal figures. The sandy ground was soft, and Rebecca was glad she'd worn sneakers. The wind kept the heat from being too much, but gusty breezes kicked up sand and sharp leaves from the scrubby little bushes. Rebecca paused to better secure her hair out of her face.

A woman with a shaggy tan dog on a leash passed them going back toward the trailhead. The woman smiled, and the dog gave a couple of friendly barks. They'd probably come from the other car in the parking lot. Once they were gone, Rebecca and Sam would be alone. She was used to a lot more people on any hiking trail, let alone one that should have been a major tourist attraction. Still, it was a weekday afternoon.

She glanced back the way they'd come. The city was spread out in a valley to the east, with a long line of purplish mountains beyond. She felt as if she could see forever.

The dog barked again, the shrill sound carrying clearly the couple of hundred feet to them. No, they wouldn't be quite alone after all. A man in a white shirt and dark pants stood up from behind a boulder. The sign had clearly said people were supposed to stay on the trail, but he must have gone up the hill to get a closer look. So many people thought rules didn't apply to them. She shaded her eyes and studied the man, but her view was mostly blocked by the woman with the dog. Hopefully she was telling the guy to obey the rules.

And hopefully Rebecca's grandfather hadn't been a rule breaker. What if they had to do something forbidden to reach the next clue?

"Let me see the map," Sam said. She passed it over. "We must be almost to the end. The two trails meet here, and there's less than a quarter-mile more after they join."

"And the end is amazing! At least, I hope so." They hurried forward.

A few minutes later, they reached a signpost marked "6."
Sam said, "I think this is the end of the real trail. It's hard to tell
for certain, what with animal trails and runoff channels and
places where people have gone off trail."

"The map shows the six at the end," Rebecca agreed.
"Though I have yet to find any of the petroglyphs they show in
the little drawings. Look, though – would you say that figure is
dancing?"

They stepped closer to a low boulder with a two-foot-high
petroglyph. The figure was either human or a humanoid spirit.
It appeared to be wearing a dress and a headdress and was
holding a long stick in one hand and an even longer staff in the
other. Below it a circle was split in half by a horizontal line, with
two dots like eyes above and a wider mark like a mouth below.

"One dancing, one smiling?" Sam said. "But with so many
images out here, it's going to be hard to say for certain."

Rebecca nodded and gazed at the other rock art nearby.
"There! I'm calling that a maze. *Amazing*, right?"

Sam shaded his eyes. "Oh, I see, on the shadowed side up
there. Huh. I can't quite make it out from here, but you're right,
it's much more like a maze than anything else we've seen." He
grinned at her. "From what I've learned about your grandfather
so far, he'd enjoy that kind of wordplay. What else do we have to
find?"

"'The end is amazing. Where people smile and dance.' I
think we have those elements. Next is 'and rock.' Everything
here is a rock."

Sam laughed. "I don't think that graffiti is five hundred
years old, but it fits."

She followed his pointing finger to some words scratched in
the rock: Redd Rocker. Rebecca rolled her eyes. "Definitely not
prehistoric rock art. But it does work with the clue. Next is
'These eyes have seen five hundred years.' That would be true
for all of the rock art here, more or less, except that modern
graffiti, right?"

"It doesn't seem too specific. What's after that?"

"Do not avoid their gaze, but meet it closely."

Their own gazes met and held. Rebecca felt a little
breathless. A gaze could certainly have power.

She pulled away. Her attraction to Sam was not helping her focus! Rebecca took a deep breath and reread the clue. "Meet it closely sounds like we're supposed to get close to one of the petroglyphs. But which one? And what are we looking for, anyway?"

Sam shrugged. "I guess we look around."

It figured. Apparently Grandpa wanted to drag her out of her comfort zone, and if she had to go off trail to explore, that would count. And if it turned out he scratched or painted the next clue on a rock in a national monument ... Well, at least he was dead.

She might as well start close. She could meet the eyes of several nearby petroglyphs without leaving the trail. She crouched and studied the eyes in one figure, then shifted to the left and looked at another.

Her feet slid in the sand and she tipped to her knees. She got a whiff of strange fragrance from a patch of weeds. The way the boulders had tumbled on this hill had created thousands of little hiding places among the rocks and plants. But so far, Grandpa's clues had been pretty specific – even if they only made sense once you got there.

Redd Rocker was to her left, the maze straight ahead and up the hill. The dancing figure and smiling face were on the same boulder to the right, a few feet off the path. She was placed as equally between them as possible. Of that group, the face was the only one that really had eyes to meet. She crawled toward it on hands and knees. She brushed past an innocuous looking bush and received several scratches on her arm from the sharp leaves. Sam had said something about the desert wanting to kill her.

She suddenly remembered rattlesnakes.

With her face about a foot from the petroglyph face, she glanced down.

Tucked among the rocks, out of sight from anyone passing on the path, was a metal box.

# *Eight*

Rebecca's hand shook as she reached for the box. It was a metal candy tin for peppermint bark. Maybe Grandpa had a sweet tooth? Or was this some random trash left by a tourist too lazy to bring it back to his car? She straightened and gazed down at the box. It had to hold the next clue. It would be too much of a coincidence – and too heartbreaking – if it were anything else.

She glanced at Sam and he nodded in encouragement, drawing close to her side. She swung open the lid. Several folded pieces of paper lay inside. A strip of masking tape on the inside lid had words in marker: "Take one and leave the others unless you are the last."

Rebecca pulled out the top piece of paper and unfolded it.

Are they witches in disguise
Or prophets of the future?
The men who came here didn't know.
They had destruction on their minds.
And they changed the world.
They ate of the flesh among bombers and bullets.
And so should you!

Then past the dead soldiers you'll find a dead end.
One is the loneliest number
Walled off from its fellows.
Pay your respects and do not forget.

Another baffling poem. Rebecca wrinkled her nose. "This one's kind of gruesome."

"No kidding. What about the other papers?"

Rebecca crouched by a handy rock – not one with petroglyphs – and used it as a table. She pulled out the papers one by one and skimmed them. "They all seem to be the same."

"We'd better double check to be sure. You read one and I'll follow along on another." They checked the five pieces of paper that way; all were identical.

"One for each of the grandchildren, I suppose. In case we weren't working together." Rebecca examined the box itself before returning four pieces of paper to it. Sophia would not be collecting her copy, but Rebecca couldn't see any point in taking it, and the note said, "Take one." Rebecca closed the box and stood.

For a moment, the world spun. She took a quick breath.

Sam's arm came around her. "Okay?"

Two more deep breaths and she could answer. "Fine now, thanks. Just a little lightheaded." She was tempted to lean into him, to relax against his shoulder. She resisted the urge. "I know, I know, drink water. Let me put this back."

She returned the box to its hiding place, picked up the bottle she'd set down while looking at the clue, and finished the water. Sam hovered closely, as if to support her if she needed help. She couldn't quite decide if she wished she needed help or was glad she didn't. She wouldn't fake helplessness, though, and the weakness had passed.

She gave Sam a bright smile. "All better now. I just stood up too fast."

He studied her intently. She hadn't realized how green his eyes were, or how the tiny laugh lines around them made him both sexy and approachable. Her heart thudded in her chest. *You keep looking at me like that, and I won't be fine.*

For a moment she was afraid she'd voiced the thought out loud. But Sam broke the silence instead. "Did it even occur to you that you could take every copy?"

"What?" It took her a moment to shift gears. She glanced at the box, hidden again for the next clue seeker. "No." She shifted uneasily. "Why, do you think I should?"

"I don't think you should do anything that will make it hard to live with yourself later. But I'll bet Arnold and Benjamin wouldn't hesitate."

That wasn't really an answer about how *he* felt. Her face heated. Did he think her a naïve fool? It wouldn't change her behavior. But it would change how she felt about him. "You're probably right. In fact, I'm sure you're right. But I won't play the game that way." She lifted her chin. "Even if it means I lose."

He dipped his head towards her and said in a husky murmur, "Good for you." His eyes sparked and his lips curved. Her heart skipped at least three beats before racing forward.

Their gazes held, and the air thrummed with awareness. He had to feel it too. She couldn't be imagining the spark between them. This was chemistry, so combustible it was ready to explode.

She wasn't ready for an explosion. She shifted away from him and gazed around at the scenery. "Now what?" Her voice came out breathy.

Sam pulled out his phone and glanced at it. "It's been a long day already, and we don't have time for another adventure like this. Let's head back and consult with the others and plan to get an early start tomorrow. We can walk back the long way and take a closer look at the other petroglyphs."

"Why, do you think there might be more clues here?"

He shrugged. "It's possible. Your grandfather did say he wanted you to get to know the state. Who knows, maybe we'll need to learn more about the petroglyphs in order to solve this clue, or a future one. But even if we don't, it seems like it's in the spirit of things to enjoy our visit."

Enjoy? Rebecca hesitated. On the one hand, she only wanted to get through this and get it over with, so she wouldn't have to worry anymore. Playing tourist could come later. On the other hand, how long had she been putting off enjoyment in order to get things done? And she was there. She had no guarantee she would ever be back. Besides, if she was going to earn her grandfather's treasure, maybe she should play by his rules.

She smiled at Sam. "Right. Let's explore."

She did enjoy the walk back. They took time to read the brochure and learn more about the people who had made the petroglyphs. To think that the rock art had been made 500 years before. What had the people been like? No one really knew what the petroglyphs symbolized. Rebecca and Sam had fun trying to identify some of them. A lizard, a turkey, and what they joked was a cow-bird.

She kept an eye out for the stranger, but he must have turned back earlier. An old couple passed them with a cheery greeting, probably locals since they didn't pay much attention to the petroglyphs. Sam pointed out a hawk soaring overhead. A small rodent rustled in the bushes. If it weren't for the backs of houses on one side of the open space, and the city stretched out in the valley below, she might have thought they were miles from civilization.

By the time they got back to the car half an hour later, she had dozens of photos on her phone, of the petroglyphs and the surrounding scenery. And if Sam happened to be in a few pictures, well, he was a part of this adventure she wanted to remember. He was so easy to be around. Despite the sexual spark, and despite the stress of the treasure hunt, she felt more relaxed than she'd been in ages. She'd actually had fun!

When they got to the gate near the parking lot, he stepped aside and put a hand lightly on her back to guide her through in front of him. She went ahead with a smile.

Theirs was the only car in the little parking lot. Rebecca's smile faded, and she came to a sudden stop.

Sam bumped against her and took her arm to steady them both. "What? Oh no."

The two tires on the side closest to them were flat. Deep gashes explained why. Sam rounded the car. He looked across at her with a frown. Rebecca already suspected what he'd found.

"This side too. We have four flat tires."

# *Nine*

Sam parked next to Erin and Drew's house. Rebecca dozed next to him, her seat partially reclined. Sam studied her in the fading light of dusk. He hated to disturb her. It had taken hours to talk to the police, get the car towed, and eat dinner while they waited for new tires. She'd tried to insist on paying for them, and he'd deflected her only by claiming that he was due for new tires anyway.

He did need new tires. In another year or so. But this wasn't her fault. Sam had wanted in on this ... whatever it was. It no longer felt quite like a game, or even simply an adventure. It was serious for the players involved, enough that someone was willing to commit a crime to slow them down. They both agreed, it had probably been one of her half-brothers, or the brother-in-law. Sam would bet on the latter – he'd taken an instant dislike to Rick Mason, Tiffany's husband. The man was too smooth, and the way he'd looked at Rebecca had rankled.

Whoever had slashed the tires, how far would that person go? Damaging a vehicle was one thing. If Rebecca had been alone, would the guy have confronted her? Found a way to slow her down physically?

His hands were clenched. He took a deep breath and relaxed.

Something moved in the window of the house. He ducked his head to get a clear view. The big orange cat, Tiger. Not someone wondering what they were doing, sitting in the car at dusk, like a couple of teenagers at the end of a date. Actually, the cat might be wondering – Sam wouldn't put it past him. But Tiger wouldn't ask questions.

Rebecca stirred and let out a faint sigh, her eyes still closed.

He'd have to wake her. Gazing at her face, sweet and vulnerable in relaxation, he was tempted to lean in for a kiss. But that would be creepy. A modern sleeping beauty would probably wake up with punches flying if some guy she wasn't dating woke her with a kiss.

He spoke her name softly and placed a hand on her shoulder. Her eyes fluttered open and she met his gaze. He couldn't see the color of her eyes in the dim light, but he knew they were brown, except when the sun hit them directly. Then the brown went almost amber, shading to green near her pupils.

Their faces were only a foot apart, and the car seemed to cocoon them off from the rest of the world. The moment grew heavy with possibility. Rebecca's chest rose and fell more rapidly. He still wanted to kiss her. He was pretty sure she'd let him, given the way she was looking at him now. But they'd known each other one day, and although they'd gotten to know each other quite well in that time, Rebecca had enough confusion in her life. She needed a friend, someone she could trust. Shifting their relationship now would only add tension.

Sam eased back. Moving those few inches felt like pulling himself out of a whirlpool. "We're home." His voice was husky, so he cleared his throat. "Erin's place, that is. Shall we go tell them what happened?"

She sighed. "That should only take a few hours." She sat up, ran her fingers through her hair, and gathered her bag. By the time Sam rounded the car, she was stepping out with her chin high and the steel back in her spine. She might still be exhausted, but she'd buried the fatigue and looked ready to go back to work – or into battle, if necessary.

Sam was on his second beer by the time they finished explaining everything that had happened. Even he was amazed, hearing it all laid out like that, and he'd been there.

Camie jumped on the worst news. "So we assume this guy you saw at the petroglyphs was the same one who slashed your tires, and is one of the Westin brothers or this Mason guy. That means they have the new clue as well, whether or not they found the first one on the computer."

"It's a safe bet," Rebecca said. "And they had several hours to follow up while we were dealing with the car."

Camie's eyes narrowed. "He made a mistake with that, though."

Erin frowned. "How do you figure?"

"Sam and Rebecca weren't trying to hide what they were doing, because it didn't occur to them that someone might be following them. They didn't take precautions. Now we know better."

Sam slumped lower in his seat. Tiger, sprawled across his lap like a twenty-pound pillow, grumbled. Sam preferred to assume the best of people, and deal with the consequences when he was wrong. That policy was coming back to bite him this time. He should have taken precautions. Camie probably would have, but then she was naturally suspicious.

"It almost makes me wish I'd taken all the copies of the clue," Rebecca said. "I'll bet they would have. But then ..." She looked troubled.

"Then you would be as bad as them," Sam finished.

Rebecca closed her eyes on a long sigh. She spoke softly, as if to herself. "If I can't do this and be true to myself, there's no point in doing it at all."

"Yeah, yeah," Camie said. "We'll take the high road, et cetera. But it's good to know what your enemy is capable of. From what you've said, I'll bet there was a backup plan anyway. Probably if someone stole the clue, the lawyer would have copies to give the rest of the group after a certain time. Sounds like your grandfather doesn't want someone to get a head start and leave everyone else behind. He wants everyone to stick with it, so he handicapped the race."

"That makes sense," Rebecca said. "So if we suspect they cheated, should we tell Mr. Ruiz?"

"I prefer to save the authorities for a last resort," Camie said. "If we get to a point where we're sure we should have found a clue, and it's not there, we can check with him. But there's no point in whining about what's past."

Sam studied Rebecca to see how she was taking this. Camie would take over if given half a chance, and Rebecca deserved to stay in charge. But she merely nodded. "That's why I didn't tell the police who I suspected of slashing the tires. For one thing, we have no proof, and it would be insulting to accuse them if we're wrong. For another, I didn't want to have to explain the whole story, and it doesn't make sense without doing that."

"I doubt the cops would have followed up anyway," Camie said. "Not if it meant going to Santa Fe and accusing respected, wealthy businessmen. Like you said, no proof, so what could they do about it?"

Rebecca nodded. "Anyway, I don't know how much a head start is going to help them. The clue is pretty complex, at least to me."

Erin and Drew were side by side on the couch, leaning over the latest sort-of-poem. "Witches or prophets," Erin said. "That's ringing some sort of bell. Let me look up a few things." She rose and wandered toward her office, muttering softly.

Camie leaned forward and plucked the clue out of Drew's hand. "Let me see that."

"It sounds awfully gruesome," Rebecca said.

"Something about dead soldiers and destruction." Sam was working from memory, and his memory was tired. "Los Alamos? White Sands?"

When Rebecca looked puzzled, he explained. "Erin could no doubt give you more detail, but Los Alamos is where they developed the atomic bomb. Still lots of military projects up there. White Sands is where they tested the bomb."

"Trinity Site," Camie mumbled, still bent over the clue. "That's where the bomb was tested. But White Sands is near there and they still do military stuff."

Drew nodded. "A lot of the airspace over White Sands is a no-fly zone, because of missile testing."

"That's right, you used to be a military pilot," Sam said. "What's your take on all this?"

"I have a couple of thoughts. The first is that these military places are restricted. You can get into Los Alamos the town, maybe some historic sites, but it won't be easy to get to the lab. Same with White Sands. It's a tourist attraction, right? But that's going to be different from the places that have active military action. You'd better hope this is talking about historical sites, because if you have to get onto an active base, you're in trouble."

"Trinity Site is only open once or twice a year," Camie said absently, her focus still on the paper. "We'd have to wait for the next open house."

"Surely my grandfather wouldn't have sent us someplace like that," Rebecca said. "Unless he really wanted us to take a long time over finding the treasure, a way to keep me in the state? But he couldn't know exactly when he would die, so planning the clues around rare events seems illogical. And I don't think – I hope – he wouldn't expect us to do anything really illegal, like break in someplace. So chances are Trinity Site isn't what we're looking for."

"Good point," Sam said. "Anything that narrows it down is a help. But this state is full of military sites, both active and historical. We could be going completely in the wrong direction. What about Civil War sites? Or Spanish or Native historical battles?"

Rebecca groaned, and Sam was sorry he'd mentioned the possibilities.

"Bombs and bullets sounds relatively modern," Drew said. "Especially the bombs."

"But wasn't there something about eating flesh?" Rebecca made a face. "Are there any stories of cannibalism?"

Drew chuckled. "If we're dealing with both bombs and cannibalism, I certainly hope that would narrow it down." He held out his hand and waited patiently until Camie passed over the clue. Sam suspected she had it memorized by now. Drew's gaze skimmed over the paper. "But there's one more thing that interests me. This bit about dead soldiers."

"A military graveyard?" Rebecca said.

"Maybe. But the term 'dead soldiers' can also refer to a bunch of empty beer bottles in a row. 'Bullets' is a term for beer as well."

Sam raised his beer in a toast to Drew. "Good catch."

"That's clever, but ..." Rebecca pressed her lips together, and then said apologetically, "I'm not sure it helps. New Mexico might have a number of military historical sites or graveyards, but there have to be even more places to get beer."

"Thousands," Sam groaned, his momentary elation at a possible breakthrough fading. "You're right, that doesn't move us forward." He pushed a hand through his hair. "Maybe it's time for some sleep. I can't think straight."

Erin came out of her office. "Found it!" She sat next to Drew and spread two books on the coffee table. He put the clue on the table and leaned forward next to her as she explained. "In Hispanic culture, owls are considered witches. I thought I remembered something like that. It's those big, round eyes, no doubt. They look like they could put a curse on you. But what's really interesting, what makes me think this is the right track, is that in Native American mythology, owls are seen as prophets."

Rebecca reached for the clue and studied it. "Are they witches in disguise, or prophets of the future? That does fit with owls. All right, so we have owls, a possible military connection, destruction that changed the world, and either real dead soldiers or empty beer bottles. I'm tired, too, but I can't blame my complete lack of understanding on that. I'm baffled."

Owls ... Beer ... All the things they'd been discussing swirled in Sam's head. He slapped a hand over his face and laughed. "You have to be kidding. It could not be that easy."

"Easy! How is any of this easy?" Rebecca's voice sounded ragged.

Sam looked at her and smiled. "I don't have the whole thing worked out yet. And maybe I'm completely wrong. But what are you doing for lunch tomorrow?"

# *Ten*

Rebecca stared at Sam, waiting for him to explain his joke, if that's what it was. He tipped back his beer bottle and then stared at it, as if baffled to find it empty. She had to smile. It comforted her to know he was tired too. She didn't think she'd ever been more exhausted in her life, but at least it was a good fatigue, born of physical and mental exertion, not anxiety and despair.

Camie said, "You really think it's the owl bar?"

Sam shrugged. "Does that make sense? Or am I hallucinating?"

*The owl what?* It took Rebecca a second to realize she hadn't spoken aloud. Even her voice was worn out

Drew said, "Let's go through it a step at a time. 'Are they witches in disguise, or prophets of the future?' Erin figured out that part; it seems to be talking about owls." He winked at his girlfriend. "Next, 'The men who came here didn't know.' Pretty vague. Didn't know what?"

Erin leaned closer to see the clue. "They probably didn't know about the meaning of owls. They would have simply seen the bar as a local restaurant."

Ah, so the Owl Bar was an actual bar with drinks, not something about stripes on owls or an owl holding a bar. Rebecca nodded. Good to get that cleared up.

"Fair enough," Drew said. "That brings us to 'They had destruction on their minds. And they changed the world.' Certainly seems to apply to the guys who designed the atomic bomb."

Erin snuggled closer to him. "They hung out at the Owl Bar while working down there," she explained. "And that gruesome line – 'They ate of the flesh among bombers and bullets. And so should you!' – It's not so gruesome if you think about the flesh being hamburgers."

"Bombers, bullets, and dead soldiers are all slang terms for beer," Drew said. "That seems like a pretty solid clue. But this last bit ..."

Camie rose and paced the room. "'Then past the dead soldiers you'll find a dead end. One is the loneliest number, walled off from its fellows. Pay your respects and do not forget.'" She made a face. "Could be something within the bar. We may not figure out that part until we get there."

Rebecca wasn't sure she'd followed everything, but the ideas seemed to make sense. Asking these particular people for help had been smart. "So–" She interrupted herself with a yawn. "I take it we have lunch plans tomorrow?"

Sam echoed her yawn and then said, "It could be a wild goose chase – wild owl chase – but fortunately the Owl Bar is only half an owl's – I mean hour's – drive from here. And at least we'll get a good green chile cheeseburger."

Rebecca made a noncommittal sound. Oh goody, more health food.

Camie frowned down at Sam and Rebecca. "Looks like you two need some sleep. Sam, you are not driving out to Magdalena tonight. Stay at my place. Got your key?"

He nodded and rose. Tiger slipped off his lap with a rumbling complaint. "Oops, sorry buddy. Forgot you were there." Sam gave Rebecca a rather sappy smile and brushed his fingers against her hair, a startlingly intimate gesture. Rebecca's breath caught in her throat. She gazed after Sam as he stumbled toward the door.

When she glanced back, Camie was studying her with narrowed eyes. Rebecca's face heated. Sam had a key to Camie's house. That had to mean something. But he'd barely acknowledged Camie on his way out, especially compared to how he said goodbye to Rebecca. That had to mean something as well, though maybe only that he was too tired and drunk to realize what he was doing.

Sam turned back and put his empty beer bottle on the coffee table. "Don't need this," he mumbled.

Drew got up with a grin. "I'll walk you to Camie's." The men left together.

Rebecca avoided Camie's gaze and cleared her throat. "I should get to bed as well."

Camie sat in Sam's vacated chair and leaned forward, her elbows on her knees. She glanced at Erin, then back to Rebecca with a smirk. "Not quite yet. I think there may be a detail or two you left out about today."

Tiger crouched in front of Rebecca and meowed. She pulled her hands out of the way as the big cat leapt up. He settled on her lap, purring, and she scratched behind his ears, glad for the distraction. Her face burned, but at least it looked like she was going to get her questions about Sam and Camie's relationship answered.

"I'm ..." Rebecca trailed off. What was she? Sorry? Only if Sam and Camie were dating, and in that case Sam was the one who should be sorry. Not interested? Ha, she wasn't a good enough liar to pull off that one.

"Sam is a great guy," Erin said.

Yes, he was. But he lived here, and she was only a visitor.

She hadn't expected to regret that. She'd had little interest in New Mexico, had only thought of it as one of those hot desert states like Arizona. Now she almost felt at home, as if she'd known this place, and these people, for years instead of hours.

Rebecca looked up at last. "I'm only here for a few days."

Camie snorted. "You can do a lot of things in a few days, believe me." She leaned back and drummed her fingers on the arm of the chair. "Whether you could get Sam to do them or not, I don't know. He's kind of a gentleman."

Erin looked amused. "Only you would consider that a bad thing."

Questions crowded Rebecca's mind. She focused on the one that seemed most important at the moment. "You and Sam, er, you aren't ...?"

"We dated for a while," Camie said. "Didn't work out. He's good in bed, though, so don't worry about that."

Rebecca's face was about to burst into flames. She did not need to know that, on so many levels. For one thing, she did not want to think about Sam and Camie having sex. And she really did not, at that moment, want to think about him being a good lover, because the fire in her face was spreading throughout her body.

She managed a breath. "So you're still friends." Duh, that was obvious.

Camie shrugged. "I know some people think it's weird to be friends with an ex, but unless they hold a grudge, what do I care? Sam and I were good as friends. We weren't so good as a couple. It's a small town, so we're going to see each other. Might as well be friends."

Good enough friends that he had a key to her house, Rebecca thought. Maybe Erin read her feelings, because she said, "I would have invited Sam to stay here, but you're in the guest bedroom. He lives half an hour outside of town, so sometimes it's easier for him to crash with one of us if he's here late."

Rebecca wouldn't have minded sharing the guest bedroom ... She shoved away the thought and tried to sound casual. "Sam was great today, very helpful in all kinds of ways." Did that sound like a double entendre? "I mean, he drove, he took pictures and video at the meeting, he helped figure out the clue, and he even noticed I was getting cranky from low blood sugar before I realized it. And he didn't get upset about the tires, he just took care of things." Wow, he really was amazing, when she thought about all that.

From the corner of her eye, she saw Erin and Camie exchange a glance. Both were smirking now. Rebecca realized she'd been gazing into space, probably with a stupid dreamy look on her face. She sat up straighter. Tiger grumbled and repositioned himself. "I really appreciate everyone's help. I couldn't do it without all of you."

"It's okay," Erin said. "No one's going to blame you for being interested in Sam."

"We just want the gossip," Camie said. "With Erin and Drew acting like an old married couple, there's not enough of that. I have to get my entertainment somewhere."

Rebecca stared at them. It wasn't really in her nature to talk about personal feelings. But then, she so seldom had the opportunity to do so. She liked the idea of having girlfriends who weren't so wrapped up in their own problems, or so busy with work deadlines, that they could actually listen to her. "I don't know how much there is to say, really. He's sweet, and he has such a nice smile."

She smiled remembering it. "And when we were at the petroglyphs, there was this moment ... Nothing happened, but we looked at each other, and it felt like ..." She shrugged. "I'm not explaining this well."

"No, I know exactly what you mean," Erin said. "That moment when something feels possible."

"That's it. But is anything really possible? Like I said, I'm only here for a few days, and we have so much work to do." Dare she tell them that she'd thought about having a fling with Sam?

"Don't worry so much," Camie said. "Let things happen and enjoy the ride. Anyway, it's not like you *have* to go back, right?"

Rebecca stared at her. She had simply assumed she would go back to Washington. Where else would she go? But she was tired of the rain, the traffic, the pressures. Even, truth be told, tired of her sister and brother-in-law. Tired of the expectations and being taken for granted. If she wanted to change her path, why not go someplace where all the choices were different?

But still ..."I couldn't move here to be with someone I've only known a few days. That doesn't make sense. And if we don't find the treasure in time, I'll need a job."

"We'll find it," Camie said. "Anyway, there are jobs in New Mexico. Maybe not a lot, but you don't know until you try."

"We're not suggesting you change your whole life for Sam," Erin said. "But maybe it's time to change it for you?"

It was too much. Rebecca couldn't think about all the possibilities. She was hardly used to having any choices, and suddenly it seemed like she had too many.

She didn't have to make decisions tonight. She took a deep breath. "I don't know. I'll think about it. Maybe I'd even like to talk it all out with you." She gave them a shy smile. "But right now I think I need to sleep on it. And tomorrow we get back to work on the treasure hunt." That had to come first. The other team must have the same clue they did and might already have solved it, including the mysterious last bit. And they were willing to play dirty.

If Rebecca found the treasure, it opened up a lot of options. How could she make choices, if she didn't know what the choices were?

She sat up straighter. "First we find the treasure."

# *Eleven*

They didn't wait until lunch after all, since Erin checked the hours and found out the restaurant opened at 8 a.m. for breakfast. Drew had to work, but the rest of them made the trip. They wouldn't arrive quite at opening, since Rebecca hadn't dragged herself out of bed until almost eight. Still, the small town of San Antonio, New Mexico, was a short drive away.

They took Camie's yellow Jeep. Rebecca sat in back next to Erin, listening to Camie and Sam debate the green chile cheeseburger as a breakfast food.

Had the other team figured out the clue? Maybe she would run into them at the restaurant. Or maybe they had already come and gone. At least her relatives lived a couple of hours away in Santa Fe, giving a drive-time advantage to Rebecca's team. Or did they live in Santa Fe? Grandpa's house was there, but Tiffany and the brothers might live somewhere else. How strange that Rebecca didn't even know where her half-siblings lived. Of course, even stranger that she hadn't known of their existence a few weeks before.

Rebecca turned to watch out the back window of Camie's Jeep. Sam had tried to check for cars following them the previous night, but it was dark and they had been so tired. He might have missed something. Rebecca would've missed one of those old volcanoes coming back to life, or Godzilla stomping across the road. She had been half asleep by the time they got to Socorro and remembered nothing until waking up to see Sam looking at her as if he wanted to kiss her.

She glanced toward him and heat flooded her. She took a deep breath to cool off and forced her attention back to the window. She needed to focus!

If no one had followed them last night, then the other team shouldn't know where Rebecca was staying. Let them figure out things on their own this time. She'd been naïve before, assuming everyone would play fair.

As they left the highway, Erin also twisted to look back through the mud-splattered window. "Anything?"

No cars got off right after them. "It looks like we're in the clear." Rebecca turned to face the front, feeling a little queasy from staring out the back as they rounded the big curve of the exit ramp. In less than a minute they were slowing down, passing a few buildings and then turning to park facing the Owl Bar & Cafe, a tan, stucco building. The town was even smaller than she'd imagined, a few buildings clustered around one intersection with a flashing light.

They entered into a short hallway with newspaper clippings on the walls and then turned through another doorway into the main bar. No windows let in sun, and the overhead lights hardly seemed to pierce the shadows. She had a vague impression of half a dozen booths with tall wooden backs, and on her right side a long bar with a tiny woman behind it.

Sam and Camie led the way to a back room which had more booths around the outside and a row of tables in the middle. They all slid into a booth, the fit snug enough that her arm brushed Sam's. The conversation about Sam from the prior night flashed into Rebecca's mind, but she quickly buried those thoughts. They had work to do.

A waitress brought menus, which fortunately included eggs and hash browns, green chile optional but not required. Rebecca was firmly against hamburgers for breakfast. They ordered and then Sam studied a framed paper on the wall. "In the 1940s, the bar started serving burgers to feed this new group of people claiming to be prospectors. They were really the scientists working on the Manhattan project. Must've been an interesting time."

Rebecca wasn't well versed in wartime history, and at that moment she was more interested in the present. She took a careful look around the room to make sure none of her relatives were hiding in a dark corner before pulling out the printed clue.

"Read it again," Erin suggested.

"'Then past the dead soldiers you'll find a dead end. One is the loneliest number, walled off from its fellows. Pay your respects and do not forget.'"

They all gazed at each other for a minute. Finally Camie said, "Huh. I guess we'll have to do some poking around and see if anything jumps out at us. After breakfast."

By the time the food came, Rebecca's eyes had adjusted to the light spread by hanging lamps with faux-stained-glass Budweiser shades, so it no longer seemed so dark. Various images of owls decorated the walls – photos, wooden carvings, macramé, and more. It was a good breakfast, even if the coffee wasn't quite what Rebecca was used to in Seattle.

They rose and began exploring. "Past the dead soldiers," Camie said. "If the dead soldiers are beers, maybe that's referring to the bar. The actual bar you belly up to, in the other room." She headed for it.

"How do you find a dead end in a building?" Erin asked. "As far as I know, there's only one entrance, so the whole building is a dead end."

Sam pointed to a nearby hallway. "There's nothing down that hallway except bathrooms, which makes a pretty good dead end. And that bit about one being lonely, walled off from its whatever. Could be toilet stalls."

Erin shook her head at him. "Trust a boy to come up with that one."

Sam grinned. "I'll check out the little boys' room."

"I'll take the ladies' room," Erin said. "I need to wash my hands anyway. They're sticky from that breakfast burrito."

Rebecca wandered through the building, studying furnishings and artwork on the walls, waiting for something to make sense but feeling fairly useless. *One is the loneliest number.* As much as she enjoyed her new friends, she wasn't part of their group. Nor was she part of her father's New Mexico family. She was close to her sister and brother-in-law, and she loved her new niece, but she wasn't part of their little family unit either. She couldn't even define herself through her job anymore.

Was her grandfather trying to tell her something? Warning her that her life path was leading to loneliness? Though how could he have known? It had to be a coincidence. Or her own tendency to over-analyze everything.

She leaned on one end of the bar, watching Camie farther down in deep discussion with the little woman behind the bar. In a moment they headed back to the kitchen. Rebecca wouldn't have had the nerve to tell strangers what she was up to, let alone poke around like that. Maybe she was alone because she didn't reach out enough.

Sam draped an arm lightly across her shoulders. "You okay?"

She nodded vaguely. They had chemistry for sure. Even better, she really liked and respected him – at least what she knew of him, which in reality wasn't much. Was she so lonely that she was imagining possibilities that weren't really there?

She shook herself out of her reverie and managed a smile. "Sorry. Just thinking."

"I didn't find anything useful back there," he said.

Erin joined them. "Nothing. Did anyone search the back room yet?"

"I wandered through it, but I wouldn't say I really searched it," Rebecca said.

"Maybe there's something hidden behind one of the owls," Erin muttered, turning away.

Rebecca sighed. "I don't know, random searching doesn't feel right. The last clue was pretty specific."

Sam nodded. "At the petroglyphs, he led us to exactly the right spot. The problem is, it only made sense once we actually saw what we were looking for."

"And I suppose I don't have enough evidence to make major conclusions about my grandfather's behavior. Still ..." Rebecca leaned on the bar. Her grandfather's comments resonated with her emotionally, but that could be mere coincidence. He didn't know her. She had to think like him, and that meant putting aside her angst about the meaning of life.

Sam glanced around the room and then said, "One!" When Rebecca only stared at him, he pointed. "This place has a tradition, people tacking dollar bills onto the walls. Once a year it's all collected for charity. Maybe there's a message on one of the ones."

That sounded promising. Rebecca followed him, but there wasn't really room for the two of them to study the patch of one dollar bills tacked to the wall, so she simply watched. "You said once a year. Do you know when?"

"No. Maybe recently, since there aren't that many bills here now."

Rebecca frowned. That could be problematic. Would her grandfather have risked his clue being taken down? He might have had some idea of when he would die, but cancer was rarely precise. A prediction of three to six months might turn into three weeks, or two years.

As Sam examined the money, she went back to the clue.

*Then past the dead soldiers you'll find a dead end.*
*One is the loneliest number*
*Walled off from its fellows.*
*Pay your respects and do not forget.*

Camie joined them. "Nothing. The owner doesn't remember your grandfather, or anyone asking for anything special like a place to hide things. There's a waitress who isn't here now, but it's unlikely Gramps told anyone here what he was doing."

Sam turned from the wall. "If there's a clue on these bills, I'm missing it. Some of them have names written on them, but nothing familiar. I'll take some pictures in case we want to study them or look up the names later."

Erin came out of the back room brushing off her jeans. "Nothing back there that I could find."

"What are we missing?" Camie grumbled.

Rebecca said slowly, "I think we're missing the point. This isn't an Easter egg hunt, where you search in the hidden corners. We have to decipher the clue."

Camie sighed. "That clue has been running through my head for the past hour. It hasn't helped."

Rebecca smoothed the paper on a nearby table. "Try looking at it instead of only hearing it or remembering it. There's a blank line between the part of the clue that got us here and the next part. What if that's important?"

Erin leaned over her shoulder. "Weren't we assuming the first part gets us here, and the next part is what we do once we're here?"

"Yes, but maybe not *here* here. It says 'Then past the dead soldiers' – like after we get here, we have to go past here." Rebecca shook her head. "I'm not explaining this well. What I mean is, maybe we have to go outside of this building to find the dead end."

Sam nodded. Camie shrugged. "Worth a shot."

They trooped outside and paused, scanning the area. They were on an intersection where the streets seemed to go on for some distance in each direction. Across the street was a produce shop, closed for the season, which according to the sign would be August through October. An art gallery stood on another corner. Not much else was visible besides a gas station, another restaurant, and a few houses.

"Maybe there's a dead-end street nearby," Sam said. "We need a map."

"I don't think the one in my Jeep will have enough detail of this town," Camie said.

"I'll pull one up on my tablet." Rebecca set her bag on the hood of the Jeep and powered up her computer. Soon they were crowded around studying a map of the area. "No obvious dead-end streets ..."

Sam laughed. "But there's a 'dead' end a block from here." He pointed at a cemetery on the map.

Rebecca groaned. "I don't know about my grandfather's sense of humor. Come to think of it, though, my dad enjoyed bad puns, so maybe it runs in the family." She checked the direction of the cemetery – farther down the street, away from the highway – and then put away her computer. "It's only a block, so we can walk."

She'd vaguely noticed a car pulling in a few spaces down. She glanced over as doors opened.

Out stepped Arnold, Benjamin, Tiffany, and Tiffany's husband, Rick Mason.

Tiffany spotted Rebecca first. Surprise flashed on her face, followed by ... could it be pleasure? But then she glanced at her brothers and looked down.

Arnold glared. "You! What are you doing here?"

Rebecca's stomach knotted and her mind went blank, but Sam gave them a friendly wave and a smile. "Enjoying a good breakfast at one of the state's premier tourist stops."

Arnold opened his mouth and then closed it again, frowning as if he couldn't decide whether to challenge them – they must be there because of the clue – or keep quiet in case they really didn't know the clue's answer included the Owl Bar.

While Benjamin stared and Tiffany fidgeted, Rick Mason stepped around the car with his toothy politician's smile firmly in place. "How nice that Rebecca is getting to see some of the state. What's next on your agenda?"

As if they would tell him! Rebecca gave him her meanest stare. Should she confront him about the slashed tires? She was ninety percent certain he was the culprit, but he was unlikely to admit it.

Sam draped an arm across her shoulders and said, "The Bosque Del Apache, of course." He gestured across the street, in a different direction from the cemetery. "Most people come in October for the cranes and snow geese, but the bird watching is good year-round. We want to make sure Rebecca experiences some of our New Mexico treasures before she heads home."

Mason gave a considering glance in the direction Sam had pointed and then turned aside, pulling out a piece of paper that had to be the clue. Did he really think they would hand him the answer like that? Or did he think Sam was making an excuse for them heading that way?

What was Sam up to? Misdirection was great, but they didn't want to go that way, and they were in a hurry.

"Well, enjoy your breakfast." Sam started ushering them into the Jeep.

Once they had the doors closed, Camie asked, "Where am I going?"

"Head toward the Bosque," Sam murmured.

Camie shrugged and backed into the street.

Were they really going touring? "What if they find the next clue?" Rebecca asked. "You know they won't leave any copies for us."

"We'll get there before them." Sam added to Camie, "Hurry, I figure we have about a one-minute head start."

Rebecca looked back. Her relatives were still standing outside of their car. Tiffany seemed to be arguing, her arms raised in exasperation. Rick grabbed the keys from Benjamin and gave a sharp look at the Jeep.

They rounded a corner and a building blocked her view. Camie said, "I don't think there are any roads that double back, and a bright yellow Jeep is hardly inconspicuous—"

Sam interrupted. "This road has a few sharp twists. Once we're out of sight, pull over. Rebecca and I will get out and hide. You keep going toward the Bosque. Once they're past, we'll head to the cemetery."

Camie nodded, and the Jeep sped down the narrow, winding road with a growl. Rebecca clutched her bag tighter, hoping no people or animals were crossing the street ahead. She hadn't even put her seatbelt on yet.

Camie skidded to a stop. "Go."

Sam jumped out of the car and pulled Rebecca out after him. Before she quite had time to process what was happening, he'd slammed the door and the Jeep sped away. Sam pulled her toward a building a few paces away and they crouched beside it. "If they go all the way to the Bosque and back, we should have half an hour. More, if Camie can keep them following her into the park."

No more than a minute later, a car sped by. "Only two people," Sam said. "That was Benjie on the passenger side. Could you see the driver?"

"No, but I saw Rick Mason take the keys as we were leaving."

Sam stood and drew her to her feet. "So Tiffany and Arnold stayed behind to work the clue. I'd like to say they don't have a chance of solving it, but they got this far. If they'd followed us, they would have been here an hour ago, so they solved it on their own. At least one person in that group has some brains, and at least one has no ethics. A dangerous combination."

Rebecca gazed at him. "Fortunately, more than one person in our group has brains. You planned all that in a matter of seconds. Do you do this kind of thing a lot?"

He wiggled his eyebrows. "Escape from evildoers alongside a beautiful woman? Only in my dreams."

She chuckled. "I'm hardly a Bond Girl."

He leaned closer. "You're better. You're the heroine here,

you know, and I'm the lowly sidekick."

Her face heated. "I'm hardly some kind of Lara Croft swashbuckling daredevil, either."

He peered around the building to check the road and then took her hand and led her forward. "It's just as well. Lara Croft has some moves, but I never got the impression she was very good with interpersonal relations."

The warmth moved from her face throughout her body. Did that mean he was interested in an interpersonal relationship with her? His hand was warm on hers. He didn't let go, so neither did she.

They walked back up the road that would take them to the cemetery. Now all they had to do was avoid Tiffany and Arnold, get to the cemetery, decipher the last bit of the clue, meet up with Camie and Erin, and get out of there. And then they would have to go through the whole clue-deciphering process again.

Rebecca grinned at Sam and gave his hand a quick squeeze. He had been right – treasure hunting was a lot of fun.

# *Twelve*

Sam tore his gaze away from Rebecca's face barely in time to avoid stumbling over a row of rocks edging the road. She was always cute, but when she smiled like that – wow! For a moment the fatigue and worry, the tightly-wound control, had slipped away, to be replaced by something startlingly like joy. A guy could get used to having a woman smile at him like that. In fact, he could make it his mission in life to get her to smile like that as often as possible.

Those were wild thoughts. She didn't come to New Mexico looking for a boyfriend. She needed kindness, support, friendship. He wouldn't do her any favors by pushing her into something more complicated, not when her life was so complicated already.

And yet ... Her hand was warm and smooth against his palm. His whole body seemed tuned to that point of contact. He shifted slightly and their fingers intertwined, as if the pieces of a puzzle had slipped into place. How could simply holding hands be so powerful? It was like being back in junior high, where being able to touch a girl – the slightest brush of skin on skin – felt like magic, like a gift.

They rounded a curve in the road and the Owl Bar came into view. No windows, fortunately, but if Arnold and Tiffany came out, they'd easily spot Sam and Rebecca. Then this convoluted dodge would be pointless. Sam needed to pay attention to what they were doing or risk screwing up this whole endeavor. Yeah, he'd really be a big hero if Rebecca lost her treasure because Sam was too busy thinking about the feel of her skin to pay attention to their surroundings.

He gestured across the road. "Let's cut across and get out of sight as quickly as possible."

Rebecca nodded and they jogged across that road, through the parking lot of a gallery, and north across the street until they were on the same side as the restaurant. If someone came out of the Owl and looked in the right direction, they might still spot Sam and Rebecca. But at least the trees that hung over the edge of the street offered some cover.

They walked quickly to the east, toward the cemetery. Somewhere during their jog they had stopped holding hands. Sam couldn't quite bring himself to take her hand again. The first time it had seemed natural. Now he was thinking about it too much to make any move natural.

They glanced back a few times but didn't see anyone leave the Owl. Two minutes later, they reached the cemetery and turned up the short dirt drive alongside it. A low wire fence enclosed an area about 500 feet on a side, less than a city block. The sign above the gate said San Antonio Catholic Cemetery. Only one person was visible, a middle-aged woman in jeans and boots weeding a plot close to the gate.

Rebecca and Sam exchanged glances and went in. They moved out of earshot of the woman before Rebecca pulled out the clue. They studied the last lines.

*One is the loneliest number*
*Walled off from its fellows.*
*Pay your respects and do not forget.*

By silent agreement, they moved slowly among the graves. Not only had the poem said to pay their respects, but it seemed right when walking among the dead. Several of the fancier graves were marked by almost-life-sized statues. One had to be the Virgin Mary. Another was a man in a draped robe holding a child. Jesus? Some saint? A few family plots were fenced in with decorative wrought iron. Other fencing was simple chain link.

Rebecca frowned slightly as she gazed around the enclosure. Several graves in a cluster were marked by what looked like two-foot-high houses. One even had a rectangle of fake grass in front, while another had a miniature latticework fence. This place was a far cry from the tidy marble headstones on acres of green grass most people probably thought of when they heard the word "cemetery."

Sam was used to the desert, which could seem barren until

you tuned into the signs of life. He was used to the particular mix of ethnic and religious influences. He loved the desert, the culture, the people. He'd been such an awkward kid growing up in Connecticut, never fitting in or understanding the usual social cues. New Mexico Tech had been filled with kids just like him. Sure, there were some rich kids with fancy cars, and even a few jocks, but most students were quirky geeks who made their own social rules. Moving to New Mexico had felt like coming home.

He paused, gazing down. In a patch of sand and scattered weeds, two headstones looked like they were molded from cement. One had a cross sitting on top of a heart; the other had only the heart with a piece of rebar sticking up, the cross tumbled beside it. The initials and dates looked like they had been drawn by hand when the cement was wet.

Rebecca had switched from her business suits to faded jeans and a T-shirt, but she was still a big city girl from the Northwest. This must seem like a foreign country to her. Probably one she wanted to get out of as quickly as possible. He wished he knew what she was thinking.

He decided to take the simple expedient of asking. "What are you thinking?"

"It's like with the petroglyphs. There are too many options for something that's alone. That fancy black marble monument is the only one of its kind I can see. The statues are all individual. And all these fences are walling off the graves from their neighbors."

Okay, so she was thinking about entirely practical matters. Good for her. "But a lot of the fences enclose family plots, so the graves aren't really alone."

Rebecca frowned. "I suppose you could argue that anyone dead and buried is alone. Though maybe it depends on your religious beliefs."

"Was your grandfather Catholic?"

"Yeah, I guess so. He was buried in a Catholic cemetery. But getting into religious philosophy seems a bit abstract for this treasure hunt. Besides, if this is a Catholic cemetery, there probably isn't anyone here who isn't Catholic."

Sam nodded. "And if there is, I don't know how we'd find them. Unless they're buried outside the cemetery, on unconsecrated ground." They both scanned the area around the cemetery. It was bordered by the dirt road on one side and the paved main street on another. The remaining two sides had thick bushes and trees growing close to the fence. They'd use up their lead time fast if they had to bushwhack through that. And if the others arrived as Sam and Rebecca found the treasure, their trick with the Jeep would be pointless.

"I'm having trouble picturing my sick grandfather trailblazing through all of that," Rebecca said. "Let's focus inside the fence first." She pointed at the miniature houses. "Those little dollhouse-type markers are walled off from their fellows. Or at least, they have walls. And maybe some of these fences only have one grave inside. We'll save time if we split up."

"I guess you're right." But he didn't want to move away from her. Talk about feeling like he was back in junior high. Sam turned away and headed to the southeast corner. He was such a geek. He'd thought he'd learned something about dealing with women in the dozen years since he first came to New Mexico as a college student, but apparently not.

No, that wasn't entirely true. He had learned that if you wanted something, you kept trying, even if you made a fool of yourself. Which you would, without a doubt. At least if he made a total fool of himself with Rebecca, she would go away and forget all about him.

Somehow that didn't make him feel any better.

Rebecca paused to take a good look around. The woman doing the weeding was hidden by the bigger monuments closer to the gate. Rebecca couldn't see anyone else, so she crouched to examine the grave markers that had reminded her of dollhouses. She tried to peek inside the little structures without touching anything. It was weird to be poking around people's resting places. But what choice did she have? This was all her grandfather's fault.

Not that the treasure hunt was all bad. She glanced at Sam, who was walking along a row of graves with his hands stuffed in the pockets of his cargo shorts. His faded T-shirt stretched across toned shoulders. Even his calves were muscular, not bulky but sculpted. A runner's legs, not a weightlifter's. He was like a model for an anatomy class, designed to show each individual muscle. No wonder she kept getting distracted!

She checked the last of the little houses and rose. Checking every potential hiding place would take all day. There were vases for flowers, loose headstones resting on the ground, and the occasional pile of fist-sized rocks that seemed random, but she had an uncomfortable feeling they might be marking graves as well.

Grandpa liked puzzles. He wouldn't want them to stumble across the clue through sheer luck, or even through hours of searching. And they might not have hours, if Tiffany and Arnold were half as good at solving puzzles as their grandfather was at designing them.

*One is the loneliest number*
*Walled off from its fellows.*

In the back corner of the cemetery, a decorative iron fence surrounded a small plot. She couldn't see any other graves nearby, unless they were hidden by the weeds. Alone? Rebecca headed for it.

She only saw one headstone inside the enclosure. From outside the gate, she couldn't read the name or date. Weeds grew both inside the fence and in front, blocking the gate. A huge, oddly-shaped cactus filled one corner of the enclosure. It looked like it was made of a bunch of prickly tubes stuck together, growing in a random mass five feet high. She couldn't resist reaching out to touch one of the hard, inch-long spines.

Sam stepped up beside her. "Cholla." When she raised her eyebrows, he explained. "The cactus, this type is called cholla. Very common around here. And very painful, so watch your step. Think this could be our spot?"

Rebecca studied the clue. "Pay your respects and do not forget. How do you think we do that?"

"Kneel? Make the sign of the cross? Pour a libation on the grave?"

Rebecca shot him an amused glance. "Guess we should've bought a bottle of whiskey at the bar. Kneeling makes sense. That's kind of like at the petroglyphs, where I had to get down to eye level to see the box hidden among the rocks."

"I'm not sure anyone has gone through the gate in years,

though." Sam lifted the latch and pulled the gate open. The mass of weeds that had seemed to be blocking the entrance slid easily out of the way. "Hey, I'm wrong! Look, you can actually see the grooves where this was opened, maybe not recently, but within the last few months."

Rebecca bent forward to look. "You really think grooves in the dirt would last for months?"

"We haven't had rain yet this spring."

That was perhaps the most shocking thing she'd heard all week. It was May! The Seattle area had had rain almost constantly since the previous September.

Sam placed a hand lightly on her lower back and ushered her through. "Careful with the kneeling. Everything in the desert bites or scratches."

"Prickly plants, prickly people," Rebecca mumbled. She glanced at Sam. "I don't mean you, or Erin or Camie. But my relatives." She crouched, keeping her knees off the ground. "It's too bad this place is so neglected. Oh! Pay your respects. Clear out the weeds?"

Sam laughed. "Brilliant. Except we don't want to make it obvious that this is the right spot, so we put them back when we're done." He poked at a prickly-looking mass with his foot. Like the weeds outside the gate, it appeared embedded in the ground but actually brushed aside easily, revealing a small box.

"And voilà."

# *Thirteen*

They exchanged grins. Something beeped and Sam jumped. "Text coming in." He pulled his phone out of his pocket. Rebecca grabbed the box and stood. Clue number three. Progress. Except she had no idea how many clues they had to find in total. Were they nearing the end or only getting started?

Sam swore and shoved his phone in his pocket. "Better hurry. They're on their way back."

Rebecca jolted. They'd only been in the cemetery ten minutes or so. "Already?"

"Benjamin and Rick must've gotten close enough to see that we weren't in the Jeep. Or else Arnold and Tiffany called them because they figured out the clue. Either way, the guys turned around, so Camie and Erin are headed back as well."

Rebecca pried open the box and pulled out a piece of paper. "Oh good grief. It's not even in English!" She handed it to Sam.

NE N JRPUJV TURTHQ GIRSQJ UM GURQ EDQ YUMWQJ DIRVQ SQQEV EDQ TIUHV IG EDQ MUMQ DQNJQJ VMNBQ

22 5-13-16-1-7-9 20-12-18-5 12-24 22 3-13-7-22-26 18-12-24-19-16-13 26-2-9-7 5-2-26 14-7-13-7 12-26 20-7-22-15-24 25-16-2 26-16 25-16-2-13 19-16-13-26-2-9-7

"These aren't words in any foreign language. Not enough vowels. Looks like a code or cryptogram. What about the other pages?"

She rifled through them. "They all look the same." Rebecca frowned at the copies. The other group was only minutes behind, minutes they'd gained by cheating, by destroying Sam's property and causing a long delay. And if that team had reached the cemetery first, no doubt they would have cheated again.

She sighed and closed the box with the other sheets of paper still inside. She placed the box on the ground and kicked the weeds back over it.

They squeezed through the gate and Sam pushed those weeds back in place. As they hurried through the cemetery, he said, "Not even tempted?"

"To take all the clues? Definitely tempted. But I'm not willing to stoop to their level." She stopped speaking while they passed the woman who was weeding near the main gate. Once on the dirt road, she added, "It's ego as much as anything. I don't want to be like them. And if I were alone, I don't know that I could resist the temptation to even the odds." She winked at Sam. "But since I have friends who have my back, I can pretend to be morally superior and still have a chance at success."

"A good chance," Sam said. "Karma pays people back in the end."

"Maybe, but sometimes the wait is excruciating!"

They paused at the main street and cautiously peeked toward the Owl Bar a block away. "I don't see anyone," Sam said. "Let's get away from the cemetery, in case they haven't figured out the clue. We can circle around the back of the bar and meet the girls at the gas station on the other side. But we'll be exposed for a block. You up for a jog?"

"I've been feeling like I need a run. Let's go."

It felt good to stretch her legs and get into the rhythm of a jog, even if it was only for a minute. They paused at the intersection to check for traffic.

The door to the Owl swung open. As one, Sam and Rebecca leapt forward across the street, angling to place a parked SUV between them and the door. They darted past the vehicle to the back of the bar. As Rebecca rounded the corner, someone shifted into view. That had looked like Arnold's shoulder, but he wasn't turned in their direction.

She stifled a relieved laugh as they trotted along the back of the bar. From the other side, they could see the little gas station, but Sam held her back and spoke softly. "We don't know if they're heading to the cemetery or waiting here for Benjamin and Rick. Better pause for a minute. I don't think they saw us."

"No, I'm sure not." Rebecca leaned against the wall, breathing hard, more from adrenaline than the exertion. It was getting warm as the sun got higher; she plucked at the front of her shirt to get a little airflow. "Now what?"

"I'll text Erin that they should meet us at the gas station." He kept talking while he did so. "If anyone asks, we've been buying fudge."

"Oh sure, that's believable."

He grinned. "It is if you know the area. That gas station is famous for its homemade fudge."

"Huh, learn something new every day." She glanced around the back parking lot. No one had come after them. "I'd like to know what the others are up to."

"Should we do a little reconnaissance?"

She nodded, and they crept around the side of the building, between the bar and the gas station. At the front corner, Sam gestured Rebecca to take a peek. Nice that he trusted her and wasn't trying to take over "the fun." She leaned forward slowly, scanning the parking area in front of the bar and across the street ahead. Arnold and Tiffany were near the front door, about 25 feet away.

She pulled back and whispered, "They seem to be waiting."

Sam frowned over that for a moment. "They might have solved the clue and be waiting for Benjamin and Rick. Or they might be stuck, or on the wrong track."

"I think we can assume they're not giving up." She gestured with her chin. "There's their car."

Rick and Benjamin pulled up. Sam took Rebecca's arm. "Come on, while everyone is distracted." They trotted to the gas station and went inside.

Rebecca peeked out the door, while Sam spoke to the sales clerk. The yellow Jeep turned past the bar and pulled up in front of the gas station. Rick got out of his car and stormed toward the Jeep as Camie and Erin got out. Trouble coming?

Rebecca glanced over her shoulder at Sam, who was handing money to the sales clerk. If Rebecca's "family" wanted a confrontation, she preferred not to do it in front of strangers. She stepped outside.

Rick glared from Erin to Rebecca. "What's going on? What trick is this?"

"What do you mean?" Rebecca spoke as pleasantly as possible.

"Them driving off! Where were you?"

"Buying fudge. I hear it's really good."

Camie came around the front of the Jeep so the three women stood shoulder to shoulder. Tiffany hurried toward them but hung back about ten feet. Benjamin and Arnold were watching from farther away.

Rick moved closer to Rebecca, his fists clenched. "Don't play games. You made us think you were still in the Jeep."

Rebecca resisted the urge to back up. The building was close behind her anyway. "I made you think? I didn't realize I had that kind of power over you."

Camie added, "Thinking's not so bad, once you get used to it."

Rick let out a wordless growl. Rebecca heard the door creak open behind her and shifted aside, never taking her eyes off the threat in front of her.

Sam came out, holding a white box. "Who wants fudge?"

Rick pulled back his arm and swung.

Someone screamed. Rebecca instinctively ducked sideways.

Sam jerked back, but the punch caught him across the chin. He staggered back and slammed into the closed door, and then he slid slowly to the ground.

Rick loomed over Sam, his face flushed and shoulders hunched in anger. He pulled back his foot for a kick. Sam slumped against the door, blinking up at him, the box of fudge crumpled in his hand.

They had to stop Rick. But how? Rebecca felt trapped in slow motion. No time to think, no time to plan.

Camie took two fast steps, twisted, and kicked out. Her foot plowed into Rick's stomach. He grunted, folding at the waist as his body jerked back several feet. He landed on the pavement in a groaning heap.

Tiffany still stood ten feet away, her eyes wide and both hands over her mouth. Arnold and Benjamin hurried toward them.

"In the Jeep!" Camie said.

Rebecca shook herself out of her stupor and grabbed one of Sam's arms while Camie got the other. They hauled him to his feet as Erin opened the vehicle's door. Moments later they had all tumbled in and Camie was peeling out of the parking lot.

Rebecca looked back. Rick was sitting up, Arnold and Benjamin looking down at him. Tiffany watched the Jeep pull away. For a moment her gaze met Rebecca's. And then the figures faded in the distance.

They neared the on-ramp to the highway. Camie said tightly, "Seatbelts on?"

Rebecca fastened hers and then helped Sam, who was fumbling with his. "Are you all right?" she asked.

"He hit me." He sounded more astonished than angry.

"I noticed." Rebecca managed a small smile, though her chin trembled. "I bet it hurt."

Sam rubbed his jaw. "Yeah. He hit me." He shook his head. He looked at her. "I've never been punched before."

"Really? I thought boys grew up fighting."

"Wrestling at recess, maybe, but no one's actually punched me in the face before."

Rebecca gently pulled his hand away from his jaw. "Let me see." She ran her fingers over his jaw and chin. Sam's eyes closed and he let out a little murmur. "I'm sorry," she said. "Does it hurt? Where did he get you?"

He put his hand over hers and shifted slightly so her fingers brushed his chin just off center. "There." His eyes opened and a mischievous glint entered his gaze. "Are you going to kiss it better?"

She chuckled, leaned forward, and placed a gentle kiss on his chin. She hovered there a moment, inches from his lips. His breath brushed past her cheek. She slowly pulled back. "Did that help?"

Sam cleared his throat. "It gave me something else to think about, anyway."

Camie said loudly, "I'm glad you're not hurt. Now are they following us or what?"

Rebecca looked out the back window. "I don't see them."

Sam ran a hand through his hair and seemed to pull himself

together. "They haven't been to the cemetery yet. They've probably figured out that we've found the next clue, so their choice is to follow us or follow the clue. I'm betting they'll follow the clue."

"What's our choice now?" Erin asked. "We should have called the police and had that man arrested for assault."

"We still could." Rebecca glanced at Sam. "Do you want to? That was totally unprovoked."

He frowned and shook his head. "It might slow them down, but it would slow us down too. Or me, anyway, while I answer questions and file a report. I hope you're not willing to sacrifice me that way. And to tell the truth, I don't really want to explain to a couple of tough police officers how I got laid out flat with one punch."

Camie glanced back. "Yeah, what's up with that?" Her voice held amusement. "I thought the hero was supposed to knock out the villain in a single swing, not the other way around. You sure you're on the right side?"

"Hey, he took me by surprise! I've never been punched before."

"Oh, right, right," Camie said. "I think I heard that somewhere."

Rebecca took Sam's hand. "I'm glad you didn't fight back. It wouldn't have helped anything to have you going all macho on us."

"Yeah." Erin twisted to look back at them. "Rick had enough testosterone for the both of you." When Sam quirked an eyebrow, she flushed. "I don't think I meant that quite the way it came out."

Sam chuckled. "Don't worry, my fragile male ego is intact. But just for the record, I've never–"

The women all joined in. "–been punched before."

"So I guess we go home and figure out the next clue," Camie said. "You did get the clue, right?"

"We got it," Rebecca said. "Grandpa threw in a twist, though. It's some kind of code."

"Oh, sounds like fun," Camie said.

Sam leaned back and closed his eyes. His palm was warm against Rebecca's, and he rubbed his thumb gently over her knuckles. She wasn't sure what this was between them, or what it could be. But for the moment, it felt good. She studied his profile and wondered how much pain he was in. It wasn't only the punch; he'd slammed back against the door and then hit the ground as well. And was he feeling more humiliated than he'd let on?

She tried to think of something to distract him. "Do you know what I find interesting?"

Camie said, "That Rick wound up hitting Sam, when for a second there I was sure he was about to hit you?"

Sam's hand tightened on hers, and his mouth thinned.

"I'm trying not to think about that," Rebecca said. "Though, sorry Sam, I have to say I'm grateful it worked out this way instead."

He opened his eyes enough to give her a sideways glance. "Me too. Because if that had happened, I don't know what I would have done. I've never hit anyone else before, either, but that would make me want to."

"Let's not think about it," Rebecca said. "It didn't happen. No, what interests me is Tiffany's reaction."

After a pause, Erin said, "She didn't exactly rush to her husband's side. That goes with what you said about your first meeting with them. Not a happy marriage."

"Could be shock, though," Camie said. "She didn't rush to stop him either."

"I feel sorry for her anyway," Erin said.

The others murmured in agreement. Then Camie said, "You know what else I noticed? Sam managed to hold onto the fudge. Guess he's a hero after all. You going to share?"

He passed the box around. It was good fudge.

They parked in Camie's garage and walked through back alleys to Erin's house half a mile away. They hadn't been followed home, but Socorro was a small town, and they didn't want to chance the other group spotting the Jeep parked outside at Erin's.

Sam's chin was starting to bruise by the time they settled in the living room with glasses of iced tea and a bag of frozen peas for Sam's face. He insisted he was otherwise unhurt, and his eyes were clear and focused.

Camie said, "Let's see this clue. You said it was some kind of code?"

As Rebecca passed it over, Sam said, "I'm thinking a cryptogram."

Camie studied it. "That's one of those puzzles where each letter stands in for a different letter, right? I'm more of a videogame girl myself."

"Give me a Sudoku," Rebecca said.

"If I had to choose a puzzle, I'd take a crossword," Erin said, "but I'd rather read a book."

Sam held out his hand. "I guess I'm up then."

"You sure you feel up for it?" Rebecca asked.

"Sure." His smile looked more natural. "A nice quiet activity is exactly what I need. That and a pencil."

Erin fetched a pencil and a blank piece of paper. Sam grabbed a book to use as a table. "Okay, we have a one-letter word. That has to be an *I* or an *a*. Assuming Grandpa is playing fair."

Rebecca groaned. "I don't know if we can count on that."

"We might as well start with the assumption, until proven wrong," Sam said. "Two-letter words are helpful as well. There are a limited number of options, such as *an*, *to*, *in*, that kind of thing. So the first words, NE-space-N, will be something like *If I* or *At a*. And of course a three-letter word has a good chance of being either *the* or *and*."

"You really do know these cryptograms," Rebecca said.

Sam shrugged. "I did them a lot when I was in junior high. Haven't done one in ages, but it'll come back to me."

They were silent for a minute. Camie started tapping her foot. "I'll bet there are computer programs that can solve a cryptogram in seconds."

Without looking up, Sam said, "That destroys the spirit of the game. This will only take a few minutes."

"Fine. Anything the rest of us can do?"

Sam shot her a grin. "Be patient and be quiet."

Camie let out a theatrical sigh. "Sure, give me the hard job."

"Maybe we should go into the kitchen and ... think about lunch," Erin said.

Sam murmured agreement without looking up. Rebecca

shrugged. It had only been an hour since their substantial breakfast, but she couldn't think of anything more useful to do at the moment.

The three women gathered in the kitchen. "We really going to talk about food?" Camie asked.

Erin pulled out a chair. "I thought we'd leave Sam in peace. And maybe ask again if we should be doing something more about that Rick Mason guy. He's dangerous."

"You're not wrong, but what can we do?" Rebecca sat with her elbows on the table and rested her chin on her hands. "Even if we convince Sam to file a complaint against him, he could claim that Camie attacked him, too."

"Guy like that won't want to admit getting his tail kicked by a girl," Camie said.

"True," Erin said, "but I still don't like knowing he's out there. If he's the one who slashed your tires, which seems likely, and now he's hit Sam – Rebecca, you need to be very careful about going anyplace he might find you alone."

"No worries about that!"

"He has a short temper," Erin added. "The question is, will he escalate? Getting his tail kicked by a girl might cause him to act out even worse, to get revenge. Or take out his anger on someone else. Someone he thinks is weaker." They contemplated that for a moment.

Rebecca cleared her throat. "Can I just say how grateful I am not to be alone in all of this? I shudder to think what might have happened if I'd been by myself at the petroglyphs with him. And I'm doubly grateful for the place to stay as well. Someplace where he can't find me."

"We'll have to make sure of that," Erin said. "Does he know who I am, or Camie?"

Rebecca thought back. "I don't see how. We didn't introduce you today, and I don't think we've mentioned your names before. And I think Sam only introduced himself by his first name."

"Good. The more privacy the better." Erin gave a sharp nod. "That man is a bomb waiting to go off, and I feel really sorry for his wife."

"So do I." It was too bad she and Tiffany weren't close

enough that Rebecca could actually do something about it. Help, offer support, encourage Tiffany to get out of the relationship. It had sounded like she wanted to leave him, but would she be strong enough to do it on her own, when even her brothers didn't support her? Rebecca sighed. Family was complicated.

Camie turned a chair around and straddled it. "You know what we should do? Write down exactly what happened today. Each of us in our own words. Then we'll have a record if it comes to talking to the police or whatever. Write it down now, before we forget or things get muddied."

"Good idea." Erin got a tablet of paper and some pens from her kitchen drawer. She tore off pages and passed them out.

Camie put down her pen five minutes later and rose to pace the small room. Erin and Rebecca wrote for a few more minutes. Rebecca was finishing up when Sam strolled into the kitchen.

He grinned. "Who wants to hear the next clue?"

# *Fourteen*

Sam watched Rebecca's face light up. Okay, so maybe he couldn't knock out the bad guy, but if he couldn't be a knight in shining armor, at least he could be a geek with sharpened pencil.

Music came from the other room. "Someone's phone is ringing."

Rebecca popped up. "That's mine." She gave a lingering glance at the paper in his hand before hurrying out.

"Let's see it," Camie said.

He hesitated. It seemed like Rebecca should see the clue first. But Camie plucked it out of his hand and read.

"At a druid's circle, formed in fire, the winged horse meets the coils of the nine-headed snake. A broken limb is a great misfortune, but here it leads you to your fortune." She made a face. "Oh, that's helpful."

"At least it makes sense grammatically, so Sam must've solved it right." Erin added quickly, "Not that I doubt you, but we didn't even know if it was a cryptogram."

"Sure." He gave her an absent smile. Rebecca's voice grew louder in the living room. Sam couldn't catch the words, but she sounded upset or annoyed. Should he give her privacy or check on her? He took a step toward the hall, debating.

Erin said, "It would be helpful if we knew Grandpa."

"How do you figure?" Camie asked.

"Well, for example, say there are five or six clues around the state. Or ten, or whatever. Is he the kind of person who would put them in a logical order, with the shortest distance between each one? Or would he send people back and forth randomly? If it's the former, that's a clue in itself. He went from Santa Fe to

Albuquerque to down here, so this clue probably leads us farther south, or else east or west, but there isn't as much in those directions. It would be less likely we'd have to head north again."

Rebecca's voice had faded to a low rumble but still sounded tense. He could go in and catch her eye, see if she looked like she needed anything. As he reached the archway to the living room, Rebecca shoved her phone back into her bag.

"What's up?"

She scowled. "Mr. Ruiz wants to meet with us. Today. Now."

"Us meaning ...?"

She led the way back to the kitchen. "My half-siblings and Rick Mason and me." She looked at Camie and Erin. "He didn't mention you, so I guess you're off the hook."

"What's going on?" Erin asked.

"That was Mr. Ruiz, the lawyer. Someone told him about our 'altercation.' He's calling us in to discuss the matter."

"Any chance he's going to come down hard on Mason?" Camie asked.

Rebecca shrugged. "He only said that Grandpa wouldn't have wanted things this way, so we have to decide what to do next. I get the impression he might call off the whole thing."

"No more treasure hunt?" The idea hit Sam hard. What would become of Rebecca if she couldn't get the money? Would she leave right away? Would he never see her again?

"I guess. Though come to think of it, could he stop it? He'd have to get to the clues before we did – no, I suppose if he knows where the final treasure is, he could go there and retrieve it." She sighed and turned to Sam. "I said it wasn't fair to make us drive all the way up to Santa Fe, so we're meeting in Albuquerque." She looked suddenly uncertain. "Or I am, anyway. I shouldn't have assumed ..."

He brushed a hand down her arm. "You can assume. Of course I'll go along." The relief and pleasure on her face made him feel ten feet tall.

Erin rose and plucked the clue from the table. "I'll make a copy of this." She headed toward her office, calling back over her shoulder, "Camie and I can work on it while you're gone."

Camie nodded. "Don't panic. Your job is to convince the

lawyer to let the treasure hunt continue. It would be nice to kick out Mason, but not if it means you lose your outside allies as well. We'll solve this clue and be ready when you get back."

"Thank you." Rebecca didn't look entirely convinced, but Camie's confidence was enough to bolster anyone.

Erin returned with a photocopy. Rebecca glanced at it, shook her head, and shrugged. "Druids and winged horses? I can't even think about this right now." She slid the clue into her bag and pulled out another piece of paper. "I have the address where we're supposed to meet at one o'clock."

Sam studied it. "Okay, I guess we should get on the road."

"Maybe I should drive, since you hit your head."

Sam studied her. She was agitated and distracted, not good qualities in a driver. "Honestly, I'm fine. I've had a concussion before – two of them, actually – and this isn't one. I get knocked around worse every time I go mountain biking."

She nodded and they headed for his car. Rebecca was silent, frowning over her own thoughts, as they drove through town and got on the highway. Sam wanted to say something to help, but what? He knew from experience that women didn't always like it when you tried to solve their problems. Camie had gone ballistic whenever he'd offered advice, which was one reason they'd only dated for a month. But Rebecca wasn't Camie, or any other woman. In some ways, he felt like he knew her shockingly well, considering it had only been a couple of days. In other ways, he didn't know her at all.

He gave a mental shrug. Trying something was probably better than doing nothing. He could ask questions and listen, if nothing else. "What's bothering you the most?"

She twisted in her seat to gaze at him, eyebrows drawn together.

Apparently he needed to be a bit more specific. "Is it the delay? Fear of losing the treasure? Or just that Mason is such a jerk?"

"Honestly? I'm afraid you're going to be in trouble."

"Me?"

"We know that Rick's attack was completely unprovoked. You never took a swing at him. And Camie was acting in self-defense, or at least defense of the rest of us. But what if Tiffany,

Arnold, and Benjamin say otherwise? What if Mr. Ruiz says we can't have outside help anymore, that only the direct descendents can continue? Even if that gets rid of Rick, they'll have a big advantage over me. I can't do this alone."

Sam wished he weren't driving, so he could take her in his arms. "You could, you know, if you had to." Much as he wanted to be needed, telling her she needed him wouldn't help, and wasn't true.

She gave a crooked smile. "Fine, I don't *want* to do it alone. When you first talked about a treasure hunt being fun, I thought you were nuts. But it has been fun." She looked away and mumbled, "With you."

It was probably good she had turned away and couldn't see his goofy grin. "It'll be all right. Mr. Ruiz seemed to have sympathy for you, and I'll bet he's not fooled by Mason's fake charm. Plus, we have the police report from the slashed tires. It's still here in the car."

She settled back in her seat. "You're right. There's no point in worrying about something before it even happens. I know that logically." She sighed. "I've gotten too much in the habit of worrying about everything."

"You need a vacation. A real one, not all this running around with high stakes." Sam tried to sound casual. "You should stay for a week or two after this is over. See the sights in a more leisurely manner."

"I'd like to ... I guess it depends on how all this works out. If I get the treasure, I'll have more freedom. If not, I'll have to find work fast."

"It wouldn't cost much to stay here a while longer. Erin will be happy to have you stay, or Camie ... or me."

A tension hung between them, from things said, and things left unsaid. Had he gone too far?

Finally Rebecca answered. "Thank you. I'll think about it." She laughed. "I have so many things to think about! For the moment, I'm going to stop worrying about next week, or tomorrow, or even today's meeting." She pulled Sam's translation of the latest clue from her bag. "But I will think about this. Because maybe I can actually do something about it."

She shot him a shy, sideways glance. "And because maybe it

will be fun."

He grinned. "Read it to me again. I was so excited to solve the cryptogram that I didn't really process what the clue was."

"The first part is: At a druid's circle, formed in fire, the winged horse meets the coils of the nine-headed snake."

"Awfully mythological for New Mexico. Sounds more like England or Greece."

She nodded. "But we already decided we weren't supposed to go out of state, probably. Certainly Grandpa wouldn't have sent us to other countries. I hope."

"Okay, let's take it one step at a time. That's worked so far."

"A druid's circle. That's like Stonehenge, right? A bunch of stones in a circle? Is there something like that out here?"

Something tugged at Sam's memory. "I think I've heard of some kind of henge thing, not stones but an art installation. Or maybe I'm thinking of the Cadillac Ranch, with a bunch of cars sticking out of the ground. But that's in Texas."

Rebecca pulled out her tablet. A few minutes later, she said, "All right, searching for henge plus New Mexico came up with Fridgehenge or Stonefridge. That sounds like a possibility."

"That's it! A bunch of refrigerators in a Stonehenge formation."

"Oh, but it's gone. Taken down a few years ago. I suppose it could still be part of the clue." She searched a bit more. "I don't see anything about winged horses or snakes there, though."

"Some formation of stones in a circle, like those volcanic hills up by the petroglyphs? Lots of volcanic remains in New Mexico, some of them national parks, I think. That doesn't narrow things down much."

"I'll check." Some time later, she said, "Nothing relevant at Capulin Volcano National Monument, or the Valley of Fires lava flows, or any of the other volcanic areas in the state."

"All right, moving on. Winged horses – that's Pegasus, right?"

"Right. I'll double check to make sure there aren't any others, but that's the famous one. Let's see ... There's a legal services company called Pegasus. And a tech company that's building a ghost town. Odd, ghost towns seem like they should be made through natural decay, not built. That would be a good place to hide a clue or a treasure, though. Except it looks like it never actually happened."

She continued searching, occasionally mumbling something. The drive up I-25 was easy, a straight shot with little traffic, so Sam had nothing to do but think. At least Rebecca had a distraction now. She might worry, but that didn't keep her from tackling problems head on. If she did need a job, any company would be lucky to get her.

Was anyone hiring in Socorro? Between the college and the associated research groups, they needed a lot of computer people. He'd have to ask about her specific skills and interests. Local jobs didn't exactly pay a competitive wage compared to Seattle. But it was cheaper to live in small-town New Mexico. And you couldn't beat the weather.

When he realized he'd spent fifteen minutes trying to convince her of the benefits of New Mexico in his own mind, he stopped. Talk about worrying about the future, rather than focusing on the problem at hand. He should be trying to solve the clue.

Rebecca pushed her hair back from her face. "All right, it looks like Pegasus is definitely the winged horse, and a nine-headed snake probably refers to Hydra, a mythical monster that Hercules fought, unless it's a group of comic book villains or one of several technology things. Given that both Pegasus and Hydra have mythology references, I'm going with that. But what Greek mythology has to do with New Mexico, I have no idea. I thought maybe a museum exhibit or statues, but I can't find anything that fits."

"Hmm, there's a place to the west of Socorro called the Enchanted Tower. It's a rock climbing area, but all the climbs have names based on fairy tales. Like Sleeping Beauty Wall has climbs called Poison Apple and Glass Coffin. I don't think there's anything from Greek mythology, but I could be wrong."

Rebecca considered a moment. "It's an interesting angle, anyway. Even if that's not the right place, it shows how names and ideas pop up where you wouldn't expect them. Seems like the kind of thing Grandpa would have liked."

"You should be able to find a climbing guide to the Tower online."

She focused back on her tablet. "I'll check it."

Nothing appropriate turned up there. They tossed around a few other ideas but hadn't come to any solid conclusions by the time they reached Albuquerque. Rebecca started to fidget as they neared the law offices for the meeting.

"We have a few minutes," Sam said. "How about a snack?"

Rebecca chuckled. "You know me too well. A latte and some food are exactly what I need before facing everyone."

They found a café. Sam called Camie to check on progress in Socorro. They hadn't yet figured out where the clue led, but at Sam's mention of rock climbing, Camie said she had an idea. He also used his phone for a quick check of his e-mail messages. Shoot, something had come up at work that he would have to deal with ASAP. He'd been hoping they could survive the week without him. He worked four ten-hour days, so he had Fridays off anyway, and he had plenty of vacation time stored up, but he still had to be on-call for certain emergencies.

First things first. He smiled at Rebecca. "I guess we turn over the clue solving to the support team. Ready for this meeting?" She nodded and they headed for the offices.

They were on time, but they were the last ones to arrive, walking in on a heated conversation. Rick Mason broke off in the middle of a sentence. He drew himself up, glared at Sam, and said, "I am only trying to protect my wife's interests." Great, no doubt he'd been telling his side of the story first and casting blame. They should have gotten there earlier.

Mr. Ruiz rose and made a show of shaking hands with both Rebecca and Sam. "Thank you for coming. I apologize for the inconvenience." Tiffany hadn't glanced up from where she sat staring at her hands in her lap. Arnold and Benjamin looked uncomfortable.

Rebecca gave the lawyer a warm smile. "I hope we can take care of this quickly. We've agreed not to press charges against Mr. Mason."

Mason sputtered. "Against me! Why I should ... I ..." He glanced at the brothers and subsided. Maybe he was uncertain they'd support him in a flat-out lie, and Camie was right that he wouldn't want to admit being beaten up by a girl.

"That's very kind of you," Mr. Ruiz said. "Though it's not my primary concern. When Tiffany called and told me how out of hand things have gotten, I had to intervene."

Sam and Rebecca both looked at Tiffany, but she didn't glance up. So she'd been the one to report the fight, and apparently not in a way that was biased toward her husband.

"It was kind of you both to be concerned," Rebecca said, her gaze still on her half-sister. "I must admit, I thought we had enough of a challenge deciphering the clues, without having to deal with fistfights and slashed tires."

"Slashed tires?" Mr. Ruiz said. "I hadn't heard about that."

"Oh yes. Someone–" Rebecca shot a pointed glance at Mason "–slashed all four of our tires at the petroglyphs yesterday."

Tiffany finally looked up, her lips pressed together tight as she stared at her husband. He shrugged. "Petty crime. Could have been anyone."

"*Could* have been," Rebecca said in a tone that suggested otherwise. Sam had yet to speak, but she seemed to be doing fine, and watching her was fun.

"Oh, dear." Mr. Ruiz adjusted his glasses and gestured toward the chairs around the table. "Please have a seat. I believe it is time to discuss the alternative option."

Sam and Rebecca exchanged glances as they took chairs. The others looked interested as well, so apparently Mr. Ruiz hadn't explained the new option yet.

He folded his hands on the table. "Mr. Westin and I discussed this treasure hunt at length. We tried to predict possible complications. The last thing your grandfather wanted was his grandchildren fighting or coming to harm." He looked at each of the siblings in turn. "So in the event of unpleasantness, I was to offer an alternative. Door number two, you could call it."

An alert tension filled the room as the lawyer paused. Sam suspected the old man was enjoying his theatrics. Finally he said, "Instead of continuing the treasure hunt, you each have the option of taking a buyout now. One hundred thousand dollars."

A gasp born of many breaths whispered around the room. Mason was the first to speak. "One hundred thousand. But the treasure is worth more than that."

"Oh yes," the lawyer said. "Ten times that. But still, as a

reward for failure, one hundred thousand dollars isn't bad. And that amount would go to each of you, the grandchildren that is, without needing to divide it as you might the treasure."

"What happens to the treasure if we agree?" Rebecca asked. "Or if only some of us do?"

Mr. Ruiz beamed as if she were a clever student. "If you all agree to take the money now, the treasure will be auctioned for charity. If two or more of you choose to continue, the treasure remains until someone finds it. Or, of course, you could work together. But at least two people must continue the hunt."

Tiffany's chair screeched as she pushed back from the table and leapt to her feet. "I want the money. I'm done!" She raced from the room.

Mason shot up. "Tiffany!" He swore and headed for the door. But he paused and looked back at all of them. "Don't listen to her. We're still in. I'll bring her back."

Several of them started to speak at once, but Arnold was the loudest. "No." When Mason stared at him, Arnold went on. "If she wants out, she's out. Leave her alone. I'm beginning to think ..." He looked at Sam, Rebecca, and the lawyer, and seemed to reconsider his words. He shook his head at Mason. "Let her go. Benjie and I will continue the game without her." Arnold looked at Benjamin, who nodded.

Mason glared. "What about me? You can't cut me out now! You wouldn't be where you are now without my help."

Arnold looked uncomfortable. "I'm not sure how much you've helped and how much you've hurt. We'll see that you get something for your trouble, but I think we're better off on our own from now on."

Mason swore again and stormed out the door.

Mr. Ruiz said to the brothers, "Please tell Mrs. Mason that she can contact me at her leisure to discuss transferring the funds. And if she should have need of my services for any other reason, I would be happy to assist her."

Arnold nodded. "I should go after her." He looked at Rebecca. "Well? What about you? You could get back to your own life tomorrow, one hundred thousand dollars richer. It's more than you deserve."

Rebecca narrowed her eyes at his dig but didn't answer.

Sam held his breath. One hundred thousand dollars was a lot of money. Not enough to live on for life, but enough to provide a nice cushion while she looked for another job. And taking the money was not only easier, it was a sure thing.

Rebecca asked Mr. Ruiz, "What about my sister? It doesn't seem fair that she was cut out at the beginning, while we get a chance to quit now and make money off of it."

"Your sister will receive the buyout sum as well. Your grandfather didn't want any of you to miss your inheritance entirely. He hoped to lure her down here where she could meet her relatives and see some of his home state, but he understood her circumstances. I should warn you, however, if you pass up this opportunity, there will not be another chance to back out and be rewarded."

Rebecca nodded and then turned to Sam. Their gazes met and held. If she was aware of her half-brothers fidgeting across from her, she gave no indication. If she backed out, those men would work together and get the entire treasure for certain – unless Mason found a way to interfere.

Her smile started slowly. At last she said, "I'm having too much fun to quit now. I'm going after the treasure."

# *Fifteen*

Rebecca couldn't catch her breath. Had she really done that? Turned down $100,000, cash in hand, for the chance at finding a buried treasure? It was so unlike her. What had happened to the sensible, cautious Rebecca, who had asked for nothing more than to prove herself through long hours of hard work? Who had never gambled, never even bought a lottery ticket, because she knew the statistics on the chances of winning? The one who had sworn at age ten that she would not be like her parents, running out of money at the end of each month, spending every small windfall on something wonderful but useless, and going hungry again a few weeks later?

What had happened to that Rebecca, and why could this Rebecca not stop smiling?

As they walked through the parking lot back to Sam's car, he took her arm to keep her from running into a mailbox. "You okay?"

She stopped and looked at him. "I may be a fool."

He chuckled. "You and me both then." He hit the unlock button for his car a few spaces away and put the keys in his pocket. He turned her toward him, stroking her upper arms. "I would have understood if you'd taken the money and run. But I have to admit, I'm glad you didn't."

"It's not completely stupid," she said. "Not like throwing money away at a casino. The odds are reasonable here, with only a few of us competing. It's a logical investment, right?"

"Sure. You have a great chance of collecting."

"And if I don't, I'm no worse off than when I started. I'm not *losing* anything, really." She made a face. "I'm rationalizing. I'm trying to tell myself I made a smart choice. But honestly, I didn't do it because it was smart." Somehow she'd edged closer. Her hands were at his waist.

"Why'd you do it?" His voice was a low rumble that set off an echoing vibration inside her.

"I'm not entirely sure. Knowing that Sophia will get some money gives me more freedom. She and her husband are basically back on their feet, and the inheritance will cover the extra medical expenses for a decade or more. Beyond that ..."

She focused on his collarbone, a curve of sexy, tan skin. She resisted the urge to kiss it. "I think part of it was not wanting them to win, especially when they've been rude and haven't played fair. And not wanting to give up. I don't like to give up, and I hate to fail."

She met his gaze. "And part of it is because the last few days have been incredible. I've done things I'd never imagined myself doing. Seen new places, made friends faster than I ever have before. Had adventures. I didn't think I was the type for adventures."

He drew her closer. "You seem pretty adventurous to me."

"Maybe I am now. Maybe I'm becoming adventurous." Her heart was racing. She had taken one wild chance. Was she about to take another? She slid her hands up his sides, feeling the toned muscles under his T-shirt. He was so male. Not macho or domineering, but sweet, gentle, and yet so essentially masculine it took her breath away. And for some baffling reason, he seemed to be interested in her.

Her logical brain scrambled for all the reasons this was foolish. She didn't even know where she'd be in a week. She didn't want a long-distance relationship. But she didn't think she could do a fling with Sam after all. She liked him too much.

The new Rebecca, the one who took chances, pushed aside those thoughts. She glided her hands up Sam's chest until she could cup his face. Then she guided his head down so their lips met.

It was a gentle kiss and couldn't have lasted more than a few seconds. And yet time seemed to spin out endlessly, as if she could feel the earth slowly revolving. Eons passed in the moment of that kiss.

This was right. She needed this.

She deserved this.

All of it.

They drew back, their gazes locked for a long moment. The world rushed back around them. Traffic noises, raised voices. Arnold and Rick Mason were arguing.

"I don't know!" Rick said. "I got out here and she was gone. She can't have gotten far. I have the car keys. You check that café. Ben, try the back of the building. I'll drive a few blocks and see if I can spot her."

"Should we get out of here?" Sam asked.

Rebecca nodded. They got into the car. Rebecca said, "I wish I could do something to help Tiffany. I don't know if she would want my help, though."

"I bet she would. You could ask."

"I don't even know how to reach her. Mr. Ruiz might give me her phone number. So long as she has her own cell phone, and Rick doesn't answer it or check her messages. I bet he would if he could. But what if she does want help? I have no idea what to do."

"Give me a minute, and I'll have a suggestion." Sam pulled out of the parking lot.

Rebecca studied him. "What's with that expression? You look like you have a secret."

He gave her a look that was probably supposed to be mysterious. "Many secrets, my dear, but only one that relates to this conversation."

"Well, are you going to tell me?"

"All shall be revealed shortly."

A rustling came from the back seat. Rebecca whipped her head around. A lump on the floor was moving. A head peeped out from under a jacket that had previously been on the back seat, and Tiffany met Rebecca's gaze. "Um. Hi."

Rebecca stared. "Hi."

"I guess you ... um ... Sorry about this. But thanks."

Sam was chuckling. "No problem. I spotted you when I got in. At least I hoped it was you. You're welcome any time."

"Sure," Rebecca said. "I mean, of course." Her brain was scrambling. Had she said anything that Tiffany shouldn't overhear? She'd been bashing Rick, which might embarrass Tiffany but shouldn't come as a surprise.

"We're a few blocks away now," Sam said. "I'd feel better if you put on a seatbelt."

Tiffany did so, keeping her head down so her hair fell to hide her face. Rebecca turned to face forward, so as not to make her any more uncomfortable.

"Did you want to go any place in particular?" Sam asked.

"Not home," Tiffany said. "I'm not sure where, but I can't deal with Rick right now. I know you don't like him, and no wonder after what he did, but he can be so persuasive. I've tried to leave him before, but if I go to a friend's house, or to my mother's, he always finds me and talks me into coming back. I need to go someplace he can't find me. A hotel, maybe."

Rebecca shook her head. "You'd have to use a credit card. Wouldn't he be able to track that?"

"I guess so. Yes."

"I'd pay for you, but my credit's not that good right now." Rebecca glanced at Sam. "Do you think there's space ..."

"I'm sure we'll be able to figure out something. For now, let's concentrate on getting out of town. Once we're on the road, you can call Erin and Camie and get an update. Don't worry," he called back to Tiffany. "You're safe now."

The silence stretched out as they got on the highway and headed south. What did one say in this situation? How on earth could Rebecca make small talk with a half-sister she barely knew who was on the run from her jerk of a husband? Not a single conversation starter came to mind.

Finally Tiffany spoke softly. "I hope you find the treasure. I really do."

"Thank you," Rebecca said. "I wish ... well, I wish we weren't all at odds over it." The hurt came back. Tiffany hadn't been so bad, and she had issues of her own to deal with. But Arnold had made it clear that Rebecca wasn't wanted, and Benjamin had followed his lead. As if her father's actions before she was even born were her fault!

Still, Arnold had finally shown some sense when he sided with Tiffany rather than Rick. Wait, Tiffany wouldn't know that part. "You know, your brothers did tell Rick to back off, after you ran out. Arnold said for him to leave you alone." She glanced back.

Tiffany had a slight smile. "That's good to know. My brothers aren't bad men, really. But they don't understand. Arnold and Rick have been friends for a long time, since high school. It's hard for Arnold to believe that Rick isn't the great guy he used to know. But it doesn't matter now. I'm leaving no matter what they say. No matter what anyone says. I have to get free." Her confident words were undermined by the tremor in her voice.

"I'll help however I can," Rebecca said. How, she didn't know. Unless she found the treasure, she wouldn't be able to help financially. At least Tiffany had $100,000 coming to her. Rebecca didn't know much about the legal end of things either. It sounded like Tiffany might need a restraining order as well as a divorce. "Mr. Ruiz said he would help too. Call him any time."

"Thanks. That's a relief."

But it was the emotional side of things that would be really hard for Tiffany. Rebecca had never been in a similar situation. She'd have to figure it out as they went along. Camie and Erin would help as well. Maybe it wasn't fair for Rebecca to dump another problem on them, but they seemed to enjoy the challenges.

"What the—" Sam exclaimed.

The car jolted, throwing Rebecca forward against her seatbelt. Something had hit them from behind.

Tiffany screamed. "It's Rick! He followed us!"

Rebecca held on as the car swerved and Sam fought for control. They veered into the dirt alongside the road before he forced the car back on the highway. The engine roared as he sped up, trying to pull ahead.

"He's going to kill us!" Tiffany's voice was shrill.

Rebecca looked back. She saw a silver car, not the one they'd seen at the Owl Bar that morning. It looked big and powerful, and it was drawing closer. She couldn't see the driver clearly, but the crumpled front bumper showed it must be their attacker.

"Don't look back," Sam said. "If he hits us again, be braced for it."

Rebecca faced forward. Her heart raced and for a moment her vision blurred. She forced herself to breathe. What could she do? Even with a seatbelt, an accident could cause whiplash. She remembered the instructions from airplanes, to cross your arms against the seat in front of you and put your head on your arms. But she couldn't lean against the dashboard with the seatbelt across her chest.

She pulled her knees up, her feet on the edge of the seat, wrapped her arms around her legs, and tucked her face against her knees. She couldn't see the road, couldn't see anything. She could only wait.

Would Sam be able to keep far enough ahead of Rick? Should she call 911? But they were on the highway, miles outside of the city. Unless a police car happened to be nearby, no one could reach them in time.

Her body slammed forward as the car suddenly slowed. There hadn't been a jolt or the sound of impact, so Sam must have hit the brakes. She lifted her head enough to glance sideways. The silver car was alongside them, sailing past. Sam gave a quick twist to the wheel.

Metal connected with a crunch as their front corner met his back corner.

Rebecca buried her head as the car fishtailed. Brakes squealed. The car vibrated as they hit the rumble strip alongside the highway.

Their car settled into a steadier rhythm. Sam blew out a loud breath.

Rebecca cautiously raised her head. The highway in front of them was clear. She leaned to check the rearview mirror. The silver car had run off the road into a field.

She sat up and put her feet back on the floor, pressing a hand to her hammering chest. After several deep breaths she cleared her throat and looked back at Tiffany.

"Are you all right?"

She nodded. "I'm so sorry," she whispered.

"It's not your fault," Sam said. "We survived, and that's what's important."

"But your car! First the tires, and now this."

"It's only a car."

Tiffany was silent for a moment. Then she smiled and shook her head. "You would not believe how worked up Rick gets about his car. I don't know what he was thinking, to risk it like that."

"Are you going to stop and call the police?" Rebecca asked.

"I've been debating that," Sam said. "On the one hand, I'd love to get Rick arrested for vehicular assault or something. And this could help Tiffany in any divorce case. On the other hand, I'm more concerned with getting Tiffany someplace safe right now. I'm certainly not going to stop at the scene of the accident with Rick in this kind of mood. And he chose a time when there weren't other cars close by, so it's not like we have witnesses. Tiffany, what do you think?"

It took her a while to answer. "I just want to go someplace, any place, away from him. I don't think I could face the police right now, and you have no idea how convincing Rick can be. Somehow he'll turn this around to be my fault, or yours. I'll pay for your car repairs, as soon as I get the money from Mr. Ruiz."

"You might want to wait to collect it until you're sure Rick can't get his hands on it," Rebecca said. "I'll bet Mr. Ruiz can help arrange things."

"We can worry about that later," Sam said. "The good news is, it will take at least a few minutes for Rick to get back on the road. If we're lucky, he'll need a tow truck. We'll have time to get someplace safe."

Rebecca said softly, hoping Tiffany couldn't hear, "Do you think Erin's house is safe enough?"

"No. She's too well-known around the college, and half the town knows Camie. If someone asks the right questions, he could probably get their names and track them down. We'll go to my place."

Rebecca remembered that he lived somewhere outside of town, which was why he sometimes stayed with Camie or Erin. It would be interesting to see his home. Hardly the most important thing on her to-do list, but it was easier to think about that than about the homicidal maniac chasing them. Had it really been only a few hours ago that she'd decided to stop worrying?

Sam took the next exit. When Rebecca glanced over, he said, "I want to get off the highway before Rick has a chance to catch up with us. We can take back roads from Los Lunas to Belen.

Maybe find a place to stop for a few minutes. I've got a lot of adrenaline I'd like to pace off."

"I'd like a bathroom." Rebecca rubbed her lower belly where the seatbelt had pressed into her flesh. Good thing her bladder hadn't been any fuller. "That was some good driving, by the way."

"I knew all those racecar driver video games would pay off someday. Okay, no I didn't – not like this. But it's nice to know my misspent youth had its advantages."

Rebecca's phone rang. She found it on the floor where it had spilled out of her bag. "It's Mr. Ruiz." She answered. "Hello?" She glanced toward the back seat and raised her eyebrows. "You're looking for Tiffany? She's disappeared and Arnold is worried?" When Tiffany nodded, Rebecca said, "Hang on," and handed her the phone.

Sam pulled off the street at a place with a big red and yellow sign that said Sonic. It was an old-fashioned drive-in, and he pulled up to a post with a menu on the sign. Tiffany was talking quietly on the phone. Sam murmured, "Let's give her some privacy." Rebecca nodded and they got out.

"I'm going to do a couple of laps around the parking lot," Sam said. "Then we can order something if you want."

"I'll see if they have a restroom." Once she'd done that, Rebecca studied one of the menu signs. Suddenly chili cheese tater tots and ice cream shakes sounded amazing. A reaction to stress, no doubt. Self-medicating with food. Oh well, if nearly getting killed didn't earn her a little comfort, nothing did.

Tiffany got out of the car and Sam joined them. A voice from the sign was asking if they wanted to order. Tiffany got an iced tea with lime. Rebecca sighed and compromised on a cherry limeade. She regretted that when Sam asked for a peanut butter fudge shake. Maybe he'd let her have a taste.

They leaned against the car as they waited for their food. Tiffany said, "I told Mr. Ruiz what happened. He said to take pictures of the damage to the car, and he'll help me with a restraining order. For whatever good that will do. Rick will ignore it."

"That's why we'll keep you away from him," Sam said. "Let's stop by the Walmart in Belen so you can pick up things for a few days. Even if he traces the credit card transaction, he can't get there in time, and maybe it will throw him off track since we're going on to Magdalena."

"All right. Thanks again." Tiffany ducked her head so her hair hid her face. "I don't know what I'd do, if ..."

A teenager on roller skates brought their drinks, interrupting what threatened to become an awkward moment. Rebecca thought of all the help she'd given her sister and brother-in-law, and before that her mother, for relatively little thanks. In some ways it was easier to be taken for granted. Having someone weighed down by guilt and obligation was uncomfortable for both parties.

Tiffany sipped her iced tea and then finally looked Rebecca in the eye. "Also, I got Arnold to agree to hold off on the treasure hunt today. It's not fair that you should be delayed taking care of me. He promised he won't go anywhere before eight o'clock tomorrow morning, if you'll agree to the same."

"Wow. I mean, thanks. I can't believe you even thought of that." She wondered if Arnold was likely to keep his promise but didn't want to ask. Then there was Rick. Him, she could criticize. "Does Rick have a copy of the clue? And is he likely to use it?"

Tiffany closed her eyes. "I don't know. If he can't find me ..." She opened her eyes and shook her head. "I'm not sure if he has the clue, but probably. There were several copies, and I'm not sure what happened to them all. We didn't get very far in solving it, though. As for the other part, yes, he might keep searching for the treasure, either to get the money, or because he hopes it will lead him to me."

Great. Now they had to solve the clue, get to the next location first, and avoid having Rick spot them anywhere along the way. The silence dragged out until Rebecca said, "Well, we'll be careful. And thanks again for thinking of asking Arnold to delay."

Tiffany shrugged and looked away. "It's the least I can do."

Awkward silence again. Sam broke it by saying, "Things could be a lot worse. We have time to get Tiffany settled, and then I need to run by work for an hour. Let's hit the store and call Camie and Erin."

"I'll text Arnold that you agreed," Tiffany said.

"Then you'd better turn off your phone," Sam suggested. "I don't know if he could track you by the GPS unless he reported you kidnapped or something, but ..."

Tiffany's face hardened. "I wouldn't put it past him."

They drove to the store, let Tiffany shop, and found a quiet corner of the parking lot to call Camie. After updating her on the day's events, Sam turned on speakerphone so they could both hear her.

"Sounds like you have your hands full," Camie said. "I don't know if delaying until tomorrow is to your advantage or not, though. It gives the boys time to figure out the clue."

"Us, too," Rebecca said. "We didn't make much progress on the drive up, and I haven't even thought about it since then."

"That's why you have Erin and me." The satisfaction came through in Camie's voice. "We figured it out. Next stop: City of Rocks."

# *Sixteen*

Looking up City of Rocks gave Rebecca something to do on the drive to Magdalena. The site had "incredible volcanic rock formations," a visitor center with exhibits, and an observatory. In pictures, the rock formations looked like large boulders. Neither the State Park page nor Wikipedia explained the mythology references, but when she added "Hydra" and "Pegasus" to her search, she found a map showing the Hydra Trail that led to Pegasus Campground. So that made sense. The druid's circle, formed in fire, could refer to the volcanic rock formations. That didn't give a very specific location, however. Maybe that was where the second part of the clue came in, about broken limbs. It might make sense when they got there.

Hopefully something would make sense. Rebecca felt off-balance, thrown by a mental vertigo. She'd felt so sure of her decision to continue the treasure hunt rather than take the money. She'd imagined the fun she and Sam could have together, getting to know each other better, seeing what developed between them.

She had not imagined Tiffany accompanying them, and she tried hard not to resent it.

Tiffany had clothes for several days, toiletries, and a prepaid cell phone, bought and activated under Sam's name, so she could call her mother, brothers, and Mr. Ruiz. She also had $300 cash from the ATM for incidentals, and several paperback novels. The shopping bags and wallet full of cash had improved her mood. The security, maybe, or simply a sign that she was a step closer to escaping her husband.

Sam and Tiffany tossed around some ideas about the future. Where she might go, what she might do. She had a teaching degree and talked fondly about the year she'd spent teaching on one of the reservations before she got married. She would need to update her credentials, but with the inheritance money, she had time to do that even if she didn't get anything in the divorce, or couldn't get it settled right away.

Rebecca hardly felt in a position to give advice, since she didn't have a job, home, or plans of her own. Her problems seemed insignificant next to Tiffany's. Rebecca did want to help, yet she couldn't dredge up the mental and emotional energy to tackle yet another problem.

Maybe she wasn't as nice as she liked to think. When she'd said she wanted to help Tiffany, had she only meant she wanted to offer a few words of encouragement and then go on her way? Was her flirtation with Sam more important than Tiffany's safety? Was the treasure?

"You okay?" Sam asked.

It took a moment for Rebecca to register his words and realize they were directed at her. She glanced around at unfamiliar scenery. The road had narrowed to two lanes, and grassy plains led to low wooded hills.

"Tired?" Sam asked.

"I guess. Hungry, maybe." She shook her head. If she couldn't even tell the difference between fatigue and hunger, how was she supposed to figure out her own future, let alone help anyone else?

"We're almost there. I have to go into work for a bit, but you two can raid the fridge while I'm gone. I got groceries a couple of days ago and haven't been home to eat anything, so you should find plenty of food."

The road curved, and they started passing a few buildings.

"Work?" Rebecca glanced at the dashboard clock. "It's almost five o'clock."

"I know. I just have to check on something. It won't take long."

They were entering a small town, with old brick buildings and a few smallish Victorian-style houses. The main street featured a bar, a rundown motel, and a boarded-up café that had clearly suffered a fire. It looked more like a ghost town barely holding on to the occasional tourist than a place where people would actually live and work. "You work here?" Rebecca asked.

"Half an hour west of here. The Very Large Array." Sam turned onto a side street.

"Huh?"

"It's an observatory – radio astronomy. There was a scene in the movie *Contact* where Jodie Foster is sitting out by these big white astronomy dishes. That's us. But we're not actually looking for aliens. We study black holes, pulsars, stuff like that." He made another turn and parked.

"Wait, you're a scientist?"

"Sorry, no." Sam got out, and Rebecca scrambled after him to hear his answer. He opened the door for Tiffany and took a couple of her bags before opening a gate in a low fence. "I'm on the engineering side of things. I work with the electricians, plumbers, IT guys and so forth, to keep things running."

Rebecca barely noticed the small house as he led the way up the porch and pushed open the front door. "You told me you were a handyman."

He shot her a grin. "As I recall, I told you I worked with plumbing and electricity, and you supplied the word handyman."

A dog, mostly golden retriever, padded in from a back room. Sam leaned down to ruffle her ears. "Hey, sweetheart. Rico take good care of you?" He glanced up. "Rico is the neighbor kid. He feeds Willow when I can't get home. This sweet old girl is Willow." The dog wagged her tail, studied Rebecca a moment, and sat.

While Sam led Tiffany into another room, Rebecca stood stiffly, hands clenched. Heat washed over her. She felt like a fool. Had he tricked her on purpose?

Sam came back, but Rebecca didn't turn to look at him. He said, "Willow, want to go for a ride?" The dog rose and headed for the door. Sam turned to Rebecca. "I'll be back in an hour or two. Make yourself comfortable." After a pause, he added, "Are you all right?"

She stared straight ahead. "I can't believe you did that."

He moved into her field of vision and put his hands on her upper arms. "What? We can't do anything until tomorrow anyway. Are you afraid to be here alone?"

She shook her head, still refusing to meet his eyes. "Not that."

"What then? I'll be back as soon as I can, but I need to take a look at the problem and approve the plan. Then the guys can do the work without me."

"You're a manager?" Rebecca pulled away from him. "Never mind. It's nothing." She was making a scene. She was ruining everything, and she didn't even know why.

"Come on, talk to me."

She took a shuddering breath and blinked back tears. Sam reached for her again but she turned and crossed the room. She got herself under control enough to speak. "I can't right now. I can't explain."

She could feel him watching her. She shouldn't have said anything. Would he believe her now if she said it was only low blood sugar making her cranky? Could she even get the words out?

"All right," he said. "We'll talk when I get back. But Rebecca ..." He waited until she turned toward him. "We will talk. If you're upset, I need to know why."

She nodded once and watched him leave.

When she turned back, Tiffany was studying her from the doorway to the next room. Rebecca waited for the questions or criticism. Tiffany gave her crooked smile and said, "I'll see what he has to eat."

Rebecca followed Tiffany into the kitchen and sat at the small wooden table. She crossed her arms on the table and put her head down with a groan. What was wrong with her? Sam had a good job. Better than she'd realized. Was she upset because he was smart and successful? That didn't even make sense.

Anyway, she'd known he was smart. She hadn't cared what kind of job he had. She'd accepted him for who he was ... But maybe she didn't know who he was after all.

For a few minutes she heard cupboards opening, the sound of chopping, and then sizzling. Finally Tiffany said, "Do you want to talk about it?"

"It's not important," Rebecca mumbled. "I'm being a fool."

She lifted her head and Tiffany slid a plate next to her. The dish was covered in some kind of red sauce and melted cheese, with two fried eggs on top. Rebecca sniffed at it and her stomach growled.

"I'm hardly an expert on relationships," Tiffany said. "But I have learned the danger of not saying what you need to say." She placed her own plate on the table and sat across from Rebecca. She toyed with her food, her bangs hiding her eyes as she went on softly. "When I first got married, I compromised on a lot of things. I told myself it was necessary. I loved my husband, and I would be happy if he were happy." She took a bite and chewed slowly.

Rebecca cut into her own food and identified corn tortillas covered in refried beans and hash browns. The red sauce was mildly spicy, and oddly, the fried eggs added the perfect touch. She wasn't sure whether she was more surprised that Tiffany had whipped up this dish so quickly, or that Sam had all the ingredients.

Finally Tiffany spoke again. "The problem was, when more important things came up, I didn't know how to talk about them. I was in the habit of giving in. And somehow, before I knew it ..." She shrugged. "Rick controlled everything."

Rebecca thought about that while she ate. She certainly didn't want a relationship like Tiffany and Rick had. But she didn't want to fight all the time either, especially over silly things that shouldn't be such a big deal. "All right, but you have to compromise sometimes, right? How do you know what's not enough, and what's too much?"

Tiffany shook her head. "Like I said, I'm no expert." After a while, she added, "Maybe what I'm trying to say is, you don't have to have a big fight with Sam if you don't want to. But if you got so upset, there's probably something you need to say."

Rebecca sighed. "So I need to figure out why I got so upset." She mopped up the last of her food. "Some of it was hunger, and I feel a lot better now. Thanks. But that's an easy excuse. I know I get more emotional when my blood sugar is low, but I don't think I completely make up the emotions. And I hate it when people use things like hormones as an excuse for their behavior."

"So you need to figure out what set you off, and if it's important, speak up."

"You know what? It's nice to have another sister."

Tiffany shyly returned her smile. "I always wanted one. What's Sophia like? And her baby?" She sounded wistful.

Sophia had been less than excited at learning their father had other children. Not upset, exactly, but she'd been uninterested in meeting a new set of relatives. Still, Rebecca said, "I have photos on my computer. Want to see?"

That gave them something to talk about for an hour. When the conversation started flagging, Rebecca said, "You don't have kids, do you?" She surely would have heard of them. It was a bit odd, come to think of it, since Tiffany was over thirty and had been married for some years.

"No. We wanted them, or at least I did. Rick has a son with an earlier girlfriend. The boy is fourteen now. I see him sometimes, but he lives with his mother, and I wanted babies of my own. But I couldn't have any."

Rebecca hesitated and finally said, "At this point, that's probably for the best. It makes splitting simpler."

"I suppose. I wanted to adopt, but Rick was afraid of what we'd get."

It took a moment for Rebecca to realize she must be talking about the quality of child. "You know, I have friends who've adopted and completely adore their children. And giving birth yourself isn't always a guarantee. Biological kids can have health problems, mental problems, or, you know, just be brats."

Tiffany chuckled. "I know. That's what I tried to tell Rick. Hey, do you think I could adopt now? They let single people adopt these days, right?"

"Yes, I'm pretty sure they do. Or there are always foster kids needing a great home. Once you're back on your feet."

"That gives me something to look forward to." They sat in silence. The room had dimmed as it got darker outside. It was probably time to turn on a lamp, but the darkness felt cozy and safe.

Headlights flashed across the windows as a car turned into the short driveway. Tiffany jumped up and stood trembling as she looked out the window. She relaxed and crossed the room.

"It's Sam. I'll fix him a plate while you two talk."

Rebecca tipped her head back and closed her eyes. "Great."

Sam flipped on a light when he came in and then closed the curtains. Rebecca wished she'd been able to stay half-hidden in the darkness. But at least she'd figured out what she needed to say.

The dog headed for the kitchen. Sam stopped five feet away from Rebecca. "Am I in trouble?"

She patted the sofa next to her. "No. I'm all right now."

He sat, his body turned toward her but two feet of space between them. "Can you tell me what happened?"

She took a deep breath and stared across the room. "I was upset because I felt like we were getting so close. When I discovered that I didn't even know what you did for a living, it was a shock." She swallowed. "It made me feel like I didn't know you at all."

Sam was silent for a minute. He took her hand and she managed to look at him. "Shoot," he said. "That actually makes sense."

She glared. "You were expecting nonsense?"

"No, definitely not! I only meant–" He peered at her. "You're teasing me."

"A little." She smiled. With his hand curled around hers and his gaze warm on her face, it would be easy to dismiss her earlier concerns. But even if she'd overreacted, maybe some part of her mind was trying to send her a warning. "Everything has been happening so fast. We've only known each other a couple of days."

He nodded. His thumb stroked over the back of her hand. "It's hard to believe it has only been two and a half days. But if you think about the amount of time we've spent together, it must be more like thirty hours." He grinned. "That's like ten dates."

"Hmm. You have an interesting idea of what makes a date."

He edged closer and slipped an arm around her shoulders. "Hey, car chases, fistfights – some guys will only take you to see a movie. With me, you live one."

She chuckled. "Just what I always wanted. Although if you think about it, I'm really the one who got us into all of this."

"You sure know how to show a guy a good time." He nestled her closer. "Look, Rebecca, you know I like you. Maybe more than I can explain logically. I don't know what's going to happen. But I feel like we do know each other on some important level, even if I don't know your favorite color or even where you went to college. I know you're smart and determined. I know you don't back down even when the odds are against you. I know you've had some tough times and deserve someone to be nice to you. I won't say 'take care of you,' because you're perfectly capable of doing that yourself. But I'd like to help when I can, and I'd like to know you better."

She eased back enough to look into his eyes. "Careful, I'm beginning to think you're too good to be true."

"I have my faults." He leaned closer, his voice a caress. "Want to stick around long enough to learn them?"

"Mmm, tempting." She brushed her fingers down his cheek. "For now, why don't you get some dinner?"

"Smells amazing."

"That's all Tiffany's doing. I think I hinted that my cooking is mediocre."

"That's okay." He rose and pulled her to her feet. "I like to cook. Living out here, there isn't much choice other than surviving on TV dinners or learning to cook. I'm not crazy about TV dinners."

"You're frighteningly perfect, aren't you?"

"Hardly that. I might as well warn you now, I have no ambition. I've worked at the same place for eight years, and I'll stay as long as they'll keep me. The work is fine, the people are great, but what I really like is working four ten-hour days, so I have more time for hiking, rock climbing, and mountain biking."

He draped his arm across her shoulders and led her to the kitchen, where Willow lay on a round dog bed in the corner. "When I came to Socorro for college, I was a chubby, awkward nerd. I discovered the outdoors, and, eventually, girls. It took me six years to graduate because I was having too much fun. Huevos rancheros!"

Rebecca jumped at that last comment. After a moment she realized it wasn't some kind of Spanish swear, but rather the name of the dish Tiffany offered him. She chuckled and sat, watching Sam enjoy his meal in between friendly questions clearly designed to put Tiffany at ease when she would have slipped out of the room. He certainly had people skills, something Rebecca lacked. She had plenty of ambition, but where had it gotten her? Easy-going Sam was the one with a job, a home, good friends, and fun hobbies.

It was funny to think of dating someone so different from herself. But maybe that was exactly what she needed. Someone who would push her to think about her feelings and recognize what she wanted. Someone who knew how to have fun.

They chatted while darkness fell outside. A dog barked somewhere in the neighborhood. Otherwise, the night was silent. They seemed cut off from the rest of the world. Violent husbands, disapproving brothers, and frantic searches for treasure did not belong here. Financial worries and questions about the future could be put aside. There was only this cozy room, a woman who was becoming a sister, and a man who made Rebecca feel at home.

Finally Tiffany headed for the guest room. Sam smiled at Rebecca. "I'll change the sheets on my bed for you."

"Um, all right. Thanks." Did that mean they were sleeping together, and he wanted the bed nice for her? Or was he changing the sheets so she could sleep alone? Had he mentioned sleeping arrangements when they first came in? She'd been distracted.

She trailed after him as he retrieved sheets and they made the bed together. She watched his strong hands pull up the blankets and felt warm all over. She wanted him. But this seemed fast, and awkward, with Tiffany right next door. Rebecca and Sam had shared a couple of quick kisses, and now they were leaning over a bed together. The room seemed too small.

Finally she decided to ask and took a deep breath. "Um, sorry if I missed something. Who is sleeping where tonight?"

His eyes crinkled. "There's a hammock on the back porch. I sleep there a lot when the weather is nice. This bed is all yours."

"Oh." She couldn't decide if she was relieved or disappointed. He came toward her. She said quickly, "Can I see your hammock?"

He wiggled his eyebrows. "You can see anything you want."

She chuckled, the tension broken, and followed him from the room. They went through the kitchen to a covered back porch. The night air was cool and soft. They must have been at the edge of town. A few lights shone off to the sides, but the small yard backed onto a grassy plain. The hammock was strung between two porch pillars.

Rebecca stepped off the porch and looked up. "Wow." She'd never seen skies that dark, and so filled with stars. She'd rarely seen the night sky without buildings blocking much of the view.

Sam came up behind her and put his arms around her waist. She leaned back against him as he murmured, "We're at sixty-five hundred feet, so the air is thin and dry. See that band where the stars are thicker?" He raised an arm in a sweep across the sky. "That's the Milky Way."

"Wow. I never knew you could actually see it from Earth so clearly."

He bent his head to rub his cheek against hers. "Where I work, the VLA, it's out in the middle of nowhere, because the skies are so clear. I'd like to take you there sometime, show you what I do."

She snuggled back against him. "I'd like that too." She rested her head back against his shoulder and gazed at the sky for a long time. "I can see why you live here." She turned and wrapped her arms around his shoulders. She wasn't sure who started the kiss.

When they finally broke apart, they were both breathing heavily. "Wow," Sam gasped.

"Uh huh."

He held her close for a moment with a hand on the back of her head. Then he eased back. "It's been a long day, and tomorrow will be another one. We'd better get some sleep."

"Uh huh." Rebecca went back inside with a smile on her face.

Despite her exhaustion, Rebecca had a buzz of energy and didn't think she'd be able to settle down immediately. It was an hour earlier in Seattle, so she called her sister. Rebecca hadn't even told Sophia about the treasure hunt yet, not wanting her sister to feel bad about skipping the memorial and missing out on a fortune. Rebecca also hadn't wanted the pressure of finding the treasure, or the disappointment from her sister and brother-in-law if she failed. She had enough pressure coming from herself.

"One hundred thousand dollars?" Sophia gasped. "That's amazing. It will make things so much easier for Lizzie." She chatted for several minutes about all the ways she could use the money. Finally she wound down. "So what was the big deal about us needing to be there? I thought that lawyer had all kinds of hints about how it would be worth our while to come in person. Unless ... you got even more?"

"Not exactly." Rebecca hesitated. The truth was complicated and would take a while to explain. But she had to do it at some point.

When Rebecca finished, Sophia said, "You passed up one hundred thousand dollars? What were you thinking?"

"It's a gamble, I know, but it's not like I have anything else I need to be doing right now. And since you're taken care of now ..."

"Oh, I'm fine, sure. I'd much rather have the money and no hassles. But it doesn't seem like you, taking that kind of risk."

Rebecca lay back on the bed and stared at the ceiling. She imagined Sam sleeping in the hammock a few feet on the other side of the wall. "It's an adventure."

"So is going to Cancun for a couple of weeks and having an affair with some sexy stranger. And that wouldn't cost you a hundred thousand dollars."

"Hey, New Mexico is kind of like Cancun. Except for, you know, no ocean. But I have sunshine, spicy food, and this guy helping me, Sam ..." How could she explain Sam in a few words?

"Oh my gosh. Please tell me you're having an affair with a sexy stranger."

Rebecca chuckled. "Not exactly. Not yet."

Sophia gave a satisfied sigh. "All right then. You get right on that. When you get home, I expect to hear a lot of juicy details. And pictures! Don't forget to take photos."

"Will do." Rebecca hung up smiling. Maybe she was crazy, taking adventure rather than a sure financial payout. But as it turned out, being crazy was a lot of fun.

# Seventeen

Rebecca awoke feeling like a whole new person. Sunshine and a fresh, cool breeze streamed through the open window. She rose and did some sun salutations to greet the day. She'd been slacking off on both her yoga and her jogging, but at least she hadn't been completely sedentary lately.

And a new day waited, full of promise. She'd see new sights. She'd hang out with Sam. They'd find the next clue – together. At the moment, she wouldn't ask for more.

She wandered to the kitchen. Willow rose from her dog bed and rested her head against Rebecca's thigh. Rebecca rubbed the dog's ears while she looked out the window. Sam was still in the hammock, cocooned in a blanket. At least she assumed it was him; she couldn't see more than a tuft of sun-streaked hair.

She started the coffee maker. While she waited, she ate a banana from a bowl on the counter. She had to be more conscientious about her blood sugar, to avoid meltdowns like the previous night's. She was glad they'd had the conversation afterward, but she could have done without the emotional crisis getting there.

She poured two cups of coffee and found some milk for hers. She'd noticed Sam took his black. Cups in hand, she pushed past the screen door. Willow followed her out. Rebecca whispered, "Good morning," and held the coffee mugs near Sam's head so the aroma wafted over him. He didn't stir. Willow flopped down on the porch and seemed to grin at Rebecca.

The smell of coffee always got Rebecca up, but apparently Sam needed something stronger. The smell of bacon, maybe. Or being a New Mexican, green chile.

She put down his mug and sipped from hers, watching the

field in front of her grow brighter as the sun rose. How could he sleep with so much light? If he was that tired, maybe she should let him sleep. But they had things to do. She checked her phone. Almost seven o'clock. They had agreed not to start out until eight, so they had some time. Patience was a virtue.

She finished her coffee. His must have cooled. She walked across the porch, letting it creak, and cleared her throat a few times. Nothing. She leaned over him, put a hand on his shoulder, and whispered his name. He shifted, mumbled something, and let out a sigh. Then he was still.

Heavy sleeper. That could be a good thing, if they ever shared a bed, since she tended to be restless. At the moment, it was annoying. They hadn't discussed their morning agenda, but they shouldn't waste time. More to the point, she wanted to get moving.

She'd have to be more aggressive.

He'd at least shifted enough that she could see one ear and his cheek. She brushed his hair back and leaned close, whispering his name. And then she planted a line of kisses from his temple to his cheekbone. He gave a murmur of pleasure, and his lips curved.

Rebecca kissed her way to his ear and gently bit at the lobe.

Sam jerked upright with a gasp. The hammock swung wildly, knocking Rebecca off balance. She stumbled and caught herself on one of the porch posts.

The hammock flipped over, dumping Sam off the edge of the porch onto the ground.

Time seemed to stop. Then it rushed back, and Rebecca darted off the porch to crouch next to Sam, who was on his hands and knees. "Are you all right? I'm so sorry."

He lifted his head and laughed. "I'm awake, anyway. I was having a great dream. Or maybe I wasn't. Were you kissing me?"

Rebecca's face heated, but she nodded. "I thought it would be a gentle way to get you up."

"Not gentle, but memorable. I'm sorry I interrupted." He shifted off his hands to sit next to her. He was wearing boxer shorts and nothing else. The heat flooded down to the rest of Rebecca's body. He said, "Care to continue where you left off?"

"You're sure you're not hurt?"

"A little fall like that? Nothing I don't do to myself every week." He leaned closer, presenting his cheek. Rebecca complied, brushing kisses across his face. As she worked her way down his neck, she said between kisses, "I brought you coffee ... but it's cold now."

"I seem to be warming up nicely without it."

Willow pushed in between them, tail wagging. Sam lay back on the ground as the dog tried to add her kisses. He laughed. "Feeling left out? Or trying to tell me it's time for breakfast?" He rose and offered Rebecca his hand. "I need a shower. A cold shower. How are we doing for time?"

"It's almost seven thirty. I'd like a shower, too, but I don't have any clean clothes."

"I can loan you a T-shirt and boxer shorts, if that helps. And I can probably find some shorts to fit. It will be hot today if we're in the sun."

"I can work with that. But I need to pick up the rest of my things today if we're going to stay here."

"Right." They went inside and Sam refreshed Willow's food and water. "I'll be quick, and then I can pack up some food while you shower." He headed down the hall. Rebecca admired the view until the bathroom door shut behind him.

Tiffany peeked out of her room. "I heard voices. Am I interrupting anything?"

Rebecca shook her head. "You missed me causing an accident and Sam walking down the hall in boxer shorts, but things are quiet for the moment."

Her eyes widened. "I'll have to get up earlier in the future." Tiffany came out wearing a long T-shirt and sweatpants. She headed to the coffee pot. "Shall I make breakfast?"

"Thanks." Rebecca glanced at the time. "I do need something more substantial than the banana I already ate, but we should get on the road as soon as possible."

Tiffany opened the fridge. "I'll make breakfast burritos. You can take them along." She started setting out ingredients.

Rebecca hesitated. "Did you want to come with us today?"

"No way. Too much chance of running into Rick. I'm not ready to face my brothers yet either. Arnold sounded very reasonable yesterday, but he might still have divided loyalties."

She glanced over her shoulder. "The idea of divorce really bothers him. It's not only religion, it's because of Dad leaving Mom. He thinks broken marriages destroy families."

Rebecca wasn't sure if she was supposed to feel guilty or not. "I'd say Rick is the one who broke your marriage, and he'll destroy the whole family if you let him."

Tiffany nodded and turned back to the ingredients. "I've decided that too." She hummed as she started frying hash browns and bacon.

A minute later, Sam came out, sniffing deeply. "Smells amazing!" He grabbed Rebecca around the waist and twirled her around the room. So bacon was indeed the secret to energizing him in the morning. He gave her a smacking kiss. "I left some clothes for you in the bathroom." He released her and greeted Tiffany as he headed to the coffee pot.

"You're out of eggs and almost out of flour tortillas," Tiffany said. "Is the grocery store close enough that I can walk?"

"We'll stock up on the way home, but feel free to use my truck – the white one out front – if you need it for any reason. Keys are in that bowl by the front door. The neighborhood is safe enough if you feel like taking a walk, and I don't see how your husband could find you here."

He bent down to ruffle Willow's ears. "This old girl isn't much of a watchdog, but she'll stand by you if anything happens. Time was, she'd love an adventure like our trip today, but now she prefers her naps at home."

"Don't worry about me and Willow," Tiffany said. "I'm looking forward to having the entire day to do whatever I want, and she'll be the perfect companion."

Rebecca went to take a shower. By the time she was ready to go, Tiffany had wrapped the breakfast burritos in aluminum foil, and Sam had packed the car with a cooler of food and a backpack that looked ready for a trek across the Grand Canyon. He was loading something like a small but extra-thick gymnastics mat folded in half.

"What's that for?"

"It's a boulder pad," he explained.

She blinked. "That doesn't really help."

"Sorry. Bouldering is a kind of rock climbing, only you don't use ropes. Instead you stay low to the ground and fall on these pads." He closed the hatchback and headed for the driver's side.

As they got in the car, he added, "I made sandwiches for lunch, since there aren't restaurants down there. We have drinks and energy bars too. You need something, grab it."

Rebecca nodded and glanced back at the pile of gear behind them. "I've seen rock climbers when I was out hiking, and I know there are a couple of climbing gyms in Seattle, but I've never tried it myself."

"New Mexico is a rock climbers' paradise. There are hundreds of climbs between here and Socorro. And City of Rocks is a popular bouldering spot."

She remembered the pictures she'd seen online, of rock formations towering ten to thirty feet high. "You don't really think we'll need to do climbing?"

Sam pulled onto the highway and headed west. "No. But Camie suggested we bring the gear. There was that bit about the broken limb. Maybe it means we need to get into a difficult or dangerous position to reach the clue. In that case, we'll be glad to have the boulder pads to fall on, and maybe even the ropes and setup gear. She'll bring her pad too, so we'll have plenty of protection if we need it."

"Wait, Camie's coming?"

"Oh, right, you were in the shower. I talked to her this morning, and she wants to come along."

Rebecca didn't respond. She'd been looking forward to spending the day alone with Sam. Funny, when she remembered her initial goal of getting Camie's help, and how she'd resented Sam worming his way in on the treasure hunt. But now she trusted Sam completely and didn't really want his ex-girlfriend along while she was trying to get to know him better.

"Is that all right?" he asked.

"Of course." She frowned. If she wanted them to know each other better, lying was not the way to start. "All right, honestly, I was looking forward to having you to myself. But I asked Camie for help, and it's perfectly reasonable that she should come."

He reached over and took her hand. "She might be useful."

"I'm sure she will be. I just feel ... a little overwhelmed when she's around."

Sam chuckled. "Many people do. But she's a sweetheart behind the in-your-face attitude. And if you tell her to back off because you want to do things your way, she will listen. The trick is to give as good as you get."

"I'll remember that. You want your breakfast burrito now?" When he agreed, she unwrapped the end and handed it to him and then got to work on her own. Hash browns, scrambled eggs, bacon, cheese, and green chile were mixed together and wrapped in a flour tortilla. "I could get used to this," Rebecca mumbled.

She could get used to Camie, too. She liked her very much, in fact. And she would *not* be jealous over a relationship that had ended. Maybe it was even good to have someone else along. Things had been moving quickly with Sam, and a chaperone of sorts would keep them on track with the treasure and give them a chance to know each other better as friends.

They finished their breakfasts, and Rebecca passed out the damp paper towels Tiffany had thoughtfully included in a plastic baggie. Sam pointed out a herd of antelope in the field alongside the road. They passed the rest of the drive into Socorro chatting comfortably.

Camie met them at the college campus, on the off-chance that someone had figured out where she lived and was staking out her place watching for Rebecca or Tiffany. She had a backpack of gear and another climbing pad, which went into Sam's hatchback.

Camie slid into the back seat and leaned forward, grinning. "Did you two have a good night?"

Sam gave her an amused glance. "Very nice, thanks for asking."

Camie turned to Rebecca and wiggled her eyebrows. "So? Was I right about him?"

Rebecca remembered Sam's advice and tried to play it cool. "About him being a gentleman? Yes, you were right."

Camie snorted and sat back. "You two are no fun at all."

"Hey, yesterday had enough excitement for an action flick," Sam said.

"And I missed it," Camie groaned. "But I'm optimistic that today will be equally exciting."

"We can only hope," Rebecca said dryly. "My major concern is Rick. What if he gets there first and takes all the clues? Even if he's not officially in the treasure hunt anymore, I don't trust him to keep out of it."

"As long as this isn't the last stop, we should be fine," Camie said. "If we're sure we're in the right place and can't find the clue, we'll call that lawyer. Assuming Ruiz knows where the treasure is, he could get there first and retrieve it before Rick arrives to steal it."

"That makes sense," Rebecca said. "Maybe I'll call him and make sure he'll be ready if something like that happens. I'm also curious if there's any news since yesterday." As they got on the highway heading south, she called the lawyer. His answering service said he had been called away for an emergency and might not be available that day.

Rebecca then checked on Tiffany. She'd been in touch with Arnold, who said Rick hadn't been seen since their meeting. "Be careful," Rebecca said.

"You too. I doubt Rick could find me, but if he's figured out the clue, you could be heading for the same place. And if he blames you for my escape ..." Her voice trailed off. "Be careful."

"I will." They said goodbye and she hung up. She twisted so she could see both Sam and Camie. "According to Tiffany, Arnold and Benjamin wouldn't say whether they'd figured out the clue, but she thinks they were still in Santa Fe when she spoke to them, so they're at least an hour behind us. No one knows where Rick Mason is. And Mr. Ruiz isn't available today, so we're on our own there."

"I'm surprised Mr. Ruiz wouldn't have some way for Tiffany to reach him, given what happened yesterday," Sam said.

"I know, but apparently something came up suddenly, an emergency."

"I'm not sure I like the sound of that," Camie said. "Too much of a coincidence."

They all considered that. Finally Sam shrugged. "Nothing we can do but get down there and see what happens. We have a couple of hours yet. Let's not worry until we know there's a reason."

It was good advice. Rebecca wasn't sure she could take it.

# *Eighteen*

The rest of the long drive passed in good-natured conversation. Camie was fascinating, and not at all hesitant to ask thought-provoking questions, including some that others might consider too personal. They discussed everything from movies and video games to politics and religion.

At one point Rebecca said, "Sam, yesterday you said something about karma, about how Rick and the brothers would be paid back for their actions in the end. Do you really believe in that?"

"If you mean karma in the Buddhist sense, that your actions in past lives decide your fate in this one, not really. Reincarnation is a nice idea, but I don't claim to know what happens after death. Anyway, I'm more concerned about this life. But I do believe in karma in the sense of simple cause and effect."

She studied his profile. She could spend all day doing that. "You mean, do good and good things will come back to you?"

"Yes, although we know good people don't always get what they deserve." He glanced at her. "But here's an example. I had a friend who needed daily cancer treatments in Albuquerque for a month. She couldn't drive there and back every day. But she had a friend who was going to be out of the country for that exact month, and offered her apartment. You could call that extremely good luck, or even a miracle. But my friend is a nice, outgoing person, who has lots of friends in Albuquerque. The timing is lucky, but the fact that she knew someone who could offer her a place to stay is based on her personality and actions, not luck."

"I guess that makes sense." Rebecca gazed at the scenery while she thought about it. What kind of karma did she have?

She had done a lot for other people in the previous two years, although she'd resented it sometimes. And while devoting herself to Sophia's family, she'd lost a lot of her prior connections.

Who would she call if she needed help? Her sister owed her but wasn't yet in a position to pay back the debt. Their mother had little money and less sense. Mom would open her home to Rebecca if necessary, but living together again would drive both of them crazy. The friends Rebecca had known from work had faded away.

Rebecca felt closer to Sam, and even to Camie, than to almost anyone else besides her sister. She could see getting close to Tiffany. Erin was quieter, more reserved, so getting to know her would take time, but Rebecca's suspected they had a lot in common. Was it simply the unusual circumstances of how she'd met all these people, or was there something about New Mexico that invited her in and made her feel at home?

She leaned closer to the window and looked up. Maybe it was the blue sky. Blue was such a peaceful, calm color. She'd had a lot of rain in her life lately, literally and figuratively. She was ready for some sunshine.

She chuckled at her metaphor and turned to glance back at Camie, who was asking a probing question about the meaning of life.

They turned onto a two-lane road through a prairie of sparse grasses, with a ring of low mountains looking purplish in the distance. At first Rebecca thought she saw a town ahead, one of low structures all the same shade of brownish gray. They passed a sign announcing City of Rocks State Park. Those were rock formations ahead, not buildings. They were clustered together in the middle of the plain.

As they drove closer, the arrangement showed as individual rounded columns. They looked like tall, thin boulders, but Rebecca remembered from her reading that they were volcanic ash deposits which had weathered into these formations.

They parked by the visitor center and a separate building of restrooms. After they all had a bathroom break, Camie went into the visitor center. Rebecca grabbed one of her emergency granola bars. She couldn't afford to have blood sugar problems this day. She was really ready for lunch, but they were all anxious about getting to the clue. Hopefully they'd find it quickly and could take a longer break after that. While she ate, she and Sam studied the cars in the parking lot. "See anything familiar?" he asked.

Rebecca shook her head. "But I'm not good with cars. What have we seen them in so far? That blue one at the Owl Bar. I guess that was Benjamin's or Arnold's. None of these are the right color. Rick had that fancy-looking silver one yesterday."

"Mercedes sedan."

She smiled. "If you say so. I don't see any cars with damage where he hit us."

"Nope. We should have asked Tiffany if any of the guys would be likely to drive something else. I saw a Prius when we went your grandfather's house. Could've belonged to one of the brothers, but it could have been Mr. Ruiz's or your grandfather's."

"I'll call her."

Camie came out with their day pass and a map of the park as Rebecca hung up the phone. "She didn't answer."

Sam put a hand on her back. "You worried?"

Rebecca hesitated. "I shouldn't be. It rang for awhile and went to voice mail. She could be in the shower or just not near the phone. I left a message so maybe she'll get back to us."

"Not much else we can do at the moment," Camie said. "She might be embarrassed if you call the police to check on her and she's getting out of the shower when they arrive." She held up the map and pointed. "This whole dotted line is the Hydra Trail, but it meets up with Pegasus Campground here. Much as I'd like a hike, especially after that time the car, we probably want to get to the next clue ASAP. Maybe then we can go for a walk while we think about the clue. Too much sitting makes me antsy."

They got back in the car and drove slowly on the loop trail that went past rock formations and campsites. Rebecca put down the window and leaned her head out. Picnic tables were tucked in among the formations. A few had parked vehicles, and she spotted a couple of tents. Some of the rock formations were taller than she'd realized, looming over even the largest vehicles and the few shaggy trees.

At the far end, a sign with an etching of a winged horse announced the Pegasus Campground. Sam paused by it. "Might as well check around the sign."

They didn't see anything tucked behind the etched stone slab. They got back in the car and drove into the campground. A flock of small birds with bobbing topknots scurried across the road in front of them. "Quail," Sam said. "They always look like they're in a panic."

They parked near the sign for the Hydra Trail. No other cars were close by. Camie said, "Either we made it here before anyone else, or they've come and gone."

Rebecca was no longer sure that Arnold and Benjamin would steal the extra copies of the clue if they found it first. Rick, on the other hand, was still a wild card.

A raven cawed from its perch on top of one of the rock formations. The wind whipped Rebecca's hair around her face, so she pulled it into a tight ponytail. The sun was high overhead and she could feel it trying to burn her skin. They applied sunscreen and drank water before moving away from the car.

Camie finished first and checked all around the trail sign. "Nothing obvious here. What's the clue again?

Rebecca pulled out Sam's solution. "'At a druid's circle, formed in fire, the winged horse meets the coils of the nine-headed snake.' That's Pegasus Campground at the Hydra Trail, so we got that far. The next part is: 'A broken limb is a great misfortune, but here it leads you to your fortune.'"

"We'll hope Grandpa didn't mean that broken limb bit literally," Camie said. "He seems to have had a dark sense of humor."

"Surely he wouldn't have put us in real danger," Rebecca said. "I'm no athlete, and frankly, I can't imagine Arnold or Tiffany climbing one of those big rocks. Benjamin, maybe. And I guess Grandpa did say something about each of us using our strengths. But it wouldn't be fair if he's the only one who could get there."

Sam glanced around. "I also don't see anything obvious to climb. Or rather, there are plenty of things to climb, but nothing right here. The Hydra Trail actually goes away from the rocks into the open desert."

"Still, we might as well check out these closest rocks." Camie trotted over to the nearest one. Within moments she had found a hold and was scrambling up onto it. The raven flew off with a caw of annoyance as she reached the top. "Not that big a deal. I didn't even need my climbing shoes."

Rebecca winced. "It would be a big deal for me," she muttered to Sam.

He put an arm around her. "Remember what we've learned so far. Grandpa expects us to use our brains. The clues always send us to a specific spot."

"Right. And usually it means something other than what it seems like it means." She smiled. "Did that make sense?"

"Perfectly. The mention of a broken limb probably doesn't mean we need to break an arm or a leg. Hey, maybe broken limb was a metaphor, and it means something will cost an arm or a leg."

They paused for thought. They were at a remote campground with nothing to buy except perhaps drinks from the vending machine near the visitor center. Even their entrance fee had been free since Camie had a state park pass.

"No, I guess not," he said.

Rebecca turned slowly, gazing in every direction. She had to think like her grandfather might. She studied the landscape of rock formations, a few trees, desert scrub land, and minimal signs of humanity. She let the words of the clue run through her mind: broken, limb, fortune, misfortune. She walked down the trail a little ways to get a different view.

She began to laugh and pointed at a tree tucked against the side of the boulder Camie was on. "There – a broken limb."

# Nineteen

"Where?" Sam hurried to her side and gazed in the direction she was pointing. He groaned. "A broken *tree* limb? That's awful."

Camie scrambled down from the boulder and they all met beside it. The broken limb was still attached to the tree, but it had peeled off partway so it lay against the ground. "Seems a bit risky," Sam said, "trusting that a broken tree limb would be in the same position weeks later."

Camie put both hands on the limb and shook it. The branch rustled but didn't pull away from the tree. "It's pretty solid. Unless the park rangers actually cut it off, I don't think it would shift much."

"The broken limb is supposed to point the way," Rebecca said. The end of the branch, where it lay on the ground, spread into several twigs which were curled like long fingers. The longest of them pointed across the road to another cluster of boulders.

Sam said, "If you look at the way the Hydra Trail angles from the campground road, those boulders are actually in a triangle between the two paths. Fits the first part of the clue perfectly."

"Good old Grandpa!" Rebecca said.

She and Camie started for the other boulders. Sam hung back. "I'll stay here and see exactly where the branch is pointing, so I can direct you."

At the other boulders, they looked back. It was hard to see the tree branch from that distance, but Sam was crouched over it. He called out, "More to the left – sorry, my left, your right. Is that dark spot on the rock a hole?"

Camie moved past Rebecca and scrambled onto the rock to squat on a ledge about three feet off the ground. "This? No, it's discoloration in the rock. There's a bit of a depression but not enough to hide anything."

Rebecca smiled. Camie could easily have checked out that place without getting onto the rock. Obviously she simply liked climbing on things.

Sam had warned that Camie would take over. Rebecca was happy to share the fun, but this was *her* treasure hunt. She passed below Camie, who was standing and running her hands over the rock higher up. Rebecca knelt by a shrub at the base of the rock and poked around.

Sam's voice came from close behind her. "This is the right area, as far as I can tell. I checked around the broken limb for any other clues but didn't find anything. It has to be here somewhere, unless we're too late."

Rebecca carefully reached between the shrub's branches toward a suspicious pile of leaves in the space where the branches split off from the base. The space didn't appear large enough for a box like the ones they'd found before, but she didn't see a better hiding place. Twigs scratched her arm. Grandpa, or whoever he'd sent to do the task, had probably been smart enough to wear long sleeves and gloves.

She brushed aside the leaves. She couldn't see clearly between the branches, but she certainly would have felt anything out of place. No box.

She scraped away at the remaining loose dirt and decayed leaves, just to be certain.

Her fingers brushed over something smooth and rounded. She freed it from the soil and pulled back her hand.

Sam crouched beside her and Camie jumped off the rock to stand over them. Rebecca held a small plastic tube in her palm.

She pried open the top and slid out the curved pieces of paper inside. "It's the next clue. And guess what? It's not in code!"

"Really?" Sam said. "Don't tell me Grandpa was getting soft."

Rebecca skimmed the note. "Yeah, real soft." She straightened, held the typed note in front of her, and recited as if she were at a poetry reading.

*You're almost there so raise a glass!*
*In this town whose name means –*
*Here you must deploy*
*To find pa—*
*In this hot black place*
*Called the mal—*
*In this landscape bleak*
*A mouth that does not –*

*If you want to scoop what's mine*
*Take a look behind the—*

They stared at her. "Is something missing from that?" Sam asked.

"There are dashes where I guess some words are supposed to be. Or maybe partial words." Rebecca smiled sweetly. "Just to make things interesting, I suppose, because *obviously* otherwise this poem would be too easy."

"We wouldn't want that," Sam muttered.

"No, we wouldn't." Camie pulled the clue from Rebecca's hand and studied it. "Huh."

Rebecca rummaged through the tube. "There are still four more copies, so I guess we're the first ones to find it."

"Excellent," Camie said. "Let's get away from here before they come. Plus, there's a guy up on the rocks over there who has a clear view of us."

Rebecca whipped around, but she didn't see anyone. "You think it's Arnold or Benjamin? Or Mason?"

"No, it's probably someone here to climb. But if people see us here, and then the guys come along asking questions, someone might point them this way. Make them do the work themselves, I say."

"That makes sense." Sam stuffed the other clues back in the plastic tube and replaced it in the shrub. "So where to?"

Rebecca studied the slip of paper as they walked toward the car. "It's going to take some time to solve this. And I'm ready for lunch."

"Let's get away from the campground and go farther along

the road," Camie suggested. "We can find a picnic table and park for a while. If we find a spot where we can see the road in, but they can't see our car, we can find out how far behind us the guys are."

They agreed and drove around the loop to a point where the boulders got closer together. Sam pulled into an unused campsite where their car would be hidden from anyone driving the loop. Then they found a picnic table where they had a clear view of the road leading to Pegasus Campground. It was a quarter-mile away, so they would be able to see cars, but people in the cars would not easily be able to identify them.

Sam pulled out the cooler and unpacked sandwiches and drinks. Rebecca studied the clue. "I guess we take this a step at a time again. First, 'You're almost there so raise a glass!' Do you suppose that means this is the last clue, and the next stop is the treasure?"

Camie leaned across the table and turned the paper so she could see it. "Could be. Or it could be a clue to the next line – 'In this town whose name means –' If this poem is supposed to rhyme, and the dashes indicate missing words or syllables, then the town name rhymes with glass."

"Something Pass?" Sam suggested. "Mass, brass, grass, um ..."

"Pass seems most likely," Camie said, "though I can't think of any names like that offhand."

"But it says the name *means* whatever the missing word is," Rebecca pointed out. "Not that it actually is the word. So even if it's a rhyme, it could be a word that means the same thing as the missing word." She frowned. "Did that even make sense?"

"Sure," Camie said. "It could be a Spanish or native word that means the same thing as the missing English word."

"Or vice versa," Sam suggested. "Or the words could be synonyms in the same language."

They looked at each other. Rebecca groaned. "All right, moving along for the moment. Next up is 'Here you must go, To find pa—' There's a dash after pa, whatever that is." She peered closer. "Hey, on some lines, the dash is separated from the word, and on some it's connected. Do you suppose that was intentional, or does it simply mean Grandpa is a sloppy typist?"

Sam put his arm across her shoulders and leaned closer to see the clue. "You're right, there's a long dash connected to *pa* and *mal*, and a space with a shorter dash after *means* and *not*. Mal means bad in Spanish, but it could still be part of a longer word. So a connected dash could indicate that it's a longer word, and a space plus a dash could mean a separate word."

Rebecca said, "If we get a dictionary we can look up words beginning with p-a. There can't be too many that also rhyme with deploy."

Camie crossed her arms and grinned. "Or we could assume pa is part of pahoehoe."

They stared at her.

"A type of lava. The word is Hawaiian. Pronounced pa-hoy-hoy, but if you only saw it written, you might think it was pa-ho-ho." When they continued to stare, she rolled her eyes. "Come on, it's a geology term."

"Oh, right, you did a couple of semesters of geology," Sam said.

"Of course you did," Rebecca said. "So we have a place we must go to find a type of lava. Does that help?"

Sam grabbed the clue. "Wait, wait, I've got it! 'In this hot black place, Called the malpais!' There's a place, a park or something, called El Malpais, with lava flows!"

Rebecca grinned. "That does sound promising. Maybe Grandpa was getting soft after all."

"El Malpais is up near Grants, though," Camie said. "In the northwest part of the state," she added to Rebecca. "Erin had a theory that if Grandpa was playing nice, he'd have you going on a circular route, or down the state, not back and forth. This would take you back in the direction you started."

Rebecca shrugged. "If it's the last clue, maybe he wanted to send us back toward the start."

"Maybe, but Grants is directly west of Albuquerque, so not exactly on the way back to Santa Fe," Camie said. "It could work if you're doing a loop, I suppose, though I think you'd have to take I-25 back up. Anyway, let's be sure before we drive five or six hours to check it out."

Rebecca read, "In this landscape bleak, A mouth that does not ... something. Speak?"

They considered. "Beak, peak, reek?" Sam said. "Speak seems the most logical answer. Wouldn't hurt to have a rhyming dictionary, though."

Rebecca paused to eat a few bites of her sandwich. What kind of mouth wouldn't speak? Someone mute, or dead, or simply unfriendly? Or was it a metaphor?

She got out a fresh piece of paper and rewrote the poem, leaving plenty of space after each line. She jotted down some of the rhyming words and added notes such as "last clue?" and "Grants?"

"We're pretty sure about the lava, anyway," Sam said. "We just need to make sure we go to the right place with lava. There were those volcanoes up by the petroglyphs, but that would really be retracing our steps."

"I'll look up some things." Camie pulled out her cell phone. After looking at it for a few seconds, she said, "Might be better reception up top." She scrambled up a nearby boulder.

Sam finished his sandwich and wiped his hands on a paper towel. "What can I work on?"

"Um, there's that first missing word. 'In this town whose name means' something that rhymes with grass. What does El Malpais mean?"

"The bad place, something like that."

Rebecca wrinkled her nose. "Can you think of a way of saying that which rhymes with glass?"

After a minute, Sam said, "Crass? That's a stretch. And if the nearest city is Grants, that's probably named after somebody named Grant. Shoot."

"Then we have this thing about the mouth, possibly a mouth that doesn't speak. I was thinking maybe a tombstone, like a dead person can't speak, but the message on their grave could. But we've already had a cemetery. I feel like Grandpa wouldn't repeat himself to that extent."

Sam frowned. "And we've already had petroglyphs, voices from the dead."

"So is it a metaphor? Something about a secret? The location of the treasure is a secret, but that's been true all along. It doesn't help us here." She reread the entire clue. "And so far, we have at best a large location. We need something to get us to a specific spot."

"Mouth, mouth," Sam muttered, gazing around. "Grandpa liked his wordplay. Maybe it's not a human mouth at all. What else has a mouth?" He flicked his finger at one of the water bottles on the table. "Mouth of a bottle?"

"The clue could be hidden in the mouth of ... of ... a pipe? Some kind of opening?"

Sam sat up straighter. "A cave! Caves have mouths, and there are caves in El Malpais, I think."

Rebecca said, "By Jove, I think you've got it." They grinned at each other.

"Camie would know for sure about caves in El Malpais; she's done caving." Sam dipped his head, brushing his lips against Rebecca's temple. "If the next stop really is our last stop, you could be a rich woman by tomorrow. And then ..." He trailed off and his mouth turned down.

Right, what then? Would she go back home? Stay a while? She'd been putting off making decisions about the future until she knew about the treasure. She might not be able to put off those decisions much longer.

Camie scrambled back down the rock. "I called Erin. Faster than trying to look up things on my phone. There's El Malpais National Monument, by Grants. That's the main thing that comes up in a search. But there's also the Carrizozo Malpais, associated with the Valley of Fires Recreation Area. That's more to the east."

"What was that name?" Rebecca asked, pen poised over paper. "Not Valley of Fires, the first part."

"Carrizozo." Sam spelled it for her. "Small town. Famous for apple cider."

"First fudge, now cider." Rebecca looked up. "Hey! Raise a glass!"

Sam chuckled and gave her a squeeze. "Could be. Now we only need to figure out the missing word, and how it can be translated to identify either El Malpais or the Valley of Fires."

"Erin is working on it," Camie said. Her phone buzzed. "And here she is." She checked the text and grinned triumphantly. "Carrizozo gets its name from the reed *grass*, carrizo in the Spanish vernacular."

"You're almost there so raise a glass, in this town whose name means grass." Rebecca laughed out loud. "I can't believe we got it so quickly! That last bit – If you want to scoop what's mine, take a look behind the whatever – that must refer to the specific spot where the treasure is hidden. We probably won't figure out that part until we're on site."

Sam said, "The part about 'you're almost there' could refer to the town itself, then – you're almost to the Valley of Fires. It might not mean we're almost done with the treasure hunt." He brushed a hand down Rebecca's back. "Disappointed?"

She leaned against him. "Not even a little bit."

"Good," Camie said. "Before we get back in the car, I need to stretch my legs. And Rebecca, you need to finish your lunch. Sam, you want to spot me?"

"Sure, if it's all right with Rebecca."

She frowned. Camie was pretty easy to spot, standing right there. Obviously Rebecca was missing something. "If you do what?"

He grinned. "Camie and I are going to play on the rocks while you finish your lunch. Okay?"

Rebecca suddenly realized how hungry she was, with half her sandwich still sitting there. "Sure."

Sam and Camie got their big bouldering pads out of the car and moved off about thirty feet. When Rebecca finished eating, Camie was hanging from a boulder halfway up. Sam stood below her, his arms raised as if giving a boost, but not touching her. Rebecca wandered over to watch. "You must be part lizard," she said.

Camie merely grunted as she swung her arm up to another hold, her muscles rippling. Sam said, "Camie is an amazing climber, but it's not as impossible as it might look. Her shoes have a sticky rubber that helps."

Camie's shoes were made of bright red leather that hugged her feet, with black rubber soles. Sam had similar shoes in gray. "Still, I doubt it's all the shoes," Rebecca said. They also both had impressively toned muscles.

Camie made a couple more moves and disappeared up the top of the rock. Sam stepped back and dropped his arms. "For this particular problem, upper body strength does come into it.

But a lot of climbing is more about balance and technique. You want to try it? We can find something easier."

"Maybe one of these days, but not right now. It does look like it could be fun." She moved closer and ran her fingers through his hair. "You know, in Seattle, people pay good money for these perfect highlights."

He slid his arms around her waist. "Hey, I pay good money – for rock climbing equipment that gets me out where the sun can do its job."

She grinned. "Saves you the cost of a gym membership, too."

Camie appeared around the side of the boulder. "Still no sign of anyone heading to the Hydra Trail."

"Are you anxious to get out of here?" Sam asked Rebecca.

"Actually, I wouldn't mind stretching my legs as well, though I think I'll do it on flat ground."

"Want company?"

"No, that's all right, you two play on your rocks." She gave him a quick kiss.

"Be careful. Watch for snakes of the human and animal variety."

"Don't worry, I'll duck out of sight if I see a car coming."

Camie slapped Sam's back. "Okay sport, you're up."

Rebecca lingered to watch Sam start his climb. He placed his right hand on a curve in the rock, though she couldn't see how anyone could possibly hold onto that. His left hand went down at waist level, pressing against the rock. A moment later he had both feet up on the face of the rock, his body at an angle. He shifted and reached up with his left hand.

Seeing him in action, she knew where he got his lean, toned muscles. She watched until he disappeared over the top of the rock formation, gave a satisfied sigh, and turned for the road.

She would never be able to climb like that. But it might be fun to try something easier. Sam would probably be a good teacher. He'd be patient and he'd make her feel safe. He wouldn't laugh, even if she was clumsy. Though she'd rather be able to impress him with her natural talent. Hah, hardly likely. She'd managed to keep in tolerable shape with jogging and occasional yoga, but how would that translate to climbing?

A raven cawed from a nearby boulder. A lizard scurried

across the road, and something rustled in the bushes, probably a bird. She passed a campsite with a parked car and a tent but didn't see anyone there. A fancy RV parked next to an especially large rock formation might or might not have been inhabited.

It did feel good to move after so long in the car. A jog would have been nice, but it was hot and she didn't have clean clothes to change into. Besides, she wasn't properly hydrated. She still felt a bit lightheaded, even after eating, and thinking back, she hadn't peed enough that day. She might not be experienced in the desert, but she'd been a runner for enough years to know when her body needed more liquid. She'd grab one of those sports drinks from the cooler as soon as she got back.

She reached a cluster of lower boulders. The rounded shapes and rough surfaces were tempting. It wouldn't be hard to climb up on one that was no taller than she was. She could see how climbing felt.

She was out of sight of Camie and Sam, and apparently everyone else. If climbing was harder than it looked, she could back down with no disgrace.

Rebecca moved off the path and ran her hands over the rock. It was surprisingly porous, with lots of tiny pockets. But then, these were ash deposits, so porosity made sense. She found a larger pocket where she could grab the edge with her hand, and she placed a foot on the slope. In a few steps, she was standing on top of the boulder. It was surprisingly satisfying.

Could she reach that larger boulder nearby? It only required enough nerve to step across the two-foot gap. Then she was on an easy slope up to the top.

Once at the top, she sat down. She was perhaps fifteen feet high, and although her position was secure, a fall would be disastrous. Even seated, it was a great view. She couldn't see all of the road, because other rock formations were in the way, but she could see for miles out over the desert.

She turned toward the visitor center, squinting to see if any cars looked familiar. Impossible to tell at that distance. She turned again, preparing to back down the rock. A flash of light on silver caught her attention. A silver car, tucked back in one of the camping spaces?

Lots of people had silver cars. There was no reason to think this was Rick Mason's. If he'd come to City of Rocks, he'd be searching for the treasure at the other end of the park. The glint she'd seen might not even be a car.

Still, she'd feel safer back with Sam and Camie. She scrambled down as quickly as she safely could. Back across the gap between the two rocks. Could she jump down from the lower one?

No, it was a little too high. Better to turn around and find the same handholds and footholds she'd used on the way up.

Don't rush it. Breathe. An accident could ruin everything.

Going down was harder than going up. She felt behind herself for the ground. There. She shifted her weight back to solid earth.

She sensed a presence behind her. Some sound or shift in the air.

She began to turn. A dark shadow moved in the corner of her vision.

Pain exploded in her head, and she fell.

# Twenty

Camie disappeared up the rock after a particularly challenging set of moves. His duties as spotter done, Sam wandered back toward the car for a better view in the direction Rebecca had walked. No sign of her.

Camie came around the boulder, dusting her hands on her shorts. "You're up."

"Rebecca's been gone a long time. You didn't see her from up top, did you?"

"I didn't see anybody except another group of boulderers over that way, and some hikers in the distance." She tipped her head to the side and studied Sam. "You really like her. Are things getting serious?"

He shrugged and headed back to the boulder. "I'm not sure what she wants. She likes me, but her life isn't here. We've only known each other a few days. How can I ask her to change everything for me?"

"Hey, I'm not sure I believe in true love, but seeing Erin and Drew together has convinced me of one thing. If the right person comes into your life, you grab hold and don't let go. So if Rebecca is the right person, what are you going to do about it?"

Sam pondered her words as he got in position. He'd done this boulder problem enough times now to know the sequence of moves. It simply took focus, preparation, willpower – and a little luck – to move his body smoothly from point to point. In under a minute, he was on top of the rock formation. He scanned the surrounding area. He didn't see anyone walking alone.

He went down the back of the boulder, an easy scramble. If

he missed Rebecca when she was gone for a few minutes, how would he survive her being across the country? Camie was right. It didn't matter that he and Rebecca had only known each other a few days. They had something special. He didn't know about true love either, but he knew what he and Rebecca had didn't come around every day. It was worth fighting for.

He smiled at Camie as he neared the boulder pads. "You're right. I want Rebecca."

"Of course I'm right. So what are you going to do about it?" She crouched on the boulder pad.

"I can't ask her to change her life for me, unless I'm willing to do the same. If she doesn't want to stay here, I'll look for work in Seattle."

Camie's eyebrows shot up. "Wasn't exactly what I had in mind," she mumbled as she turned to the rock and placed her hands on the first set of holds.

"I have a great job, a great life," Sam said. "But that doesn't mean it's right for her. We'll have to find something that works for us both." He couldn't believe he hadn't thought of that sooner. How selfish was he, to assume that Rebecca should be the one to move, simply because she didn't have a job. She was cautious. She might not want to change everything just to be with him. But if they had enough time together, he was sure they could work out something great. He'd take that chance.

Camie shrugged. "At least try asking her if she'll stay before you uproot everything." She moved up the rock like a dancer. Sam was still smiling over his new plan when she reappeared and said, "We have that one. Want to look for a new problem?"

"How long have we been doing this? I lose track of time on the rock." Sam checked his phone. "I'm not sure what time she left, but it's been an hour since we sat down to lunch. She must've been gone twenty, maybe thirty minutes."

"You worried?"

"Yeah." He didn't try to explain all the reasons buzzing in his brain. The dangers of the desert for someone not used to keeping an eye out for rattlers, the human dangers from unfriendly half-brothers and a guy who'd shown himself willing to use violence. And Rebecca had been focused on the puzzle. As much as Sam wanted her to relax and enjoy her New Mexico experiences, he didn't think she was the type to get distracted for too long when she had a goal. A ten-minute walk to stretch her legs, sure. But half an hour? Not likely. So where was she?

"Let's start packing up. If she's not back by the time we're done, we'll hunt her down." Camie checked her own phone as she removed her climbing shoes. "Text from Erin. She's given us directions – Valley of Fires is about three and a half hours by way of Las Cruces and Alamagordo, or a few minutes longer if we take I-25. Then an hour and a half back to Socorro. Makes for a long day, but no reason to put it off until tomorrow. If Grandpa's 'almost there' does mean this is the last stop, your girlfriend could be rich by tonight."

"I just want her to be safe," Sam said as he shoved the cooler into the car.

"Hey, don't worry until we know we have a reason to worry." Yet Camie hurried to retrieve the boulder pads.

Sam dragged a hand through his hair. "Should we start driving and see if we catch up to her? But what if she's already on her way back through the middle of the rocks. What am I thinking? I'll call her." He fumbled for his phone. He shouldn't be so worried. Camie was right, everything might be fine. But he wanted to hear Rebecca's voice and *know* everything was fine.

He stared at his phone. "I don't have her number. Why don't I have her number?" Because she'd hardly been out of his sight for the last few days. He hadn't needed to call her.

"I do." Camie's phone rang and she glanced at the readout. "And here she is."

Sam gave a sigh of relief and edged closer so he could hear.

"Howdy!" Camie said. "We were starting to wonder–"

The voice that interrupted her wasn't Rebecca's. It was a man. "I've got Rebecca."

Rick Mason's voice. The world seemed to drop out from under Sam. He grabbed the edge of the picnic table to steady himself.

Camie switched to speakerphone. "What do you want?"

His voice sounded hollow and fuzzed by static. "I want my wife! So here's what we're going to do."

Sam sank onto the bench. Camie put a hand on his shoulder and held his gaze.

Rick said, "Meet me at the next stop. Bring Tiffany. I'll trade Rebecca for my wife."

"You mean meet where this clue says to go?" Camie asked. "Why there? It would be faster if we went back to Socorro."

"We meet where the treasure is," Mason said. "And that treasure better be at the next stop."

"Oh, so it's not really about your wife." Camie's voice dripped disdain. "It's about the money."

"She's my wife! You'll try to take Tiffany away from me again. We need to go away, start a new life—"

Sam broke in. "I want to talk to Rebecca." He hoped Mason couldn't hear the tremble in his voice.

"She's ... indisposed right now. I won't hurt her – any more – if you do as I ask." He muttered, "It's more than she deserves."

"We'll need some time," Camie said. "Tiffany's not with us, you probably know that. And we need to solve the clue."

"Don't think you can play me. You know the clue goes to Valley of Fires. I have Rebecca's notes and I'm already on my way. I'll be waiting – somewhere I can see you before you see me. You have four hours before I start hurting her. No police, no strangers, or your friend will be sorry." He hung up.

Camie put the phone down and swung a leg over the bench to sit facing Sam. She held him by both shoulders and looked into his face. "We'll get her back."

He nodded. He couldn't form words yet. Mason had implied that he'd already hurt Rebecca. What was he capable of doing?

He couldn't think about that. If he did, he'd be no help at all. "What do we do? We can't give Tiffany to that guy." He was almost tempted, if it would save Rebecca. Give up Tiffany, and get her back later. But it was too risky. Some lines could not be crossed.

"No," Camie said. "But we should call her, let her know what's happening. We might need her." She rose. "Come on, get in the car. I'm driving."

Sam followed in a daze. He had to think, come up with a plan. But his mind felt numb. He could only picture Rebecca, frightened, maybe injured. He had failed her.

Camie drove the rest of the loop a little too fast. She pulled into the parking lot by the visitor center and sat, drumming her fingers on the wheel. "The first thing we need to do is decide whether we're going to report this officially."

Sam dragged his thoughts away from visions of Rebecca being tortured. "It will take time."

"Yes, too much time, I think. The park rangers here can't do anything but alert other authorities, and if we stop in some town to talk to the police, we won't get there in four hours. He was smart to say that."

"So we're on our own."

Camie gave him a fierce smile. "Exactly how I like it."

A car pulled into the parking lot. Arnold and Benjamin got out.

Sam was out of the car and halfway to them before he realized what he was doing. He pulled up a few feet away. "You!"

They both looked startled. Benjamin took a step back. Arnold said gruffly, "I suppose you already found the clue. Did you leave us a copy?"

Sam stalked closer. He wanted to lash out, to pummel someone, and the real cause of his anger wasn't here. "Your friend Mason kidnapped Rebecca."

"What!" Arnold and Benjamin exchange glances.

"That piece of dirt you call your brother-in-law took Rebecca and wants to trade her for Tiffany." Sam couldn't get any more words out.

"How do we know you're telling the truth?" Arnold asked.

Sam swung around. "I don't have time for this." He stormed away.

"Wait!"

Sam paused and they converged on either side of him. Camie joined them.

"Tell us what happened," Arnold said.

When Sam didn't immediately answer, Benjamin added, "If it involves Tiffany, it's our problem too."

Camie briefly explained. "We're not trading Tiffany, so don't worry about that. But we need to save Rebecca."

The brothers looked at each other for a long moment. Arnold said, "We'll help," as Benjamin said, "What can we do?"

"I'm not sure yet," Camie said. "But we should get on the road. Let's take one car so we can discuss it. Grab anything you need and come on."

The brothers had a quick conversation as they hurried to their car. A minute later, Arnold was back. "Ben will drive our car so it doesn't get stranded here. He'll be right behind us and I'll keep him posted by phone."

Soon they were all pulling out of the parking lot, Camie still driving. Sam slumped in his seat, the first rush of adrenaline fading and leaving him queasy. Surely together they could take care of Rick Mason. And Rebecca was smart; she'd hang on until help arrived. It would be okay.

It had to be.

# Twenty-One

Rebecca groaned. Her head throbbed and her stomach heaved. She was surrounded by vibrating darkness. She hadn't lost consciousness, but she'd been too stunned to fight back when Rick Mason loomed over her. He'd slapped duct tape on her mouth before she'd thought to try to scream. She had blurred memories of him flipping her face down, binding her hands, and hauling her to his car trunk. Had she even struggled? She thought so, but maybe she was only remembering her desire to fight back.

She closed her eyes against the darkness and tried to breathe back the nausea. The only thing that could make this worse was vomiting all over herself. Only with the duct tape on her mouth, it wouldn't be all over herself. She'd choke to death.

Panic flooded her. She twisted and kicked and tried to scream, the sound escaping through her nose in staccato howls. But her wrists were bound behind her back, more duct tape it felt like, and her ankles were bound together too, so she could only flop like a landed fish. They bumped over rough ground, swung in a turn that sent her sliding, and finally settled down onto a smoother road.

The trunk was stifling and hot, but she breathed deeply through her nose, squeezing her eyes tight against tears. She tried to draw on her yoga meditation techniques, but this was a far cry from savasana on a yoga mat.

Finally, endless minutes later, the worst of the panic receded to a numb calm. She wasn't dead or unconscious. She hadn't thrown up. Other than those slivers of silver lining, the situation was about as bad as it could be.

She'd faced bad situations before. Nothing like this, but

there had been times when she'd wondered how she could get through another exhausted night, and she'd survived.

And this time she had a team on her side. She pictured Sam, called out to him in her mind. He'd worry when she didn't come back quickly. He and Camie would find her.

But what was Mason's plan? Where were they going? They'd been driving on smooth road, without turning, for some minutes now. Were they back on the highway? Where could he be taking her?

Not that she could do anything about it regardless, but she'd like to know how long she'd be stuck in the trunk. With her hands taped behind her back, she was lying awkwardly on the front of one shoulder, her head twisted so her neck ached. The heat was getting worse and the stale air made her lightheaded. Would she run out of air eventually? No, the trunk couldn't be sealed that tightly. Could it?

The panic threatened to rush back in. She closed her eyes – somehow the blackness wasn't so threatening when she wasn't trying to strain against it – and counted backward from one hundred. She stumbled a few times in the nineties, even that simple task too much for her rattled brain. But by the time she got to the forties, she felt in control again.

Sam and the others would come after her. In the meantime, she could do her part by trying to escape, or maybe leaving some kind of trail.

She had to get her hands free. Then she could get the tape off of her mouth, and maybe even get out of the trunk. Modern trunks had latches so you could open them from the inside, right? She wasn't keen to jump out of a moving car on the highway, but at least she could signal for help, maybe get out and run if he slowed down.

First, her hands. She strained and wriggled and pulled until her wrists burned, but the tape held. She needed something to cut through it. If she could get a piece started, she might be able to tear through the rest.

Rebecca shifted around in the trunk, feeling behind herself for any loose tool, any sharp edge. The trunk seemed empty. If only she could see! But she couldn't, so deal with it. She backed up and felt the surface behind her. A piece of metal stuck out from the wall about an inch, curving back in a U-shape. It wasn't sharp, but it was the best thing she'd found. She pressed the edge of the tape against it and pushed.

The tape slipped off the metal piece and her hands banged against the wall. She winced, squirmed into a better position, and tried again. And again. And again.

She thought she had a notch in the edge of the tape but couldn't tell for certain. Sweat ran down her face, dripping into her eyes and stinging. Her nose ran, making breathing even harder. The tape over her mouth felt hot and slimy. She rubbed her face against the floor but the tape wouldn't pull free. Rebecca rested for a moment, woozy and nauseated. Was it the blow to her head, the heat and stale air, or a combination?

She couldn't risk falling asleep. Besides the danger of a concussion, the idea of Mason finding her in that vulnerable state was sickening. She went back to work.

Arnold was arguing with Tiffany over the phone. Finally he hung up with a frustrated sigh. "She insists on coming out. I told her she doesn't need to, no way we're giving her up to that guy, but she thinks she should be there."

"She's probably right." Camie said what Sam was thinking but hesitated to say out loud. She added, "If Mason wants a trade, he might insist on seeing Tiffany before he shows us Rebecca. We'll keep them both safe, I promise."

Arnold grunted. "She's taking your truck to Socorro to meet up with Erin. They could get to Valley of Fires before we do. What then?"

"Take the I-25 route," Sam said. It would add less than ten minutes. Even that seemed like forever, but they'd still make Valley of Fires in under four hours, and they'd pass through San Antonio. "I'll tell Erin to wait for us in San Antonio. We'll do the last part together."

Rebecca's wrists moved a little more freely. She tried to pull them apart, but she was so tired, her arms aching from the awkward position and the strain. Back to the piece of metal. She made promises to herself. *A little more work, and you'll be through. You can pop the trunk then, get fresh air. Lovely, delicious air.* And *Sam is coming. You want your arms free to hug him, don't you?*

Finally the tape broke. She jerked her hands apart, ignoring the pain as the tape tore off her skin. She rolled onto her elbows and knees and tore the tape from her mouth. She rested for a moment, forehead on clasped hands, simply breathing. The air was still hot and stale, but at least she could draw in enough of it. When the wooziness receded, Rebecca peeled off the tape clinging to her wrist and wadded it into a ball.

Her feet were still bound, so she went to work on that tape. Fortunately some of it was over her socks, and once she found the end she could peel it off rather than trying to break it. With her limbs free, she felt better, even if she was still trapped.

Now to open the trunk. She didn't care if Mason saw it open in the rearview mirror. She didn't care if they were going down the highway at 75 miles per hour. She wanted air.

She felt around the trunk where she thought the emergency release should be.

Nothing.

She tried again. She wasn't sure what she was looking for; no doubt there were different mechanisms. She needed to find something – anything – that moved. A handle. Something to twist or pull. It had to be there.

She ran her hands back and forth, from the top of the trunk to the floor. Textured fabric, felt maybe, covered the upper part of the trunk down to where it opened, with plastic below.

To one side, a flap about six inches wide pulled up. She yanked it off and blinked at the sudden light before focusing on wires and pieces of plastic. It must be part of the brake lights. She vaguely remembered a story about a kidnap victim knocking out the brake lights and sticking a hand through the hole, waving at other cars and being rescued. But this didn't look like something easy to break through, with different hard plastic pieces screwed in.

At least she had light. Probably not much, in reality, but it seemed like a beacon after her long stretch in darkness. She found the other brake light cover and tore it off as well. With the light, she could look around her prison. And was it her imagination, or was she getting more air through the brake light openings?

She still needed to blow her nose. Did she have a tissue in her pocket?

Her cell phone! It had been in her pocket ... But now it was gone. She searched the floor of the trunk in case it had fallen out but found only the remnants of tape. Either her phone had fallen out at City of Rocks, or Mason had taken it. At least she did have a tissue. Talk about small favors. She blew her nose and then wiped her face on her T-shirt. Sam's T-shirt, actually. She tried to inhale his scent, but her own sweat dominated.

Half an hour after they left City of Rocks, everyone appropriate had been notified. Sam had called Erin, who had contacted Drew. He was trying to wrap up his job early so they'd have the helicopter available. For what, no one quite knew yet, but it seemed best to prepare for anything. The helicopter could land almost anywhere, and it could travel faster than their cars.

Erin had also called some police officers she'd met during their previous treasure hunting adventures. Those officers were contacting the local officers in Carrizozo and trying to get some state police into the area. Going through official channels was taking time, to explain the situation, convince them it was real, and make a plan. But at least people were aware of the situation.

Since they didn't know what Mason was driving, they'd have a hard time spotting him before he got to the Valley of Fires. And they couldn't risk Mason seeing police cars when he got there, or he might simply keep driving.

Their plan involved a lot of chance and hope. Sam closed his eyes. *Hold on, Rebecca*, he thought. *We're coming. We won't let you down. I can't lose you.*

How long had she been trapped? It felt like hours but was probably less than one hour. Sam and Camie would definitely have realized something was wrong. But would they be able to do anything, other than report her missing? She still had to escape on her own, if she could.

She had one advantage; Mason wouldn't know she'd freed herself. She might be able to take him by surprise when he opened the trunk. Assuming he did open it. What if he was planning to abandon the car someplace, or even roll it off a cliff?

She shuddered. Best not to think about that. She had to focus on what she could control.

She might be able to get through the brake lights, but without a screwdriver to undo the screws, or something to smash up the plastic, it would be tricky. She explored the trunk carefully, checking again for any kind of release, or a tool that might be useful. She puzzled over two circular units in the roof, close to the backseat of the car, before realizing they must be radio speakers. That wouldn't do her much good; even if she broke them out and made a hole, she'd only have access to the back seat, with a hole too small to get through.

What about that little thing she'd used to break through the tape on her wrists? She squirmed around so a faint light fell on the panel that divided the trunk from the back seat. There seemed to be a separate panel, with the metal thing – a latch? – in the middle. Maybe it let the back seat down! Not the direction she wanted to go, but it would get her out of that horrible trunk.

She tested the latch in different positions but couldn't get the panel to move. It must require doing something from inside the car. Oh well, she didn't really want to be in the back seat anyway. What would she do, sneak out and attack Mason while he was driving?

She swallowed her sour grapes and kept searching.

Sam got off the phone for what seemed like the hundredth time. "Tiffany is with Erin. They're going to go to the airport and meet Drew. He'll fly them to Carrizozo to stand by. Mason has never seen Drew, so if they can get a car, he can go to Valley of Fires and pretend to be a tourist. No rental car places in Carrizozo, though. Maybe one of the local police officers can loan him a private car."

The car slowed. The brake lights flashed into the trunk, and Rebecca braced herself as the vehicle turned. She hoped Mason was a good driver. The trunk was not where she wanted to be in an accident.

They resumed speed. Maybe she should be paying attention to the movement, to try to track their progress. But without her phone, she had no idea how much time passed between their few turns. And she didn't know the state well enough to know what a left turn meant anyway. Better to focus her energy, what she had left, on escaping the car. She'd worry about where she was once she got out.

She turned her attention to the floor. She could peel the carpet covering up from the edges. There would probably be a spare tire underneath – and maybe tools?

The carpet was stiff and hard to maneuver in the small space, but she managed to scramble over it as she bent it back. A piece of hard plastic covered the spare tire, but she got that up through contortions that would have earned her a spot in Cirque du Soleil. Attached to the tire cover was a metal bar, the thing for taking off the tire.

Rebecca smiled. She was still trapped, but she had a weapon.

# Twenty-Two

Maybe she could use the tire iron to smash the brake lights and get more airflow. She tried to wriggle into a suitable position, curled on her side with her feet braced against the back of the car. The small trunk didn't give her a lot of room to maneuver. She tapped at the hard plastic of the brake lights a couple of times with no results. She needed a lot more force.

Rebecca drew the tire iron back over her shoulder. She closed her eyes and turned her face away. Holding her breath, she rammed at the light. The force of the blow jolted her shoulder. The tire iron bounced back, narrowly missing her head. Something stung her hand.

She opened her eyes and peered at the light. The plastic had cracked and a chip was missing, probably the piece that had nicked her hand. The majority of the light was still firmly in place.

Maybe this wasn't such a good idea. She had enough trouble without injuring herself. She imagined explaining to her friends, and the police, how her black eye or cracked cheekbone had not been caused by her insane kidnapper, but rather her own clumsiness.

If only the trunk weren't so hot and stuffy. But then, it would be hot outside as well. And she wouldn't get much airflow from the back of the car, without a vent at the front to draw in outside air.

She sighed and lay back. Nothing to do but wait and try to think of pleasanter things.

The car slowed, stopped, and pulled forward again. Rebecca startled into full wakefulness. Had she actually dozed off? It seemed impossible, in the circumstances, but her panic had faded into exhaustion. Maybe it wasn't dozing off so much as passing out from the heat, the fear, the blow to the head. She was still far too warm, with not enough fresh air. Every muscle ached and she felt bruised from lying on the hard, uneven floor of the trunk while the car vibrated and jostled.

She found the tire iron and, biting back a groan, got into a position where she could more easily spring up. But the car kept going at a smooth, steady pace, back to highway speed as far as she could tell. Where were they? How much farther did he plan to take her?

She couldn't risk her attention wandering again. She needed the element of surprise if she was going to escape. But there wasn't much she could *do*, and trying to distract herself by daydreaming about Sam had led to drifting off in the first place. With a sigh, she began to explore her limited space again. Maybe she had missed something useful.

The carpet that had covered the floor still lay half-rolled and half-crumpled at the back of the trunk. She'd been using it as a pillow. She hadn't fully explored the floor under that covering. She felt around the spare tire. Could she release it and throw it at him when he opened the trunk? No, too awkward. The tire iron was better.

She imagined Mason opening the trunk and herself swinging the tire iron. If she hit him in the body, it would hurt but probably not delay him for long. She'd have to go for the head. She winced at the image that brought up. What if she killed him? Even in self-defense, even if he'd attacked her first, she didn't want to live with that. But she did want to live.

She left the tire in place and felt around the rest of the floor. Then she turned her attention to the roof above her. It was covered with fabric, something slightly rough like felt. Could she pull that off? There probably wasn't anything but metal trunk above it, but she wouldn't know unless she explored.

Using her fingers and the tire iron, she peeled off the felt, popping plastic rivets as she went. She shoved the felt along one side wall. She was making her prison even smaller.

But the top of the trunk was more interesting than she had expected. An odd metal unit had a slender rod or cable sticking out of it. What was that for? She poked at it, trying to understand with her fingers what her eyes could barely see in the dim light, and then tried pulling on the cable. Her fingers slipped off. She rubbed her hands on her shorts to dry them and tried again, tugging this way and that.

With a dull thunk, the trunk lid popped slightly open.

Rebecca froze, staring at the tiny sliver of light around the lid. She'd actually done it. She'd found the trunk release and got it open. What a stupid place for an emergency trunk release, hidden like that. Was the car manufacturer trying to torture her before offering escape? But finally she realized it must be the automatic release the driver could use to open the trunk from the front seat. She'd never thought about *how* pulling a latch under the front seat translated to a trunk popping open, but apparently it was through wires attached to that unit above her.

You learned something new every day. Whether or not you wanted to.

She eased the trunk open a half inch and pressed her face close to get at the fresh air. The road rushed by beneath the car and Rebecca flinched back. No way could she jump out at that speed. She got a look back down the highway, but no other cars were visible behind them, so she couldn't signal for help. They were on a two-lane road, with grassy fields on either side. No signs of humanity anywhere.

If she opened the trunk wide, Mason would see it in the rearview mirror. He might pull over and stop, giving her a chance to jump out, but he would be warned and could get ready for her. Certainly he would make sure they were someplace secluded before he stopped, so no one could help her or witness his crime.

No, her best option was to keep the trunk mostly closed and hope Mason didn't notice that it wasn't fully latched. Then the next time he stopped, or even slowed down enough, she could jump out. With luck, they'd be someplace with people. If not, she'd have to run.

Rebecca spread out the carpet on the floor to make room and provide a more comfortable surface. Then she lay on her back and worked her arms and legs, gently stretching and flexing to keep the blood flowing and her muscles ready.

The minutes passed. She couldn't maintain a state of alert preparedness forever. Who would have imagined the horror of being locked in a trunk could ever turn to boredom? She didn't know how long she'd been in the trunk, but her stomach was claiming it was time for food, and therefore maybe three hours since lunchtime. What would happen if her blood sugar dropped too low? She'd be useless, barely capable of making decisions, let alone acting on them.

She thought again of Sam. How much more pleasant it was to daydream of him than to worry about her current situation. The sexual tension between them was nearing the explosion point. If she got out of this alive, she wouldn't hesitate any longer. She wanted him. She thought back to their morning kiss and imagined it going a whole lot farther.

She shook herself out of the daydream. It was a lovely way to pass the time, but she couldn't afford the distraction. Mason must have *something* planned, beyond simply driving forever. What did he want? To hurt her? No doubt. He'd shown that when he tried to run their car off the road, and he probably blamed Sam and Rebecca for helping Tiffany. He wanted to control Tiffany. He wanted the treasure. He wanted to punish everyone who had challenged him. But what precisely he was doing about it, and how kidnapping Rebecca played into that, she couldn't guess.

The car slowed again. Finally! She had to take the next decent opportunity, no matter how risky. It couldn't be worse than staying in the trunk, where she risked falling asleep, or getting into an accident, or letting Mason take her someplace where she couldn't escape.

She rolled onto her elbows and knees, gripping the tire iron in one hand and bracing the trunk in the other, so it wouldn't either latch closed or swing open before she was ready. The car was slowing quickly, but it still felt like they were going too fast. She'd lose her balance the moment she tried to stand up.

The brake lights flashed on, shooting startling red light into the trunk. Rebecca spread her knees wider for balance as the fast deceleration threw her toward the front of the car. Before she'd quite caught herself, the car stopped, tossing her in the other direction.

Her heart hammered and her vision grayed for a moment as the sudden surge of adrenaline threatened to overwhelm her. She had to move now!

She shoved open the trunk. The sunlight was blinding, stabbing her eyes with white-gold pain. She scrambled out, half falling since she couldn't see clearly. She squinted and looked wildly around. They were still on the two-lane road, with no traffic in sight. He'd pulled off to the side. The land around them looked black and uneven.

Rebecca pushed the trunk down and looked toward the front of the car. Mason was getting out, outrage widening his eyes as he spotted her.

She leapt for the side of the road and took off running.

The ground was rocky and uneven. She dodged bushes and boulders, leaping from one outcropping to another. As her vision adjusted to the bright light, she could see her surroundings better. The rocky ground was black, sometimes crumbled into rough chunks and sometimes forming slabs or mounds with a rippled texture like waves.

Part of her brain registered the word *lava*. They must be at the Valley of Fires. But she couldn't ponder what that meant. Her focus was on escape.

She brushed past a prickly bush that scratched her leg and dodged one of the tall cacti with the thin arms. As she crossed a large, bare outcropping, she dared glancing back. Mason was coming after her, but she'd put good distance between them. She couldn't run forever, though. She had to find either friendly strangers or a place to hide.

Her lungs burned, her throat was on fire, sweat stung her dry eyes. Her legs turned rubbery and she struggled for each step. Rebecca's mind screamed *faster, faster*, but her body wasn't obeying.

She jumped over a gravelly slope toward the next outcrop but landed short of her goal. Her foot slid in loose gravel, her ankle turned, and she slammed onto the rough rock on her hip. With a whimpering gasp, she pushed herself up.

She looked back again as she staggered to her feet. Mason was perhaps a hundred yards behind her. Rebecca forced herself onward. She passed a hole, maybe fifteen feet deep, where a slab of lava had collapsed. The overhanging edges might make a good hiding place, but not if Mason saw her go into it. She needed to get out of his sight.

She had to keep most of her focus on the ground right ahead of her, to make sure she was planting her feet solidly. And she needed to glance ahead, to ensure she didn't run into a dead end. It wasn't easy to examine the farther distance at the same time.

She hit a bare slab that extended for about fifteen feet and took advantage of the sturdier footing to scan the area around her. Was that a building up ahead? If so, it was impossibly far away. And it might or might not offer help. It could be empty.

The land seemed to rise in a small mound toward the left. If she could get out of sight around that, maybe she could find a hiding place. She shifted direction. She was slowing, her whole body shutting down. Her head pounded and her dry throat rasped with each heaving breath. She hadn't had food or water in hours, and her energy reserves were bottoming out. The mound didn't seem that far away, but it didn't seem to be getting any closer, either. She choked back a sob. She couldn't afford the breath to cry.

Finally she neared the mound. Up and over, or around? Her brain was too tired to even make a decision, so she stayed on her current path and struggled up the shorter distance to the top. As she started down the far side, she looked back again. Maybe Mason had given up. No, he was still coming.

Her run down the far side of the mound was more like a barely-controlled fall. And then she hit loose gravel. Her feet skidded out from under her. She landed on her backside and slid down a steep slope, hitting the ground at the bottom with a force that reverberated through her whole body.

Rebecca lay sprawled on her side. For a moment her mind was blank. But Mason was still out there. She was in the bottom of what seemed to be a collapsed cave, ten or twelve feet below the normal ground surface. It wouldn't be hard to scramble out, but it would take time.

A deep shadow to one side showed where a piece of the cave roof had settled into a position that protected a shelf underneath. Rebecca scrambled toward it and stretched out in the shade. She couldn't see out of the hole, so Mason should not be able to see her unless he came down. He might see the signs of her fall, though. She had to hope he didn't know the exact path she had taken, and wouldn't look in the right place. If he did …

She didn't have much fight left in her, and she'd lost the tire iron somewhere along the way. She curled her hand around a fist-sized rock, but she hardly had the energy to lift it.

The air was delightfully cool in the shade. Dirt and moss cushioned her. Her stomach ached with hunger and her whole body shook with fatigue. A fly buzzed around her face. But for the moment, at least, she had some illusion of safety.

# Twenty-Three

Sam followed Camie to the visitor center at Valley of Fires. Arnold had paused to wait for Benjamin, who had pulled into the parking space next to theirs. Sam wondered if Mason was watching, as he'd promised. He might note Tiffany's absence, but if he knew the others had arrived, they could get this negotiation started.

As Sam and Camie entered the small building, Tiffany looked up from her seat by the counter. Erin was standing with her hand on Tiffany's shoulder, while Drew paced, muttering into a phone.

Tiffany rose and gave Sam a hug. "I'm so sorry."

"It's not your fault." He squeezed back, but the hug made him wonder when – or if – he would ever hold Rebecca in his arms again.

Drew lowered his phone. "Police are alert. There's a car pulled off the highway, a few hundred feet to the east of the turnoff here. No sign of anyone in it at the moment. They're running the plates." Drew shrugged. "Could be our guy, too cautious to take the road down here where he'd be trapped, but it could be a tourist who stopped to take photos."

Camie lowered her own phone. "Mason didn't answer. I left a message that we're here."

Sam nodded. "I guess now we wait." As if the long car ride hadn't been bad enough. At least then they'd felt like they were making some progress, if only in physical forward momentum. What was Rebecca suffering right then, at that moment? Did she realize her friends were waiting, ready to do anything to rescue her? Or had she given up hope? It had been over four hours since Mason had grabbed her.

Arnold and Benjamin came in. They surrounded Tiffany and after quick hugs led her back to a corner where the three talked in low voices. The room felt too small. Sam wanted to go outside and pace, but he had to be there when Mason called again on Camie's phone. His stomach grumbled, but he was too wound up to eat. He crossed to the drinking fountain and took a few sips, mainly for something to do.

It had been hours since Rebecca had eaten lunch. Unlikely that Mason was feeding her. With her blood sugar issues on top of everything else she was going through, she'd be in bad shape. Sam needed to remember to feed her the moment they found her. They had a couple of sports drinks left in the cooler. That would be just the thing. If he got her back, he'd give her all the pampering she deserved.

Rebecca's stomach growled. Her throat and tongue felt swollen. Even her hunger faded in comparison to her thirst. She had to move. It would be too ironic to escape a kidnapper and then die of thirst, hidden in the desert.

But was he still out there? She listened, hearing nothing but the faint sound of wind murmuring in the bushes. Or was it wind? Could that faint rustling be covering up a person's breathing, a man's movement?

How long had she been hiding? It could have been a couple of minutes or an hour. Time seemed to have lost meaning.

She had to take a chance. Rebecca rolled onto her hands and knees and waited for the world to stop spinning. She eased toward the edge of her hiding spot, trying to move silently, scanning the ground above as more of it came into view. She blinked to moisten her dry eyes, but it didn't work.

No one was waiting on the rim of the hole, as far as she could see. But Mason could be standing directly above her. She wouldn't know until she moved into his line of sight.

Rebecca closed her eyes and rested her forehead on her clasped hands for a moment. She tried to gather reserves of energy, but the thought of running was laughable. Plus, she had to climb out of the hole first. If Mason was waiting, even if he didn't know exactly where she was, he'd likely be able to reach her before she scrambled up the slope to the top.

She had no choice. As much as she wanted to rest, she doubted sleep would make her stronger, unless she had water, and ideally food, first. If she waited too long, say until dark, she might not be able to function at all. She had to take a chance. If Mason did find her, she'd make him carry her back to the car. At least then she wouldn't have to move under her own power!

She crawled into the center of the hole, quickly, whipping her head around to check the rim above her. Even on her hands and knees, her dizziness and wooden limbs combined to throw her off balance, and she slumped to one side.

She lay for a moment, panting. No sign of Mason, or anyone else. But she could only see the slope down into the hole and the land immediately around its edge. Anyone standing twenty feet back would be hidden.

Rebecca shifted back to hands and knees, wincing as sharp volcanic rocks dug into her skin. She couldn't crawl all the way across a lava field with bare knees. She had to stand.

Her mind balked at the thought. It sounded impossible. She whispered, "If I get out of this ..." What would she do differently? How would she reward herself?

She would appreciate every little thing about her life, from the taste of plain water to the ability to walk. She would celebrate every day. And she would focus on what really mattered, not financial security, but the people who cared about her, who would care for her in times of trouble.

She nodded once. With a deep breath, she grabbed the lava slab that had been sheltering her and hauled herself to her feet.

Camie's phone rang, a jarring funk beat. Everyone jumped except for Drew, who merely tensed and looked even more serious. Camie took a deep breath and lifted the phone.

"Let me," Sam said.

She shook her head. "You're too emotional. I'll put it on speakerphone, but everyone be quiet." She answered the phone. "Hello?"

They gathered close, barely breathing. Mason's voice sounded ragged, though maybe that was poor cell reception. "Where's my wife? And the treasure?"

Camie said, "We don't even know if the treasure is here. We

might have to go through several more clues to find it."

"Don't play with me. I saw the note. The last clue said 'you're almost there.' This has to be it."

Camie looked around at the group, her expression considering. "Maybe. We'll see. But before we do anything else, we need to talk to Rebecca."

"Well, you can't. Give my wife the treasure, and once she brings it to me you'll get your friend."

Drew shook his head. Camie said, "No way. You're not getting anything until we know Rebecca is all right."

For about thirty seconds, they heard nothing but rough breathing. Mason sounded as if he'd been exercising hard – or his thin thread of sanity was fraying. "She's fine," he said at last. "You have my word."

Camie rolled her eyes. "Not good enough."

Tiffany murmured, "Let me," and held out her hand. Arnold and Benjamin stiffened, but Camie pondered a moment, shrugged, and passed over the phone.

"Honey, it's me," Tiffany cooed. "You don't need to do this. I know you were upset, and I'm sorry. I needed some time to think, but it's all right now. Let's put everything behind us and work together. We can all go after the treasure."

The response came through garbled. She frowned. "What? I'm sorry, I didn't catch that. Let me see if I can get better reception." She brushed past the group, and before anyone could stop her, slipped outside.

Sam was the first one after her. She stopped about ten feet from the door. As everyone piled out of the building, she motioned them to wait. Apparently she'd turned off the speaker option, since she held the phone to her ear. They could barely hear her end of the conversation over the wind that murmured across the parking lot, but she kept talking in a low, soothing voice.

"She wouldn't really ...?" Camie muttered.

"No," Arnold said. "She's trying to trick him. But we can't let her meet him alone."

"We'll protect her," Sam said. He could barely breathe. He felt like he'd been punched in the gut. If he could do nothing else for Rebecca at the moment, he would protect her half-sister. But he wanted, needed, to do so much more.

Why wouldn't Mason put Rebecca on the phone? Was she unconscious? She couldn't be ... dead. Mason wouldn't have killed her and risked the exchange. Not intentionally. But an accident?

Sam wouldn't let himself believe it.

Then Tiffany's eyes widened as she looked at Sam. "What do you mean, you don't have her anymore?"


Rebecca headed toward the building she'd seen earlier. Now that she was closer, and a little higher on the landscape, she spotted smaller structures. Green roofs on posts might be picnic shelters; a smaller stucco building could be bathrooms or a guard shack. A few cars glinted in the sunlight, and an American flag whipped in the wind near the largest building. She didn't know what was at the Valley of Fires, but it was a national park or monument or something. This could be some kind of visitor center. Where there were people, she could find help.

At first she concentrated only on moving toward that vision, but then something caught her attention. A glimpse of movement, a sound that stood out against the wind, she couldn't be sure. She glanced to her right and blinked to focus her dry, stinging eyes.

Mason. Of course. She didn't even have the energy to be surprised.

He was still a few hundred yards away, hardly closer than the building she was struggling to reach, and at a ninety degree angle. Under normal circumstances, she would have no trouble getting to safety before he caught her. But her legs threatened to collapse with every step. It was all she could do to maintain some kind of forward momentum.

Her hip throbbed and her knees stung from her fall. At some point she'd twisted her ankle, she wasn't even sure when, but that pain was starting to shriek louder than all the others.

She called up some reserve of energy she hadn't known she had. If she got close enough to other people, she could cry for help. She opened her mouth to test that theory, and a dry croak came out. She'd have to do better than that.

She forced herself forward, simultaneously trying to work

up enough saliva to swallow and ease the burn in her throat. She couldn't give up now, not when she was so close. Even if she didn't see how she could succeed, she had to keep trying.

Sam walked away from the others, trying to contain his emotions. He had failed Rebecca. She might be dead. He would give anything to see her again, to hold her, to tell her how he felt.

He blinked, the blackened lava fields swimming before his eyes. Something was moving, coming toward them. A person. Too far away to make out more than brown hair, gray shirt, tan shorts.

His heart twisted painfully. It couldn't be.

The small figure vanished behind a bush. Sam shook his head. It was wishful thinking. He was hallucinating.

It reappeared, stumbled, came onward in jerky movements. Sam took a few steps forward, his heart battering his chest. "Rebecca!"

He started toward her. The lava field was rough terrain, the undulating black slabs broken by pits where lava tubes had collapsed. Some of the holes were small enough to jump over, while others had to be skirted. Prickly bushes and spiky yucca-type plants added to the obstacle course. Every tiny delay seemed like a curse after all that waiting and worrying.

As he got closer, Sam could tell that Rebecca was limping. Had Mason hurt her? Sam's relief gave way to a surge of anger.

Another spot of movement on the lava field caught his eye. Someone in dark pants and a white shirt, maybe a business suit without the jacket, was racing toward Rebecca.

Mason.

While Rebecca seemed to fight for every step, Mason moved much faster. Sam had thought he'd been running as fast as he could. He discovered that wasn't true. He had to get there first, before Mason could reclaim his hostage. Sam didn't know whether the man had a weapon, but his hands alone could do damage, and Rebecca clearly was not up for a fight.

Sam raced surefooted across the lava. His years of rock climbing helped him judge the terrain at a glance. He could land solidly on angled slabs and boulders and push off again before his weight had even settled. The rough lava surface gripped enough that he didn't slide, so long as he avoided the slopes of small, broken rocks.

Rebecca stumbled and dragged herself back up. She raised her head. Sam was close enough to see her mouth drop open as she spotted him. But Mason was drawing near as well. Sam would not let him touch Rebecca again.

A smile lit her face. Sam knew in that moment she was thinking only of him. Then she glanced toward Mason, flinched, and put on a burst of speed.

Sam almost had her. Rebecca reached forward, toward Sam, as if he were her savior, her lifeline. In moments she could be in his arms. But Mason was going to get there at the same time.

Sam veered slightly, ducked his head into his shoulder, and body-slammed Mason. The man went flying as Sam tumbled to his hands and knees. The fall stung, but he'd had far worse from bouldering or mountain biking. Mason howled. Sam was not at all sorry to see that the swine had landed against a cholla cactus.

Sam had had his own run-ins with cholla, and they were the worst of the cacti. Not only were the thin branches completely covered with spines more than an inch long, but the spines had microscopic barbs that tore the flesh on removal, leaving wounds that oozed and hurt for days. He rose with a satisfied smile. "Stop trying to move, you'll only make it worse."

As Sam turned, other people were rushing up to them. But he had eyes only for Rebecca as he wrapped her in his arms. "I've got you," he whispered.

She clung to him, trembling, and then her legs must have given out. He supported her as he eased to the ground and pulled her into his lap. Her head was tucked against his neck, so he kissed what he could reach of her cheek. "You're safe now."

She sighed and relaxed against him. "I know."

# Twenty-Four

Rebecca woke in darkness. She thrashed, gasping for air and struggling against the bonds trapping her limbs.

Something moved beside her. "Hey, you're okay, you're safe." She recognized his voice, hoarse with sleep, before he added, "I'm here – Sam. I'm going to turn on the light."

She settled back, panting. A moment later, a small bedside lamp flashed on. Rebecca blinked against the sudden brightness, but her nightmare receded as her eyes confirmed that she was not still locked in the trunk; she was back in the cozy guest room at Erin's house, trapped only by tangled sheets.

Sam shifted a pillow so he could prop himself up against the wall and gently drew her towards him until her head rested on his shoulder. She rubbed her cheek against his bare chest and breathed in his scent. He'd showered after their adventure, as she had. She'd been rank after the hours in a hot car trunk and her exertion, but he hadn't hesitated to hold her even then, carrying her to the visitor center as an ambulance arrived.

"Want to talk about it?" he murmured.

"I'm not sure there's much to talk about. It's over, but my body doesn't quite trust that yet, apparently."

"Not surprising." He brushed her hair back, avoiding the lump where she'd been hit. "I know my suffering was nothing compared to what you went through, but believe me, I would have traded places with you in a heartbeat. In some ways, that would have been easier."

She smiled. "I know. I'll be all right. No serious damage done." They'd checked her out at the hospital and declared her "lucky" in her head injury. Mason hadn't been trying to kill her, but a blow to the head could easily wind up fatal. She'd ducked enough that the damage was mainly superficial. Beyond that, the doctor had diagnosed bruises, scrapes, a mild ankle sprain, and heat exhaustion. They had treated her for dehydration. Everything else would heal in a few days.

She'd talked to the police, too, and Mason was in custody, after his own trip to the hospital to remove the cactus thorns. Given the howls from his nearby room, he had a worse time of it there than she had, which gave her some satisfaction.

"Anything I can get you?" Sam asked. "Water, juice?"

"I need to pee." She chuckled. "Guess that means I'm hydrated again." She shifted to the edge of the bed and stood, testing her weight on her ankle, which was wrapped in a cloth bandage for support.

Sam moved as if to get out of bed. "I can carry you."

"No." She took a couple of steps. "I can handle this. It's not bad, really. Mostly I feel stiff all over." She hobbled to the bathroom. She groaned a bit while sitting down and standing back up, but it wasn't any worse than after running a half marathon. She studied herself in the mirror. Her hair hid the lump on her head, and other than some dark circles under her eyes and chapped lips, her face was unmarked. The bruise on her hip was an impressive burst of purple, and her knees were scabbed, but no one glancing at her in passing would guess what she'd been through.

She could go back home, tell people she'd had an interesting New Mexico vacation, and no one would be the wiser. Only she would know the things she'd suffered, and how much she'd changed. She could take up her old life and pretend none of this had ever happened. But she wouldn't.

She returned to the bedroom and smiled at Sam as she slid into bed. "You should see my hip, it's a festive purple."

For a moment his eyes warmed, and she thought he was going to say something flirtatious about seeing her hip. But he sighed and gazed at her soberly. "I can't joke about it. He hurt you, and he could have killed you. And I couldn't stop it."

She raised her palm to his cheek. "You told me once that I could do this, this whole treasure hunt thing, by myself if I had to. That meant a lot to me, knowing you believed in me. But do you know what meant even more? Knowing that you were out there looking for me. You and Camie, Erin and Drew and even Tiffany, were on my side. But especially you. I knew you wouldn't stop until you found me. No matter how bad things got, I took comfort in that."

He laid his hand alongside her face. "I'm glad you realized that. And I'm here now, while you deal with your injuries and nightmares. I'll be here for as long as you need me." He gave a crooked smile. "Longer, probably. Maybe I should say, I'll be around as long as you'll put up with me."

She snuggled down in the bed. "My whole life, I've been worried about security. I grew up poor, with parents who couldn't seem to understand money. I thought if I had enough in the bank, I would be safe, no matter what happened. But the last week has taught me that there's a different kind of security that's more important."

She drew his face down for a kiss before she went on. "Having friends you can count on. People who will be there for you no matter what. I'd trust you with my life."

He held her gaze, his incredible green eyes filled with emotion. "I'm honored. I was afraid after what happened, you'd want to get away from here and forget all about us. I was ready to follow you – um, not in a stalker kind of way, not if you didn't want me to ..." He shook his head. "What I'm trying to say is, I think we have something special. I don't want to lose you. When this is all over, and you figure out what you want to do next, I'd like to be there too. Wherever that is, whatever you decide."

"No need to wait, I've already decided." She yawned. He was looking at her anxiously, and she couldn't resist teasing a little. "I'll tell you all about it in the morning."

She saw his struggle, saw him swallow before he said, "Of course. You need rest."

She chuckled. "I'm playing with you." She rolled onto her side, so their bodies touched from chest to knees, and slid an arm around him. "And I want to keep playing with you. Outdoors and indoors, day and night. Nothing is keeping me in Washington now. I'll want to go back often, to visit my family, but they don't need me. And what I need is here. Not the treasure – I don't care about that anymore. It's time to start focusing on what really matters."

Sam let out a long breath and drew her close, holding her as if his life depended on it. She ran her hand lazily over the smooth skin of his back. It was their first night in bed together, not that they'd had energy to do anything more than talk and sleep. She tried to think of a sexual position that wouldn't cause more pain than pleasure in her current condition. Maybe if she hooked a leg over his hips, as they lay now on their sides.

But she was already drifting off, her body demanding rest and her mind finally at ease. She had no doubt that their passion would be explosive, but exploring it could wait.

They had time.

When Rebecca woke again, sunlight streamed through the curtains. Sam was sitting up beside her with a book in his hands. His T-shirt and slightly damp hair suggested he'd showered. When Rebecca shifted to sit up, he closed his book and leaned over to give her a quick kiss. "Good morning. How do you feel?"

She pushed her hair out of her face. "All right." Rumpled and decidedly unsexy, but he'd already seen her in worse shape. There was some comfort in knowing she didn't have to worry about making a good impression.

He handed her a glass of orange juice. She took a sip and teased, "Thanks, but isn't coffee the traditional greet-you-in-bed drink?"

"You're probably still dehydrated. And I wanted to make sure you didn't have to face the world today with low blood sugar."

She beamed at him. "If you're trying to get the award for best boyfriend ever, I think you've nailed it." She finished the juice and handed him the glass. As he turned to put it on the bedside table, she snuggled closer.

He turned back with a hum of pleasure. "Well hey there." He ran his hand down her body. "Much as I'd like to spend all day in bed cuddling, people are waiting."

She winced. "People?" Not more police, hopefully. She'd have to testify against Mason someday, unless he plea bargained, but she could use a break from rehashing all that.

"Everyone wants to know how you're doing. And we have a few details to discuss about the treasure."

Ah, "people" must mean Camie, Erin, and Drew. Maybe Tiffany. As for the treasure, she'd given up on that. Her memory of the events at Valley of Fires were a bit muddled, a whirlwind of flashing lights and people yelling and her guzzling a sports drink. But she definitely remembered seeing Arnold and Benjamin there. They must have found that clue, and maybe the treasure itself by now.

It didn't matter. Funny, after all the energy she'd put into finding it, and worrying about finding it, the treasure no longer seemed important. She'd only wanted the money for what it could give her – a new life. And she was going to take that regardless, so in a way the treasure had done its job already.

Still, she would have to explain that to everyone. And her stomach was hinting that a glass of juice was not enough for breakfast. Rebecca yawned, stretched, and got out of bed. "I'll shower and be down in twenty minutes." As she bent over her suitcase to pick out some clean clothes, her body complained at every movement. A hot, steamy shower would feel good. "Make it half an hour."

By the time she headed downstairs, she felt much better, less stiff and more awake. Voices rumbled from the kitchen and dining room, so many she couldn't pick them apart. They generally sounded cheerful, though, the chatter interspersed with laughter.

She hesitated when she saw Arnold and Benjamin seated at the dining room table with Sam. What on earth were her half-brothers doing there? Sam rose and reached out a hand to draw her closer. He kissed her cheek and whispered, "When they heard you were in trouble, they did what they could to help." Louder, he added, "I'll give you all a minute," and he headed into the kitchen.

Rebecca simply stared as Arnold and Benjamin came around the table toward her. She was still trying to process what Sam had said. Arnold and Benjamin had been at the Valley of Fires not for the treasure, but to help her?

Benjamin's lips twitched in and out of a nervous smile. Arnold huffed out a long breath. "We owe you an apology."

Since "Yes, you do" seemed like a rude response, Rebecca stayed silent.

"Tiffany has been telling us about you and your sister," Benjamin said, "the things you shared with her the other night. I hope that's all right."

Rebecca couldn't decide how she felt about that.

"We realized we've been letting childhood jealousies get the better of us," Arnold said. "We acted as if you stole our father from us which is ..." He shrugged. "Plain stupid, frankly. You didn't make him leave us, and you didn't have an ideal life because he was with you."

They weren't saying anything Rebecca didn't already know, but it was nice that they understood it now. She still wasn't sure what to say, but she managed to smile and it felt almost natural. "Why did you change your mind?"

Benjamin said, "Yesterday, you looked awful."

"Ben!" Arnold exclaimed.

He flushed. "I'm sorry. It's just, you looked so exhausted and hurt. When we first found out about you, we didn't want you to exist. We didn't want you ever to have existed."

Arnold groaned and put his hands over his face. Rebecca had to smile.

"I'm saying this badly," Ben admitted. "The point is, we didn't actually want you hurt, not like that. Seeing what Rick had done to you, what maybe we could have prevented if we acted differently, it showed what jerks we were being."

Arnold nodded. "There aren't a lot of women who could escape like you did. Or men, for that matter. And to think I let Tiffany stay with that monster, even encouraged her." He made a face and shook his head. "We owe you both an apology, and whatever we can do to make amends." Arnold held out a hand. "I hope you'll be able to forgive us. We are family, after all."

Rebecca took his hand. "I've never had a brother, but from what I've heard, their job is to harass their sister – and to step in when other people harass her. I guess you've done that." She smiled, for real, and Arnold's jowly face seemed much nicer as it split into a grin.

Benjamin took her hand and leaned in to kiss her cheek. He ducked his head shyly but his smile looked sincere.

Tiffany had been hovering in the kitchen doorway. She hurried out and grabbed Rebecca in a hug. "Oh, I'm so glad you're all right! And you three have made up." She beamed at them all. "Now sit down. I've been instructing Erin in the best way to make huevos rancheros for a large group."

Erin, Camie, and Sam each came out of the kitchen holding two plates smothered in cheese and red sauce. "Hot stuff, coming through!" Camie said as they all scrambled for places at the table.

By the time Rebecca sat back with a full belly, her face hurt from smiling. The group wasn't entirely at ease, as they were still getting to know each other. But it felt good to be more comfortable with her blood relatives, and wonderful to be hanging out with her new friends.

Finally Sam used a break in the conversation to announce, "Okay, time for business! We still have a treasure hunt to finish."

"Oh, right," Rebecca said, "what happened at Valley of Fires? Was it only another clue?"

"We don't know yet," Sam said.

Tiffany reached over to place her hand over Rebecca's. "We were waiting for you."

When Rebecca glanced at Arnold and Benjamin, the latter said, "We'd like to help you find the treasure, if that's all right."

She frowned. "I'm not sure I understand."

Arnold said, "Ben and I didn't really care about the treasure." He looked uncomfortable and cleared his throat. "We didn't want you to have it. Otherwise, we might not have even bothered hunting for it. We both have businesses to run."

Benjamin said, "Do you think Grandfather knew that? It would be just like the old devil to set us up that way."

Arnold shrugged and nodded. "I think his goal was to help us get to know each other, whether we wanted to or not, and he's done that. And we've gotten to know ourselves better, too, I suppose. We won't claim any of the treasure. We've already told Mr. Ruiz."

"Oh!" Rebecca had forgotten about the lawyer. "Is he all right? Mason didn't do anything to him, did he?"

Tiffany said, "He's fine. Mason tricked his answering service into giving out that message. Mr. Ruiz was actually at home all day yesterday. He sends his regards."

Arnold nodded. "Anyway, after what you've been through, you've earned the treasure. So we left the next clue where it is. I'm pretty sure it is another clue, and not the actual treasure, from what Mr. Ruiz said, but it may be the final clue. When you're ready, we'll all go out together to find it. If you'll let us. We'd like to be there with you."

Rebecca blinked back tears. "Thank you, that sounds lovely." She grinned at Sam. "I guess the treasure hunt isn't over after all."

# Twenty-Five

Rebecca was grateful to be in the back seat and not in the trunk for this trip. Even being in a car made her heart race, but she was comforted by the warm bodies on either side of her and the cool air blowing back from the vents. Sam held her hand, playing lightly with her fingers. Come to think of it, his presence might also be partly responsible for the speed of her heart.

Arnold was driving to the Valley of Fires, with Benjamin in the front passenger seat and Rebecca tucked between Sam and Tiffany in the back. Erin and Camie had both claimed they needed to work, though the wistful look in Camie's eyes suggested she'd much prefer to be going on their field trip. Maybe she'd only claimed prior commitments so they could all fit in one car and have "family time" together.

At least Sam seemed to count as family. He had such an easy way with people, he kept the conversation going. With the friendly chatting and occasional laughter, one would hardly guess at the previous bad blood between Rebecca and her half-siblings, except in a few awkward moments. As they passed the Owl Bar, Benjamin said, "Maybe we can stop for hamburgers on the way back." His chuckle died away into uncomfortable silence, as memories of their last encounter there crowded the car.

Sam said, "Or try the Buckhorn across the street. Great debates break out in Socorro over which place has a better burger. You should all come down for the Festival of the Cranes in November. Thousands of snow geese and sandhill cranes come to the Bosque. There are lectures, photo workshops ..."

Benjamin perked up at the mention of photography, and he and Sam had a long discussion about cameras and photo editing programs.

As they drove east, the landscape spread out in grassy plains. Rebecca had seen some of that when she first got the car trunk unlatched and peeked out. She closed her eyes and took a few deep breaths. She was safe now. She could not let the mere sight of fairly dull scenery send her into a panic.

Sam lifted her hand and brushed kisses over her knuckles. Rebecca shivered, but with pleasure rather than fear. She managed to loosen her grip on his hand. She hadn't even realized she'd tensed up and was clinging to him.

"Look!" Tiffany exclaimed.

Rebecca jumped. Following Tiffany's pointing finger, she saw a dozen small antelope grazing near the road. "So this is where the deer and the antelope play."

They chuckled dutifully, either not noticing or ignoring Rebecca's strained tone. One of the antelope bounded off with high hops. It looked so free, with miles of grasslands and hills all around. Rebecca had to remember that – the desert was, in general, a place of freedom. Her own experience was the anomaly.

They passed between some hills and a while later, the land opened up again ahead of them. In the distance, a black streak crossed the landscape from left to right. It might have been mistaken for a dark forest.

"Those are the lava fields." Sam squeezed Rebecca's hand and whispered, "How are you doing?"

She met his gaze and managed to smile. "All right." Focusing on his green eyes, she felt a rush of emotion that had nothing to do with fearful memories. He had to be the sweetest man in existence. How had she gotten so lucky? She wasn't naïve enough to think he could be perfect, but he was perfect for her. He might not be ambitious, but he would support her emotionally.

With the money she got from the treasure, she could start her own business. She had some great app ideas, and she could work on them from home, living in a small town. She couldn't give up working – she'd be too bored – but it would be nice to have more control over what she did and when and where she did it.

And it would be wonderful to share her life with someone

who would encourage her to get outside and appreciate the beauty of the world. She'd get back in shape, learn to climb, maybe try mountain biking. If they decided to start a family, Sam would be a great, hands-on father.

She was getting ahead of herself. Classic avoidance technique, since she didn't want to think about the fast-approaching scene of her traumatic experience. But she didn't need to plan out her whole life. It was enough to appreciate this moment, and the possibilities for the future.

A few minutes later they turned off the main road at the Valley of Fires. The narrow pavement cut through the black lava fields all around them. When Arnold pulled up to a pay station, Benjamin got out, fishing in his wallet for cash. Rebecca pressed her lips together to hold back a nervous giggle. She hadn't paid the day before. Had she technically been trespassing when she ran from Mason's car?

"Let's get out and walk." Sam gave her hand a squeeze and opened his door. To Arnold and Tiffany, he added, "Meet you by the visitor center."

Rebecca climbed out after Sam. It felt good to stretch her legs, and even better to be out of the confines of the car. She paused to stare out over the lava fields. Undulating black rock, dotted with bushes and spiky plants, stretched into the distance. She had hidden out there, somewhere. It had been both a refuge and a place of terror.

Sam slipped an arm around her shoulders and led her farther into the park. The narrow paved strip on top of the lava held a few buildings and picnic shelters. She recognized the flag near the visitor center whipping in the wind. Once they passed it, Sam turned her so they were looking out over the lava. He said softly, "Tiffany was on the phone with Mason and he said he no longer had you. We didn't know what had happened. I walked away, my heart breaking. And then I looked out there and saw you." He pointed.

She was trembling, and he gathered her close. "We would have gotten you back," he said. "But you got away from him on your own. You were very brave and very resourceful." He grinned suddenly. "I'll get you one of those 'self-rescuing princess' shirts."

She quirked a smile. "Thanks, but I'm not sure I need the reminder." She wrapped her arms around his waist. "I did know you were coming after me. I never doubted that." Her smile grew as her tension faded, and she teased, "I just got tired of waiting."

"Fair enough." He gave her a quick kiss and said, "Ready to track down the next clue?"

They walked ahead and met up with the others. After a pause to put on sunscreen and drink from water bottles, Arnold asked, "Where to?"

He was deferring to Rebecca. Weird. She tried to focus on the task ahead. "What was the last part of the clue again?"

Sam pulled out a piece of paper. "If you want to scoop what's mine, take a look behind the–" He lowered the paper. "Last word missing."

Rebecca nodded. "Grandfather seemed to want us to actually explore the places he sent us. I think our best bet is to act like tourists and check out the place. Maybe something will make sense."

Tiffany pointed down a slope that was covered with more vegetation than the surrounding area. "It looks like that's the main trail."

A cement sidewalk made switchbacks down the steep part of the hill and then split when it reached the flatter area dominated by black rock. Rebecca randomly chose to go left. It wouldn't matter, since it looked like the trail formed a loop. They walked slowly, pausing to check out the scenery and read signs that described the geology, plants, and animals.

The lava formed mounds and lumps, with loose boulders scattered across the ground. In some places, ripples showed where the lava had been flowing as it cooled. Low bushes and cacti grew wherever a little dirt had settled. One common plant had lots of thin, sword-shaped leaves coming out of the base, with a tall flowered stalk that shot up about eight feet from the center. Some kind of yucca or aloe, maybe? A few lizards scurried away when the visitors got too close.

In several places large slabs of lava had collapsed into holes ten or fifteen feet deep, like the place where Rebecca had hidden. A sign explained that these were former lava tubes.

Liquid lava had flowed out of the center while the surface above hardened, leaving a tunnel or cave. Over time, some of these collapsed. Thank goodness they had, and Rebecca had found one. Still, she shivered a little in the warm air as she remembered the terror that had driven her to crawl under one of the thick black slabs.

Arnold paused by a cave-in close to the path. "There are an awful lot of hiding places around here, with all these holes." It took a moment for Rebecca to realize he was talking about the treasure. She was probably the only one who saw them as hiding places for a person. Or maybe not, since Sam drew close and stroked her back.

Tiffany asked, "Are we allowed to leave the path?"

"I was wondering the same thing," Ben said. "I haven't seen any signs saying to stay on the path."

Arnold glanced around and then took a couple of steps onto the rocky soil beside the path. He crouched and peered into the hole.

Rebecca hesitated. It felt strange to be sharing information with her former competitors. She didn't even have a contract stating their obligations. Still, they'd made a verbal promise in front of witnesses. That was sort of an implied contract.

She shook her head. She shouldn't be worrying about legalities. She'd already decided she could live without the treasure. She could live without her half-siblings too, but she preferred to have a friendly relationship with them. For that matter, she preferred to find the treasure.

In any case, they were all there together, so wasting time didn't do any good. "In Grandpa's previous clues, the last part only made sense when we were out there and saw the right spot, but then it was obvious. I don't think he expected us to search every nook and cranny in the entire lava field."

Arnold rose. "Good point. I have no idea what we're looking for, with that missing word, but maybe we'll know it when we see it."

"If you want to scoop what's mine, take a look behind the–" Benjamin murmured. "Not a lot to go on. Behind the sign? But which one? Behind the line? Could mean anything."

They continued along the path. Benjamin took some

pictures with his phone. They read signs and discussed the landscape, almost like normal tourists. The words ran through Rebecca's mind, but nothing jumped out and grabbed her attention as a possible hiding place.

Sam paused to read one of the signs. "Hey, it says you can hike from here to that peak way off in the distance. Guess that means it's okay to go off trail!"

Rebecca groaned. "And that means our search area is a lot bigger."

Sam gave her a squeeze. "No, I think you're right. Your grandfather wouldn't have made it too difficult. The fun is supposed to be in unraveling the clues, not searching randomly." She nodded and they walked arm in arm down the path.

Arnold and Benjamin lagged behind, studying the landscape carefully, apparently unable to take a chance of missing something. A few paces ahead, Tiffany was reading the next sign. "This is interesting. I thought those were yucca, but they're actually in the lily family." The sign had a drawing of one of the spiky plants with the tall flowered stalks.

"They don't look anything like the lilies I know," Rebecca said.

"It's called a spoonplant," Tiffany added. "They can be fermented into alcohol, and you can make spoons from the base of the leaves."

She crouched by a dead plant next to the sign. The leaves, over a foot long and about an inch wide until they tapered to a point, had turned brown. "I can't quite picture how they do it." She poked at a dried leaf. "It's stiff, so I guess if you cut off the base, you'd have a sort of–" She shot to her feet and turned to stare at Rebecca. "A scoop!"

"What?" Rebecca glanced at the plant and then the sign. She grinned at Tiffany as her meaning sunk in. "A spoon to scoop up something!"

The others gathered around. "Take a look behind the *sign*," Benjamin said. He knelt next to the sign and peered at the back of it. "Nothing written or attached here."

They scoured the surrounding area but found nothing of interest.

Arnold helped Benjamin to his feet. "Either that was a false alarm, or somebody else stumbled on the clue and removed it. I don't see how we could miss it if it was here."

Rebecca said, "Maybe the scooping bit was only a hint that we're getting closer. We've done, what, two thirds of the trail now? Let's finish, and if we haven't found anything, check out the rest of the park. But I have a feeling we're getting close."

Excitement ran high as they moved down the path. Rebecca could see it in the others' faces and feel it bubbling in her own blood. She hadn't really wanted to return to the Valley of Fires, and she still hesitated to leave the safety of the paved path for the rough lava. But maybe this experience was exactly what she needed to start putting her nightmare behind her.

Rebecca and Sam were in the lead. They approached a bench near one of the tallest trees Rebecca had seen all day, though it was still no more than ten feet high. "Need a rest?" Sam asked.

His hand tightened on her shoulder and he froze. Rebecca glanced at him in confusion. "I'm all right, how about you?"

"A pine."

"Huh?"

"That tree, it's a piñon pine. Pine rhymes with mine."

"That's a pine?" It didn't look anything like the towering evergreens in the Northwest. The twisted trunk had a kind of beauty, like an overgrown bonsai. But she wouldn't have even recognized it as a pine if Sam hadn't said something.

She grinned. "Let's check it out."

The cement ended under the bench, in front of the tree. But now they knew they had permission to leave the path. Rebecca stepped onto the rough black ground and over one thick branch that grew out sideways. Bushes crowded close to this tree and a cholla cactus blocked one side entirely. That narrowed the search area. At the back of the tree, the twisted trunk grew over a rock the size of two fists.

Or did it? Rebecca grabbed the rock and it easily came away from the tree. In the space behind was another little plastic tube. She rose, grinning, and held it up. From the other side of the tree, Benjamin took a picture of her framed in the branches.

She rejoined the others on the path and they crowded around as she opened the tube.

*The path was long*
*I hope you had fun*
*To finish this quest*
*And see what you've won*
*Go back to the start*
*The place it begun*

Tiffany winced. "I hope he knew that should be *began*."

"A poet he was not," Benjamin murmured.

"So where did it begin?" Arnold asked. "Does that mean back to the petroglyphs? But there are no other clues to narrow it down from there."

Images swirled through Rebecca's mind. Getting the phone call about the death of the grandfather she never knew. Attending the funeral. Seeing her half-siblings for the first time. Meeting Camie, and the initial annoyance with Sam butting into the so-called adventure. Watching the video of her grandfather, and finding the first clue.

"No," she said. "It began at his house." She gazed around at all of them. "That's where we found out about the treasure hunt, and that's where we found the first clue."

Arnold groaned. "You mean the treasure was there all the time?"

"But where?" Ben asked. "We looked all over the house when we were looking for the clue. I don't remember anything unusual, anything that could be considered a treasure chest."

Rebecca shrugged and smiled. "I guess we'll have to go back to Santa Fe and see what we find."

# *Twenty-Six*

They headed back to Socorro, passing up green chile cheeseburgers in favor of an enchilada casserole at Erin's house. Given the drive time back to Socorro, and then on to Santa Fe, the group agreed to postpone the final stage of the adventure until the following day. Rebecca suspected she wasn't the only one still recovering from the previous day's exertions and stress.

Arnold and Benjamin headed home that evening, taking Tiffany with them. Rick Mason was in custody and unlikely to make bail, which had been set at a half million dollars for the crimes of assault and kidnapping. Since New Mexico was a joint property state, and Tiffany wasn't about to turn over the deed to their house, Mason would have difficulty finding anything to use as collateral. No bail bondsman would want to take on a debt they might not be able to collect, and Rick was a flight risk.

Rebecca and Sam spent the night at Erin's house again, where Rebecca had an excuse to go to bed early. If she and Sam didn't sleep right away, well, that was nobody's business but theirs. And if she woke in the night trembling and turned to the man next to her for comfort, only he had to know about it.

Rebecca couldn't hide her smile when she headed downstairs in the morning. Erin gave her a knowing glance. "Sleep well?"

Rebecca could feel herself blushing as she headed for the coffee maker. "Fabulous. I'm hardly sore at all today." When she realized how that could be misinterpreted, she hurried on, "I mean, after all that running around two days ago, and the bruises from falling ..."

Erin chuckled and lifted her coffee mug in a toast. "Here's to a good night's sleep."

Rebecca toasted back and then hid her smile behind her mug. She hoped the afterglow would fade before they reached Santa Fe. It seemed unlikely that her half-brothers would suddenly start taking their fraternal responsibilities seriously enough to interfere in her sex life, but the topic was still more personal than she was ready to share.

The two-hour drive to Santa Fe might have covered the same ground as the first time they made the journey, but the experience felt completely different. Rebecca and Sam talked the entire time, sharing dreams and plans. She'd head back to Washington in a couple of days to start packing. Sam would join her the following weekend to meet her mother and sister, and then help drive her car with a rental trailer down to New Mexico.

"I can't believe this is happening so fast," Rebecca said.

Sam glanced at her and reached over to squeeze her hand. "Too fast?"

She considered and shook her head. "No, it feels right. It just doesn't entirely feel like *me*. At least, not like the old me. But the new me is ready."

She'd called Sophia the night before to fill her in. Rebecca's sister was cautiously supportive, though she clearly thought Rebecca had gone completely nuts. "But maybe it's time for you to go a little crazy," Sophia had said. "You've always been wound too tight." Fair enough.

They pulled up to the house in Santa Fe. "How does it feel to be back?" Sam asked.

"Fine. Good, even. It's hard to believe we were here only a few days ago. It feels more like weeks. Everything has changed."

They got out of the car and headed up the walk. Time to focus on the clue. They were back to the beginning, but what would they find there? Did the house and yard look different, or was it simply her mood? The place was welcoming now, not intimidating.

Mr. Ruiz opened the door to them. Arnold, Benjamin, and Tiffany came out of the kitchen with friendly greetings. Different indeed. "Coffee?" Arnold asked, lifting his own mug. "Or do you want to get started? And I hope you have some ideas, because we've drawn a blank."

Rebecca glanced at Mr. Ruiz. He smiled like a friendly but mischievous gnome. She'd hoped that all they had to do was show up, and he'd say, "Ta da, here's the treasure!" Apparently not.

"Did you notice anything different outside or on the porch?" Rebecca asked. "I couldn't tell, but I'm not that familiar with the place."

They shook their heads. "Nothing stood out," Benjamin said, "but I wasn't really paying attention. Shall we look now?" They spent several minutes exploring the yard, the covered porch, and the foyer, with no luck.

Rebecca murmured, "Go back to the start. The place it begun."

Tiffany winced. "*Began.*"

"Hey, maybe that's a clue!" Benjamin said. "Began, begun … something about guns? Grandfather never kept guns in the house, did he?"

"No," Arnold said. "But maybe something in a painting? A depiction of a gun?"

"But we searched behind all the paintings the first time," Benjamin said. "No hidden safes, no messages taped to the back."

Rebecca left them discussing the question and wandered into the sitting room where they'd had that first meeting. She'd first heard her grandfather speak on that recording. She closed her eyes and tried to bring back that day. She'd resented him then, putting her through so much time, expense, and trouble for her inheritance. But it had turned out far better than she ever could have imagined. A simple cash settlement would have changed her financial situation. Instead, he'd changed her whole life.

Not with the money, but by introducing her to new places, new people, new ideas. She wished she'd known him in life. She wished she could somehow touch his spirit.

Rebecca opened her eyes and glanced around. The others had joined her in the room. Sam watched her, his eyes warm with affection. Arnold and Benjamin were wandering, looking at the various pieces of art. Tiffany sat on the sofa with a shrug. "I'm just here to see how it ends."

Mr. Ruiz sat and fiddled with some of the objects on the coffee table. The challenge had begun with him there, starting the recording. Had her grandfather said anything to provide a clue to this part? Something they had missed way back at the beginning?

Rebecca cast back her mind. How had his speech ended? He'd told them to work together, to think about the past and the future. She couldn't remember the details. At some point Grandpa had reached forward to end the recording, and Mr. Ruiz had turned off the TV. Then they'd gotten into arguments and discussions, and started the search.

The recording. The disc had stayed in the player, unless Mr. Ruiz had removed it later. Maybe they could listen to the speech again.

Or maybe they hadn't heard the entire recording after all.

She smiled at Mr. Ruiz and took the remote control he was casually twirling in his hand, no doubt trying to draw their attention to it without being too obvious. Rebecca turned on the TV and pushed play. Grandpa's face filled the screen again. "So you made it," he said, smiling.

Gasps and shuffling noises filled the room, but Rebecca's gaze was locked on the figure on screen.

"Some of you or all of you," he continued. "All of you, I hope. I hope you learned something about this amazing country we're in. I hope you learned something about yourself. But most of all, I hope you had fun."

Rebecca glanced at Sam and smiled. Despite everything, she *had* had fun.

On screen, her grandfather took a deep breath, while the watchers held theirs. He folded his hands and nodded. "And now for the treasure. It might not be quite what you were expecting. I fudged a little bit when I described it. It's not buried after all. It's right here." He spread his hands. "Whoever followed the clues to the end gets this house, and everything in it."

Someone gasped. Someone else swore softly. Arnold groaned and said, "The house!"

On screen, Grandfather winked. "Not a chest, exactly, but full of treasures. My old friend Mr. Ruiz will take care of the details from here. Enjoy, and God bless."

The recording ended for real and the screen went blue. Rebecca turned off the TV and collapsed on the couch. For a moment she stared at nothing. The house? She didn't need, or particularly want, a house in Santa Fe. And would this sabotage the budding friendship with her half-siblings? The house wasn't merely a thing with financial value; it had history and memories.

Sam sat beside her and took her hand. She glanced at him and he gave her an encouraging nod. Rebecca took a deep breath and turned to study her half-siblings, now seated side-by-side on the other leather sofa. They didn't look angry, anyway. Confused or shocked, maybe.

Tiffany smiled. "Now you can stay in New Mexico. Right?"

Rebecca shook her head. "I mean, yes, I was planning to stay anyway. But not *here*. This is too much. When you agreed to give up the treasure, none of you knew it would be this house."

"Doesn't matter," Arnold said gruffly. "For one thing, you were ahead of us the whole way. If Rick hadn't slowed you down, you would have gotten to the treasure first anyway."

Rebecca said, "But if you'd known ..."

"I should have noticed the house wasn't mentioned in the will. But after we heard about the treasure ..." Arnold shrugged. "I guess we were distracted. Grandfather probably meant for that to happen."

"I for one don't need another house," Benjamin said. "Though if you decide to sell things rather than keep them, let us get a bid in, all right? I don't mind you having it all, but I'd rather not have everything sold off outside the family."

Arnold nodded. "There are a couple of paintings I'd like to have, but I'll give you a fair price."

Rebecca shot to her feet. "I need to think for a minute." She strode out of the room, blinking back tears. In some ways it would have been easier to handle the situation if her half-siblings weren't being so kind.

Wandering through the house, she let memories wash over her. Of the last few days, of her childhood, of the dead man she'd never met in person, who seemed determined to make her part of his New Mexico family. When she returned, she felt more balanced. She had a plan.

She glanced at Mr. Ruiz as she took her seat. "I assume that some of the items in this house are fairly valuable."

"I'd say you could get several hundred thousand dollars, easily, for some of the artwork and artifacts," the lawyer confirmed. "That doesn't include furniture, electronics, and so forth. The house itself is paid off, so there are no expenses beyond property taxes and upkeep. Any sale would be almost pure profit."

Rebecca turned to her half-siblings. "I'd like to convert some of the pieces into cash so I can pay off my credit cards and start my own business. Say twenty thousand upfront, with more in the future as needed. And I promised my teammates a portion of the treasure, so we'll have to turn some of it into cash, or let them choose art they'd like. But if there are items that any of you would like for sentimental value, they are yours, no charge."

As the others thanked her, Mr. Ruiz broke in. "Might I suggest that if an item has a value of more than one thousand dollars, or if the total value of all items going to one person is more than five thousand dollars, you negotiate a payment in exchange? Simply to make sure there are no hard feelings or questions of propriety."

Before Rebecca could say that such stipulations were unnecessary, her new family had agreed. So she moved on. "As for the house itself, I don't want to live here, but I don't want to sell it either, at least not anytime soon."

"It shouldn't be left empty." Arnold frowned. "You'll rent it then?"

"I was thinking about finding a caretaker. Tiffany, would you be interested in the position?"

Tiffany answered by sliding over to Rebecca's couch to give her a hug. "It's the perfect place for me to find myself again," she whispered. "I'll take good care of it, and I hope you'll visit often."

Rebecca hugged her back. "I'd love that."

"I'll draw up some paperwork to clarify everything," Mr. Ruiz said. "Your grandfather would scold me for being so lawyerly, but it's best to have everything in writing. Good fences make good neighbors, and proper contracts keep peace in families, I always say."

Rebecca glanced at Sam, remembering how she'd wanted to put their arrangement in writing. While she still agreed with Mr. Ruiz in principle, no contract contingency could have accounted for the realities of their experience.

Sam squeezed her hand. "You took care of all that quickly. Now what? We were on the road a long time ..."

She picked up the hint. "Lunch. Absolutely. I'll buy."

Tiffany jumped up. "Oh! Let me cook in my new kitchen! Your new kitchen that I get to use, that is."

Rebecca grinned. "I'll be chop chef and you can give me some pointers. If I'm going to be living in Magdalena, away from takeout and all-night groceries, I need to brush up on my cooking skills."

"Hey, you don't need to cook if you don't want to," Sam said. "I'm a great cook."

Rebecca raised her eyebrows. "Can you cook anything that doesn't involve cheese and green chile?"

"Sure, but why would I want to?"

"That does narrow the menu," Tiffany said. "Someday I'll teach you to make tamales the way my grandmother does. But let's keep it quick and simple today. We may have to send the boys for groceries, since I think the perishables have been cleared out."

Everyone got to their feet. Sam and Rebecca lingered for a kiss as the others headed out of the room. "Happy?" he asked.

"Couldn't be happier. I have a whole new family!" She snuggled against him. "But most of all, I'm happy that my family now includes you."

**Dear Readers,**

Thank you for reading *Valley of Gems*. Please leave a review at Amazon or elsewhere to help other readers discover new books!

*Valley of Gems* is the second book in my treasure hunting series, following *Desert Gold* (previously published as *The Mad Monk's Treasure*). Book 3 is Camie's story, *Silver Canyon* (previously published as *The Skeleton Canyon Treasure*).

If you enjoyed these adventures, please keep an eye out for my other books. To learn more, please visit my website at www.krisbock.com or sign up for the Kris Bock newsletter: sendfox.com/lp/1g5nx3.

If you'd like to learn more about New Mexico and the surrounding states, visit my blog, "The Southwest Armchair Traveler" at swarmchairtraveler.blogspot.com/. I share book excerpts, Southwestern travel tidbits, recipes, quirky historical notes, and guest posts.

**Kris Bock**

## Ordinary Women,
## Extraordinary Adventures

**Kris Bock** writes action-packed romantic suspense, often involving outdoor adventures and Southwestern landscapes. Camie and Erin make appearances in *Valley of Gems*, while Camie and Tiger star in *Silver Canyon*.

Kris's other romantic suspense novels include *What We Found, Whispers in the Dark*, and *Counterfeits*.

Kris also writes the Furrever Friends Sweet Romance series, which features the workers and customers at a small-town cat café, and the adorable cats and kittens looking for their forever homes. Each book is a complete story with a happy ending for one couple (and maybe more than one rescued cat). These sweet romances will leave you with the warm, fuzzy feeling of cuddling a purring cat.

If you need a sweet comfort read, try *Coffee and Crushes at the Cat Café*, followed by *Kittens and Kisses at the Cat Café*, *Tea and Temptation at the Cat Café*, and *Romance and Rescues at the Cat Café*.

Sign up for the Kris Bock newsletter and get *Lions and Love at the Cat Café*, a 35-page novella, for free! This novella features a second-chance romance with a woman who works on big cat rescue. You'll also get a printable copy of the recipes mentioned in the cat café novels, news on new releases and special offers, cute links and ferret photos, and scenery of the Southwest. Sign up for the Kris Bock newsletter: sendfox.com/lp/1g5nx3.

You can also learn about my other books and read sample chapters at www.krisbock.com or on the Kris Bock Amazon page.

## *What We Found*

22-year-old Audra Needham is back in her small New Mexico hometown. She just wants to fit in, work hard, and help her younger brother. Going for a walk in the woods with her former crush, Jay, is a harmless distraction.

Until they stumble on a body.

Jay, who has secrets of his own to protect, insists they walk away and keep quiet. But Audra can't forget what she's seen. The woman deserves to be found, and her story deserves to be told.

More than one person isn't happy about Audra bringing a crime to life. The dead woman was murdered, and Audra could be next on the vengeful killer's list. She'll have to stand up for herself in order to stand up for the murder victim. It's a risk, and so is reaching out to the mysterious young man who works with deadly birds of prey. With her 12-year-old brother determined to play detective, and romance budding in the last place she expected, Audra learns that some risks are worth taking – no matter the danger, to her body or her heart.

## Praise for *What We Found*:

"Another action-packed suspense novel by Kris Bock, perhaps her best to date. The author weaves an intriguing tale with appealing characters. Watching Audra, the main character, evolve into an emotionally-mature and independent young woman is gratifying."

"This book had me guessing to the end. Well written characters drive the story. Good romance. Exceptional and believable plot twists and turns. I loved it!"

"This is a nonstop suspense. Love the characters and how real they seem with every episode played out. This is a love story and suspense all in one."

## *Whispers in the Dark*

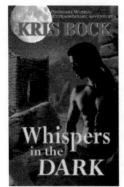

Young archeologist Kylie Hafford heads to the remote Puebloan ruins of Lost Valley, in the Four Corners area, to excavate. Her first exploration of the crumbling ruins ends in a con-frontation with a gorgeous, angry man who looks like a warrior from the Pueblo's ancient past. If only Danesh weren't so aggravating . . . and fascinating. Then she literally stumbles across Sean, a charming, playful tourist. His attentions feel safer, until she glimpses secrets he'd rather keep hidden.

The summer heats up as two sexy men pursue her. She finds mysteries – and surprising friendships – among the other campground residents. Could the wide-eyed woman and her silent children be in the kind of danger all too familiar to Kylie?

Mysterious lights, murmuring voices, and equipment gone missing plague her dig. A midnight encounter sends Kylie plummeting into a deep canyon. She'll need all her strength and wits to survive. Everything becomes clear – if she wants to save the man she's come to love and see the villains brought to justice, she must face her demons and fight.

*Whispers in the Dark* is action-packed romantic suspense set in the Four Corners region of the Southwest.

### Praise for *Whispers in the Dark*:

"This book was a delight from start to finish!"

"Whispers in the Dark has a hefty dose of adventure and mystery, as well as a strong main character."

"This book kept me turning pages until the end. The plot was full of twists and turns, always keeping the reader rooting for the heroine. Excellent read!"

### Counterfeits

*Counterfeits*
Kris Bock

Painter Jenny Kinley has spent the last decade struggling in the New York art world. Her grandmother's sudden death brings her home to New Mexico, but inheriting the children's art camp her grandmother ran is more of a burden than a gift. How can she give up her lifelong dreams of showing her work in galleries and museums?

Rob Caruso, the camp cook and all-around handyman, would be happy to run the camp with Jenny. Dare he even dream of that, when his past holds dark secrets that he can never share? When Jenny's father reappears after a decade-long absence, only Rob knows where he's been and what danger he's brought with him.

Jenny and Rob face midnight break-ins and make desperate escapes, but the biggest danger may come from the secrets that don't want to stay buried. In the end, they must decide whether their dreams will bring them together or force them apart.

#### Praise for *Counterfeits*:

"*Counterfeits* is the kind of romantic suspense novel I have enjoyed since I first read Mary Stewart's *Moonspinners*, and Kris Bock used all the things I love about this genre. Appealing lead characters, careful development of the mysterious danger facing one or both of those characters, a great location that is virtually a character on its own, interesting secondary characters who might or might not be involved or threatened, and many surprises building up to the climax." 5 Stars – Roberta at Sensuous Reviews blog

Ms. Bock also writes for young people as **Chris Eboch**. Her novels are appropriate for ages nine and up.

*The Eyes of Pharaoh* is a mystery set in ancient Egypt. This story of drama and intrigue brings an ancient world to life as three friends investigate a plot against the Pharaoh.

In *The Well of Sacrifice*, a Mayan girl in ninth-century Guatemala rebels against the High Priest who sacrifices anyone challenging his power. *Kirkus Reviews* said, "[An] engrossing first novel ... Eboch crafts an exciting narrative with a richly textured depiction of ancient Mayan society ... The novel shines not only for a faithful recreation of an unfamiliar, ancient world, but also for the introduction of a brave, likable and determined heroine."

*The Genie's Gift* is a lighthearted action novel that draws on the mythology of The Arabian Nights. Shy and timid Anise determines to find the Genie Shakayak and claim the Gift of Sweet Speech. But the way is barred by a series of challenges, both ordinary and magical. How will Anise get past a vicious she-ghoul, a sorceress who turns people to stone, and mysterious sea monsters, when she can't even speak in front of strangers?

The Haunted series follows a brother and sister who travel with their parents' ghost hunter TV show and try to help the ghosts.

In *The Ghost on the Stairs*, an 1880s ghost bride haunts a Colorado hotel, waiting for her missing husband to return.

*The Riverboat Phantom* features a steamboat pilot still trying to prevent a long-ago disaster. In *The Knight in the Shadows*, a Renaissance French squire protects a sword on display at a New York City museum.

During *The Ghost Miner's Treasure*, Jon and Tania help a dead man find his lost gold mine—but they're not the only ones looking for it.

*Bandits Peak*:

While hiking in the mountains, Jesse meets a strange trio. He befriends Maria, but he's suspicious of the men with her. Still, charmed by Maria, Jesse promises not to tell anyone that he met them. But his new friends have deadly secrets, and Jesse uncovers them. It will take all his wilderness skills, and all his courage, to survive.

Readers who enjoyed Gary Paulsen's *Hatchet* will love *Bandits Peak*. This heart-pounding adventure tale is full of danger and excitement.

Learn more or read excerpts at www.chriseboch.com.

Printed in Great Britain
by Amazon